Charms & Chocolate - Immortalized in Iron

Jenny Swan

JENNY SWAN

CHARMS
&
CHOCOLATE

IMMORTALIZED
IN IRON

III

The Witches World-Folds Saga

- Volume 1 "Awakened with Fire"
- Volume 2 "Carried by Wind"
- Volume 3 "Immortalized in Iron"
- Volume 4 "Protected by Water"
- Volume 5 "Connected by Earth"

Prologue

(approx. 30 years ago)

Valerius ran through the gloomy vestibule of the old mansion, his little steps echoing throughout the large room. Karla, his constant companion and spirit animal, followed close behind. The next day was his fifth birthday and he was really excited.

Would Nanna blow up all the balloons like the nanny had the year before? Would she fly glitter across the birthday table and make his stuffed animals sing? The voices of his fluffy friends would bring him comfort, since he hadn't been allowed to invite children this year and the halls were empty.

"The others don't understand us, nor do they like us. We're a family and other people don't matter." This was the reasoning that he'd been hearing from his father from the time he could barely speak.

He was looking for this year's Nanna, and it seemed as if he'd been running through the garden and large estate forever. The only thing that cut through the gloom was his laughter. His father and the few household servants thought he didn't notice the darkness and evil, but he did, and he laughed all the more so as to drive it away. He couldn't let it get to him, to catch him by surprise while he was playing. It couldn't overpower him from behind and devour him forever. In the evenings when he closed his eyes and couldn't laugh anymore, Karla would curl up next to him and send him many beautiful thoughts and tender feelings so that he felt safe.

But no matter where he looked, he couldn't find his Nanna anywhere. He'd been lying awake late the night before and had heard a cry resound through the estate. But then he'd listened more intently and it had been just as quiet as any other night. Did it this have something to do with her disappearance?

He came across the room he was never allowed to enter and ran right into his father, who was just coming out the door.

"Daddy, have you seen Nanna anywhere?"

"She's gone, child."

"Is she out buying something for my birthday?"

"No, she no longer works here."

"Like the Nanna before?"

"Something like that, yes."

"Why didn't she say goodbye?" Tears welled up in his eyes, but he quickly wiped them away. He knew his father never wanted to see him cry. He'd heard him often say, "He who cries is weak!" So Valerius did his best to make him happy.

His father peered down at him thoughtfully. "Have I ever told you why we live in such seclusion?"

"Because other people say we're evil even though we're not, right?"

"Yes, but what I mean is, why do they think we're evil? Do you know that yet?"

With a serious expression on his face, Valerius shook his head and looked attentively at his father, who bent down to take him by the hand. Then he pulled him into the room that Valerius had never been allowed to enter. His heart pounding, the boy crossed the threshold and peered around anxiously.

The room seemed even gloomier than the manor itself. It was dominated by a large wide table in the center and there were shelves lining the walls. There were so many books that Valerius would have needed more than a lifetime to count them all. They appeared to be old and didn't seem to have many pictures.

In one corner was a table with a large old book on it. It almost seemed to be calling out to Valerius, but his father pushed him toward a small couch.

"Come, sit down. It's time you learned the truth."

The boy obediently crawled onto the dark sofa, which was so cold he would have preferred to jump right off again. But his father would not have liked that, so he remained seated, without speaking a word.

"Many, many years ago there were witches and wizards. They were all united by the same power, yet there were five families that were the strongest."

"Was our family one of them?"

"Of course, child, we were the strongest."

"Who were the other families?"

"The de Rochats, the Montgomerys, the De Fontes, and the von Flammensteins."

Valerius's eyes shone. It was the first time his father had taken the time to tell him a story. "Then what happened?"

"It's always important to have a leader who makes sure everyone is okay, but the families battled over who was the strongest and who had the right to rule the world of magic."

"And we fought too?"

"Our ancestors did it for us. Our forefather, Melchior von Eisenfels, was alive at that time. As the fighting got worse and grew bloodier, he advocated for dividing the witch world into five covens."

"The Fire Circle, the Earth Circle, the Water Circle, the Air Circle, and the Metal Circle." Valerius enthusiastically rattled off what his tutor had taught him when he had been just three years old. He felt a little pride in knowing some of the history that his father considered so incredibly important.

"Yes, those were the five circles. That's the way it was supposed to be. But Melchior, and thus our entire family, was betrayed. Although the other witches agreed to give us a coven, they deceived us and performed the ceremony of dividing the ancient magic without us."

"Oh, that wasn't nice!"

"Right, it wasn't nice at all! Melchior joined in when it was almost too late, so only a little bit of the old magic remained, barely even noticeable. All the witches felt guilty and immediately agreed that Melchior was entitled to what was left."

"But that wasn't fair, was it, Papa?"

"No, my son, you've understood correctly. So then why do you think we're called the wicked ones?"

Valerius shrugged his frail shoulders. "I don't know."

"Neither do I. But we can't put up with it. Our family has been insulted and treated unfairly and that's why we have to get even with the others."

"Get even? But isn't that being mean?"

His father's eyes darkened and immediately he knew he had said something wrong. Beneath this glowering gaze, he made himself very small.

"We have been wronged, and it's important to

resolve it. What was done to us wasn't right. They were mean first. So, should we just put up with it?"

"Never!" the little boy replied swiftly, knowing that this was what his father wanted to hear.

"That's right. And that's why I have to leave tonight to settle this matter once and for all. But if all goes well — and I assume it will because your father is one of the strongest wizards these days — I'll be back in time for your birthday."

The boy swallowed hard. "You're leaving too?"

He pulled out a gold pocket watch attached to a long delicate chain. "Here."

Valerius's eyes widened. His small hands clasped the heirloom. "You're giving it to me? But you always said I couldn't touch it. It belongs to the head of the family and has for many generations."

"Take care of it until I return."

With sad eyes, Valerius peered up at his father. "When will you come back to me, Papa?"

"When you wake up tomorrow and the little hand is on the three and the big hand on the twelve, I will be back."

"But who will celebrate with me then?"

"Didn't you hear me? I'll be back in time. And then your birthday will go down in history as the day the von Eisenfels family finally assumed its well-deserved right to be at the top of the witch world."

"But I thought we were sharing the power with four other strong families."

"No, we won't. The time has come for us to show what we are made of."

Valerius nodded dutifully. "Okay, Papa. And you're sure you'll be back tomorrow?"

"I am. Then we'll celebrate, my son — oh, will we celebrate!"

Chapter One

It was late afternoon and the sun was casting its brilliant rays across the garden of Donnersberg Castle. The heavy walls were covered in ivy and roses, the blooming branches of the lush lilac bushes swayed in the mild wind, and a blackbird perched on a branch in one of the tall oaks was chirping its song. Maya stood amidst all of this on the mowed lawn, her face pale and her sweaty hands clasping a scraggly broomstick.

"Grandma, are you sure this rickety thing is fit to fly?"

"Absolutely certain. Now up you go. Hesitation equals failure."

"Impatience seems to run in the family," Georg murmured to Violett, who was standing together with him in the shadow of the castle tower, watching Mayla's first flying lesson with a mixture of trepidation and amusement.

Melinda von Flammenstein stepped back from her granddaughter and put her small hands on her hips. Anyone who didn't know her would never have guessed that this petite old woman with snow-white curls and a red cloak had been one of the most powerful witches of the past centuries. "Concentrate, Mayla. That's what makes or breaks everything. Remember that. Now up you go, we have other things to do today."

"I know, but I would have preferred a sturdier model." She looked skeptically at the slender handle and the gnarled twigs tied around the end with a simple string. It didn't give the impression of being particularly solid.

"Be glad Angelika lent you her old brushwood broom. Otherwise, we would have had to go to the forest to make one for you. That would have taken even longer."

"What? There aren't any stores?"

"Of course not. Like wands, witches' brooms are personal items you have to ask nature for and awaken the magic in them."

"Will this thing even work if it's not my broom?"

"It will do for this flying lesson. Sooner or later, you'll have to make your own. Enough chitchat, Mayla, get your butt in the air."

"Okay, okay." She closed her eyes. Sure, she'd been dying to learn how to fly a broomstick, but now that the time had come, she broke out in a cold

sweat. Heavens, how could anyone trust such a scrawny and rickety thing as it zoomed through the air several feet above the ground?

Steady, Mayla, steady. You are a von Flammenstein, after all!

She visualized herself lifting off the ground and gliding serenely through the air. The longer she waited, the more difficult it became. The only thing that worked was to close her eyes and go for it!

"Vola!"

She immediately shot up on her broom, and the grass, the garden, her grandma, and Georg and Violett grew smaller so swiftly that her eyes flew open in horror. Before she could cry out, a feeling rushed through her stomach as if she were on a roller coaster and she whooped loudly. "I'm flying!" Laughing, she stretched her face upwards, let the wind blow around her pointed nose, and felt numerous strands of hair escaping the clip at the back of her head. Flying felt fantastic!

Her grandmother had explained how she could steer the broom with gentle pressure. Mayla leaned forward a bit so that she sped up and flew twice around the tall oaks. Her pumps grazed a leaf that ended up sailing leisurely to the ground. Intoxicated with excitement, she made three loops around the tower and ventured a short lap beyond the castle grounds over the deep ravine and natural landscape traversed by the Rhine. She darted back again and flew toward Violett, who was grinning. Georg was standing next to the red-haired witch, beaming at her and clapping his hands, cheering her on.

"Great, Mayla! One more lap!"

She gingerly released one hand from the broomstick and waved to the two of them before darting around the oaks again and flying toward the tall mighty peaks around Donnersberg Castle. She circled the old firs growing on the mountainside and zoomed back toward the castle.

She could fly on like this forever, but if she was correctly reading her grandmother's expression from up there, she'd already been in the air longer than planned. Just one more lap. She whizzed past the oaks again over the deep ravine, enjoying the pleasant shiver that ran down her spine in the face of the dizzying heights. The wind whistled in her ears and her short jacket whipped around her waist as she dove toward the castle garden to land.

"Slow down, slow down!" Melinda, Violett, and Georg cried in chorus, waving their arms excitedly.

Surprised, Mayla tugged on the broomstick and slowed down as best she could, but she was too close to the ground. Her heels dug long furrows into the manicured lawn before she somersaulted headfirst and landed on the seat of her pants, the brush broom buried into the ground beneath her. She held her head in her hands, dazed.

Georg bent over her worriedly and wrapped an arm around her shoulders. "Are you hurt?"

"No, I'll just have a few bruises. What did I do wrong?"

"Rookie mistake," Violett commented. "Flying is so exhilarating that you perceive speeds differently."

"I noticed that. Why didn't you warn me?" she asked her grandma, who just shrugged.

"At times, I forget you're still missing a few basics. Usually, you'd have learned that in kindergarten." With a wave of her hand, the lawn was immaculate again.

"Except for the landing, it wasn't at all difficult." Groaning, she rose and held her back. "Still, I think that's it for today."

"Now gather your strength," Melinda ordered, "and meet me in the library in half an hour." Before Mayla could ask where she was going, Melinda disappeared into the castle through a side entrance. The last they saw of her was the red cloak fluttering behind her.

"Tough lady, your grandma." Georg grinned. "I bet lessons with her aren't much fun, are they?"

"Makes you long for a certain lovely witch who had been your teacher, the one who taught you your first spells — am I right?" Violett winked at her mischievously.

"Lessons with you were great, Violett, but my grandma's lessons are a revelation. Sure, she's strict and impatient, but I've learned more from her during these last four days than I would have ever thought possible."

Since they had freed her grandma from the von Eisenfels' country estate, all the members of the Inner Circle, as well as Georg, had been staying at the castle. On the first day, not ten hours after Melinda had awakened from her comatose state, the old witch had started giving Mayla lessons.

"We've lost way too much time already!" Melinda had said emphatically when Mayla had tried to get her to rest. Less than an hour later, they'd found themselves in the library.

"Grandma, any number of things can break in here," Mayla had cautioned, casting a worried glance at the marble busts, the bronze statue, and all the precious books. "I still find myself carelessly throwing my hands up and accidentally blowing things up."

"Then it's high time you stop being so sloppy. This library should provide a proper incentive to keep your magic in check and only cast it intentionally. Now get to it."

On the first day, Mayla demonstrated all the spells she had already mastered. Her grandmother had given her a few pointers to make better use of her potential. Clearly, in order to master the mighty powers of the von Flammensteins, it was best for her to learn from another member of the family who had headed the Fire Circle.

"You must always remember that magic resides in all living things. A fraction of it is hidden in animals, in plants, and even in people. All life is fed by this energy. If you close your eyes and sense not only yourself but also the things around you, you can feel it. Perceive this presence and your energy flows more freely. Once your thoughts merge with the currents of magic, not only does your own power flow through you, but the fullness of life does, too."

As spiritual as this explanation sounded to Mayla at first, she nevertheless opened herself up to Melinda's suggestions and soon felt what her grandmother meant. And the more she practiced, the easier she was able to access to her own capabilities.

From then on, she found it much easier to learn all the tricks, maintain her concentration, and control her magic alongside her grandmother. There were moments when she thought she could feel a muscle deep in her heart flexing more and more easily to her will.

Melinda also taught her a lot about fire magic. Lighting candles or fireplaces was just kids' stuff in comparison to the spells her grandmother shared with her. She showed her how to create and extinguish walls of flames with her breath, generate lightning, and melt things. It was an intensive course in the truest sense of the word, since she'd never imagined she'd learn so much in such a short time.

Mayla had insisted on the flying lessons. Ever since she had learned that witches could actually ride through the sky on brooms, she had been itching to try it out. Now that her grandmother was there, Angelika and Artus von Donnersberg had taken a step back, and Melinda encouraged Mayla to ask any questions that came to mind and learn any spell that seemed useful. She'd cleverly suppressed the fact that she'd made it through the first flying lesson with more or less serious injuries.

Holding her aching backside, she shuffled into the castle with Georg and Violett. "So, what have you been doing all day while I've been studying, studying, studying? Just hanging around?"

Violett swept her slender arms through the air, her many bracelets jingling. "Yeah, right. Artus summons us to the hall of the castle before eight o'clock every day, and after eating a far too insubstantial breakfast, we plan and discuss, puzzle and ponder."

"I'd like to join you," Mayla pointed out. "It's about stopping Vincent von Eisenfels, after all."

"That's why you must strengthen your powers," Violett said, repeating von Donnersberg's words.

"I know, I know. As I said, learning is amazingly fun, but your planning is also tremendously important."

"Incidentally, I'd also prefer to go off exploring

like Anna, Manuel, and Susana are doing, though I can honestly say that hearing how many witches and wizards have disappeared since Vincent has been on the loose scares me. There are now ten times as many people missing, and it all happened so quick! We've absolutely got to do something!"

"Have the three of them figured out yet where those who are missing are being held?" Mayla asked.

"Not since the last time you asked this morning," Georg replied sadly.

"And have any of you heard from Andrew Montgomery in the meantime?"

"No." Violett shook her head, her red long hair bobbing around her shoulders. For the past few days, she'd been blow-drying it into big waves, which really wasn't necessary; Mayla thought she was downright pretty as it was. "We haven't seen or heard from Andrew since he left three days ago for his circle's headquarters."

Georg rolled down the sleeves of his plaid shirt. "He'll probably have to stay there for a while to bring order to the coven and make sure those who were in cahoots with Vincent von Eisenfels are excluded from the council."

"That may well be the case. So, what's going on with you today? Will you join the others to work on how to stop von Eisenfels?"

"I'd rather have them help me figure out how we can use my former position as chief detective to expose the traitors within the ranks of the police and convince those who aren't corrupt that the outcasts aren't responsible for the atrocities committed by the hunters. I need to open their eyes."

"And have you made any progress?"

He nodded. "Tonight, I'll go incognito to my favorite pub where many of my colleagues enjoy their after-work beers. You know it — we went there for dinner when we first met. Could you please lend me your amulet key for that?"

Violett looked at him with concern, and Mayla did too. "Sure, but isn't that too dangerous? You are, after all, a cop on the lam!" Mayla fiddled with the thick chain hidden under the collar of her blouse and pulled it over her head. The gold protective amulet hanging from it sparkled in the sunlight. Georg accepted it gratefully and put the chain around his neck with the precious pendant hidden under his blue shirt.

"If it were up to me, I would have done it four days ago. But I'm aware that I'm the new guy and I can't expect everything to instantly go my way."

"Hear, hear!" Mayla laughed.

Georg jokingly nudged her shoulder. "Unlike you, I'm merely a simple water wizard who can't afford to put on any airs."

"Don't underestimate the possibilities your insider knowledge provides us," Violett remarked from the side, unusually sheepish and directing her gaze at the tips of her boots.

"That's right. You've already provided a lot of valuable information. I'm glad you finally trust the group unreservedly."

"It's a lot easier for me to see everybody's sense of purpose and sincerity since that good-for-nothing isn't a part of this group anymore."

Mayla felt a jolt in her heart, as if somebody had plunged a dagger into it. Georg put his hand over his mouth since, like Mayla, he hadn't mentioned Tom in days. But now the name had come up — though this wasn't the first time he'd appeared in Mayla's thoughts.

Tom. He was Vincent von Eisenfels's son. His real name was Valerius and he had supposedly defected to the hunters. Eduardo and Matthew claimed he was only spying and eavesdropping on them, but his tip about her grandmother had been correct. Without his insistent warning, they might not have freed Melinda the same night Vincent had broken out of his prison, and at that point, she would have been lost for good.

Ever since Tom had given them the lead with the help of the message spell, they had not seen or heard anything from him. Nothing.

Nothing...

Mayla's stomach contracted painfully, reminding her that she'd hardly eaten anything in days. Normally, she would have drowned her sorrows in chocolates, but since the three packages lying in her room were from their trip together to Ulmen City, she hadn't been able to touch the boxes. One look at them was enough to bring up the memory of their morning together in the confectionery, the kisses, and especially the passionate night before. How close they had been...

"Do you think he's all right?" Violett asked. Her face showed worry, causing Mayla's chest to tighten even more.

"We don't have to worry about that anymore," Georg replied fiercely.

Seemingly indifferent, Mayla shrugged, though there was actually a big lump in her throat that prevented her from speaking.

"I'm wondering if he was only here to get information out of us," Violett mused. "He was always extremely secretive and taciturn, yet somehow, he didn't look mean or conniving. I find it hard to imagine that..."

Mayla felt like she was running out of air. "Could we please change the subject?" she asked. The group was awkwardly silent as they marched into the great castle hall. She was having the same thoughts as Violett, but brooding wasn't going to help. And it didn't bring her any closer to the truth, either, and instead just increased the pressure on her heart, which was getting to her more and more with each hour she spent without him.

In the castle hall, Pierre, Nora, Artus von

Donnersberg, and Eduardo were all sitting at the large table, surrounded as always by the smell of peppermint.

"You look much better," Mayla said to Nora, who, like Thomas and Pierre, had been hit with the Pressa curse during the rescue operation and nearly choked to death on it.

"Thank you, I feel like I've been reborn." The Swede beamed at her, stroking the long blonde braid from which not a single hair strayed. One look at it was enough for Mayla to be reminded of the vivacious trip she'd taken on the broom. With practiced hand movements, she loosened the clip at the back of her head, combed her tousled hair with her fingers, wound the dark brown strands together, and pinned them neatly up.

Pierre was still a little pale around his big nose, but he was sitting upright at the table — in contrast to Thomas, who was still lying in his room being nursed back to health with the healing potion. Here too it became apparent that women were the stronger witches because neither of the two men were back on their feet as quickly as Nora.

When Mayla thought about how quickly Tom had recovered from the curse when the policemen had struck him down with it, she wondered why it hadn't occurred to her then that he had enormous powers. Oh, well, at the time, she simply hadn't had any idea, which was why she hadn't thought anything more of it.

"How was your first time flying?" Pierre asked.

"Phenomenal — I just have to work on my landing."

"Came in for a landing too fast?"

Violett laughed. "That pretty much sums it up."

Mayla said goodbye to her friends with a wry grin and went to meet her grandma in the library on the second floor, eager to find out what fascinating things she would be learning that day.

Chapter Two

"Today, we're devoting the last hour to defensive spells," Melinda told her a little later when they met in the castle's venerable library.

"I really don't need to practice that anymore. Look!" Mayla thought, *Tutare,* and immediately a shimmering bluish shield appeared around her. "I've practiced it with Violett for so many hours, it's coming out my ears by now."

"I don't mean that spell. Today, I want to show you a trick only we can do."

Mayla's chocolate brown eyes widened and she listened intently to her grandma. "Which one?"

"Without using much strength, you can throw around yourself a protective ring of flames that hardly any curse can penetrate."

"You mean it's stronger than the Tutare spell?"

"Not only is it stronger, but you need virtually

no energy to form and maintain it. In the battles ahead, this spell will be indispensable to you!"

"That sounds fabulous, but why didn't Violett or the other fire witches show me the trick? Or use it?"

"Because only we von Flammensteins have mastered it."

The words sent goosebumps scurrying down Mayla's spine. Anything to do with her family and special magic gave her a mixture of excitement and butterflies in her stomach.

"What do I have to concentrate on?"

"I'll show you. Similar to the Tutare spell, you imagine a protective wall and as you spin in a circle, you blow the ring of flames. Watch." Melinda took a breath and as she spun once like a dancer, she blew gently, and a high wall of fire was blazing around her in seconds.

"Watch out for the books!"

"Don't worry. Controlling the flames is simple for us." She blew again and the flames of the fire vanished as quickly as they had appeared. "The more you practice, the quicker you'll build up the shield. Now you try!"

"All right." She tilted her head to the sides, stretched her fingers and hands, shook out her shoulders, and imagined a wall of flames. Hopefully her hair wouldn't catch fire! Even though the others, especially her grandmother and Angelika, had emphasized several times that it was virtually impossible to be burned as a fire witch, she couldn't quite believe it — after all, her first attempts at witchcraft had resulted in a few scorched strands of hair. She concentrated on the magic, spun in a circle, and blew. Flames immediately rose in front of her. She saw a bolt of lightning rushing toward her and then bounce off the ring of fire.

"See?" her grandmother cried out. "A simple curse can't get through."

"How convenient." Enthusiastically, Mayla blew out the flames before any of the precious books or dark wood shelves could catch fire. "And would this fire shield also ward off an attack from Vincent von Eisenfels?"

"As always with magic, everything depends on your concentration and energy levels. Your powers are far from their peak, but they are rapidly intensifying — I'm delighted to notice this every day So, not long from now, you'll also be able to fend off an attack from them."

Them. Her grandmother meant Vincent and Tom. Mayla made no reply. She couldn't imagine Tom attacking her. Or did she simply not want to admit it? Had he just been playing a game with her? Had he been spying for his father and his family? Or had he turned his back on them and not revealed his name to anyone only because no one would believe he wasn't hungry for power? Mayla wanted to believe in him, in the good in him, but immediately the voices of the others filled her head about how naive she'd been to trust him.

"I also had no idea who he was," her grandmother remarked abruptly, her tone unexpectedly gentle.

Surprised, Mayla glanced up and saw compassion in her expression. "Do you also believe he was spying on us?"

Contrary to her nature, Melinda settled into a chair rather gloomily. "I like Tom and at no time did I read anything treasonous in his heart. I want to emphasize that I don't assume he was spying on us! But events didn't turn out the way he planned. The fact that his father has been released will throw him off his game... and push him to his limits. I'm not sure how he will act now that his father is at large and we know who he is."

"At no time did you even suspect he was not..."

"...Tom? Well, I knew he was keeping something from me that had to do with his past. I suspected that Tom Carlos was not his real name. And it's one of my foremost principles to trust my instincts — as you apparently do too — so I'm convinced I wasn't wrong about him. I don't know where the unexpected events have driven him or will drive him, nor do I know how the inevitable reunion with his father — if it hasn't already happened — will affect him. I am firmly convinced that his original plan was not to deceive me. Still,

I'd be lying if I said I wasn't disappointed by his lack of trust."

"So, do you still trust him?"

At a loss, Melinda swayed her head back and forth. "We have to be careful. With Vincent's escape, it's a whole new game. And it's time for us to find out who's on our team!"

Frowning, Mayla looked up. "What do you have in mind?"

"Tomorrow, we're going to the Fire Circle Council."

Her eyes lit up with excitement. "To our headquarters? That's wonderful! For ages, I've wanted to know what it's like there and who runs the council. For a long time, I've suspected the council members of having something to do with your disappearance."

"Me too!" Full of energy, her grandma clenched her small fists. "We have to clean house by taking a good look at every member. Every traitor must be exposed or we won't be safe."

Mayla tapped the tip of her nose with her index finger thoughtfully. "They don't know about me or my existence yet — I'm curious how they will react."

"We must be careful because the traitors may have already heard about you. When we get there, we'll have to closely watch how they react to both our arrivals. I'll be damned if I can't even manage to clean up my own coven!"

They practiced for a while longer until equally satisfied and exhausted. Mayla was about to leave the library around seven o'clock when she noticed the tome her grandmother was pulling off the shelf, "Tatjana von Flammenstein, The Foundation of the Four Circles." She peered over her shoulder with interest. "Tatjana von Flammenstein? Who is she?"

"She's your great-great-great-, oh, this is taking too long. She lived from 1617 to 1701."

Awestruck, Mayla peered at the red, leather-bound tome. "And she wrote a book about the founding days of the covens?"

"Among other things, yes. She was a historian and a specialist on that era."

"When exactly were the four covens founded?"

"In 1402."

"Wow, so over six hundred years ago." She sat down with her grandmother at one of the study tables and looked at her expectantly. "I'd love to hear your thoughts on what happened to the von Eisenfels family back then."

"You want another history lesson?" Melinda peered at the large grandfather clock. "There's only enough time for a rough summary. What do you know so far? And how?"

Mayla's throat went dry and her pulse quickened as she remembered the day Tom had brought her to Donnersberg Castle. That had been about five weeks before. They had walked along the

Rhine together and he'd explained the covens to her for the first time and also told her about the time of the founding. He had revealed to her that Vincent von Eisenfels had killed her real parents — though he'd omitted the fact that it had been his own father. To be fair, she had to admit that he had asked her to read for herself what had happened back then and to form her own opinion. But there had never been enough time for that. Didn't this confirm that her trust in him was not naive at all, but well-founded?

Taking a deep breath, she pushed back the thought and remembered what he'd said. "Tom told me about it after I discovered I was your grand-daughter. Regarding the time of the founding, he only briefly mentioned that the de Rochats founded the Earth Circle, the De Fonte's the Water Circle, the Montgomerys the Air Circle, and our family, the von Flammensteins, the Fire Circle. But the von Eisenfels family was just as powerful as the four founding circles, which was why they wanted to establish a fifth coven. According to Tom, it was democratically decided for the von Eisenfelses to not be granted their own coven. There has been friction and wars over it ever since."

"An extremely condensed account of the events of that time..." Melinda opened the book and pointed to a drawing. It depicted a large circle with four smaller circles inside that almost completely filled the outer one. Melinda traced it with her finger. "This outer circle symbolizes the natural power that every witch and wizard held before the covens were founded. For a variety of reasons, the powerful families in the early fourteenth century decided to divide the combined magic. Look!" She pointed again to the drawing and to the four smaller circles of equal size. "These are the four elements on which natural magic is based."

Mayla listened, her eyes shining. "Fire, water, earth, and air."

"Exactly. There is no element left. Magic was separated and divided equally among the four families. That was why the von Eisenfels family was denied it own coven. What's written about their character isn't nice, which suggests there's good reason to applaud the decision. But we mustn't forget that these books we have here were written by people who supported the decision. I have not read a single book or other document by Melchior von Eisenfels, the head of the family at that time. Was he honestly such a monster or was that the doing of the historians to justify the decision?" Her grandmother shrugged her narrow shoulders.

"I see what you mean. So what about the secret coven that he or Vincent von Eisenfels founded? And where did they get their power to rule metal?"

"Look, here." She pointed to the core of the outer circle and drew a small dot in the center with her finger. "There was a small remnant of the original magic that could not be distributed among the four circles. The power of metal. The founding families decided to grant this small part to the von Eisenfels family. This provided them a special position compared to the other witch families, but the power was not enough for them to have their own coven."

"But apparently it actually was... And somewhere, the family came across the knowledge of the spell for starting one."

"For a while now, I've suspected that the hunters shared a connection beyond mere zealousness. Five weeks ago, when I went to explore the hidden world fold — where I was ambushed and captured against all odds — I wanted to get to the bottom of that suspicion. And I was right. The von Eisenfels family had founded its own coven, possibly hundreds of years ago. Perhaps even back when the other circles were created."

"How were you actually overpowered in Southern England? I mean, Vincent wasn't there and the hunters aren't a match for your powers."

A delicate hint of pink flashed across Melinda's cheeks. "To my shame, I must confess that I don't really know. I was surprised and attacked by the hunters and while I was defending myself, I was attacked from behind. To this day, I cannot understand how they managed it. But I'm not going to let that sideline me, believe me!"

Mayla nodded thoughtfully and peered at the drawing in the book. Her thoughts returned to the balance of power and the founding era. "Apparently, it was no longer enough for Vincent to run his coven in secret..."

"I believe so too. He wants this fifth circle to be recognized — even by force, if necessary."

"Then why is he robbing other witches of their powers? Why does he want to wipe out the founding families?"

"The motive is always the same: power and revenge."

Involuntarily, Mayla wrapped her arms around her body. "We must stop him! Georg and Violett told me that he has been in hiding since his escape. Have you heard from him yet?"

"No." Melinda brushed one of her white curls from her face. "But I'm sure we won't have to wait much longer."

Chapter Three

A little later, Mayla left the library and headed to her room. She wanted to freshen up for dinner and needed a few minutes to rest. The lessons with her grandmother were always intense, and she always had to be alone for a while afterward. Today, Melinda's stories added to Mayla's worries.

She knew a confrontation with the von Eisenfels family was imminent and she knew the danger posed to all who were not at Donnersberg Castle. Her grandmother and Angelika had put a strong protective spell around the old walls so that no one who was not allowed could enter. Still, they worried about anyone who couldn't find shelter at the castle and those who went scouting — mostly Anna, Susana, and Manuel.

Exhausted, Mayla entered her room and closed the door. She was about to flop down onto the bed when she noticed there was a little someone sitting on it. When she recognized the little black cat that was her spirit animal, her grin stretched practically from ear to ear.

"Little Karl!"

It was the first time he'd been with her since being born. She hadn't seen him since she left Tom's cabin in the Pyrenees. Stunned, she noticed the little cat was already stable on his feet and quite robust even though he was only a few days old. It was probably because of the strong magic within him. But didn't he still have to be with his mother?

"Sweetie, are you okay? Are you truly strong enough to be this far from Kitty?"

Little Karl meowed in his high voice and jumped toward her. Overjoyed, she picked him up and stroked his tiny head. He was still small enough to fit in her palm. A warm, genuine feeling of love surged through her chest to then envelop her.

"My darling, I love you just as much."

For a moment, they continued cuddling until little Karl started squeaking excitedly and jumped back onto the bed. He nudged something small and brown lying on the blanket with his black nose and curled the tip of his short tail.

"What do you have there? Did you bring that?" She sat down next to him on the bed and even before she picked it up, she knew what it was there waiting for her on the blanket.

It was a praline. But not a real one. She could smell that immediately. This one must have contained a message.

There was only one person who could have sent it to her. Considering he could no longer jump onto the castle grounds because of the protection spell, he'd had to find another way to contact her.

Finally...

Her heart sank into her stomach. She sat still, pale, staring at the fake chocolate. What did he want? Why was he sending her a message? How dare he contact her through such a stupid spell? Then again, why hadn't he gotten in touch with her at least once during those past few days?

"Meow, meow," little Karl cried, breaking the silence. He sensed what was going on inside her. He tiptoed excitedly onto her lap and rubbed his fore-head against her hands, which were resting help-lessly on her legs. She slowly fought her way out of her trance and stroked the little cat's velvety soft fur.

"Don't worry, sweetheart, I was just scared." Although she already knew the answer, she asked, "Who gave you the chocolate?"

An image floated through her mind and she saw little Karl lying in a basket, snuggled up against Kitty's stomach. A large shadow fell over them, and then a sinewy hand appeared, holding a praline out to little Karl. "Take this to her," whispered a deep voice unaccustomed to talking. Then, the image and the voice vanished like a fleeting memory.

Tom.

As she brought the fake chocolate slowly to her lips, she felt hot and cold simultaneously, as if she had a case of the chills.. She'd soon find out what he had to say to her. But could she take anything he told her at face value?

Yes, yes, yes, screamed her inner voice, and she brought the praline to her lips faster than intended and whispered, "Aperi!"

The chocolate floated away from her across the stone floor before it expanded. A dark shape stirred in its center, growing larger and larger until Tom was standing in front of her. Although his appearance was slightly translucent, Mayla involuntarily flinched. Had he gotten even taller? His dark, almost black hair was hanging in short strands across his forehead, his cheeks were sunken and pale, and his black stubble and green eyes were the only color on his face. It was as if he were enveloped in a cloak of sadness, of the horror of the past few days. Had he already faced his father?

As always, his gaze was serious and determined. He looked directly at her as if he were actually standing in front of her with his long arms crossed in front of his chest. She almost heard his leather jacket squeaking with the gesture.

"Mayla..." He cleared his throat. Was it hard for

him to get out what he wanted to say? Did he miss her? Was he sorry for the way things had turned out? Or had everything gone as planned? "I need to speak to you. Please come to our meeting place tomorrow evening at ten o'clock. If you still trust me, come alone. If not, bring your grandmother with you — nobody else. I promise you have nothing to fear from me. I... I'll see you tomorrow."

As soon as the words were spoken, the praline popped loudly and vanished into thin air. Horrified, Mayla jumped off the bed and tried to hold onto it, but it was too late. Nothing was left of his message, nothing of his appearance. Such a terse message — with no way to replay it, darn it. His image was gone, the words erased forever.

Darn it. Darn it.

Tom.

What was his original plan? Was he trying to escape his family? Or had he been spying to help free his father as Eduardo and Matthew pointed out on a daily —actually, almost hourly — basis? No, she had to trust her instincts just as she always had. Tom wasn't the enemy — even though Georg and many of the members of the Inner Circle called him that.

Tomorrow evening at ten o'clock, she would see him again — she had already decided to go to the meeting. Full of hope, her heart was tempted to beat excitedly, but she suppressed the happy feeling, fearing disappointment. At the same time, she had absolutely no idea how to pass the time until then...

Half an hour later, she entered the huge hall with mixed feelings. She'd resolved not to tell anyone about the message. The... appointment was so late in the evening — she could easily retire to her room beforehand and use her amulet key to jump to the meeting point unnoticed.

Perhaps Tom had considered that when choosing the time. She had to go about it as quietly and inconspicuously as possible so that no one was the wiser. Georg in particular could always tell when something was weighing on her.

Squaring her shoulders, she gave as easy a smile as possible and joined Violett at the big table.

"Well, how was the lesson?"

"Great. I had a history lesson too."

Violett raised her red eyebrows and peered at her questioningly.

"My grandmother told me about the time when the circles were founded and the drama surrounding the von Eisenfels family."

"Yes, yes, the eternally misunderstood, poor, oppressed von Eisenfelses. I hope she also told you what Melchior von Eisenfels and his ancestors were up to, which is why they were denied their own coven."

"No, but she noted that we've never considered the situation from their point of view. I'm curious to find out what happened next. Where's Georg?"

"He left a long time ago."

"He's already gone? Where? To the pub to meet his former colleagues? I thought he was going to meet his coworkers there after work, we've just got..." She glanced at the large grandfather clock standing to the side with its long swinging pendulum, and her eyes widened in disbelief. "It's almost half past eight?"

Violett laughed. "Well, the class must have been amazing if you didn't even notice the time." Her forehead furrowed. "I hope he's careful."

"Don't worry," Mayla said, trying to comfort her. "I told him about the cops who were there when I left the police station with..." At the memory of Tom, she gulped. "I gave Georg a description of the police officers who might have met the hunters during their lunch break. I'm sure he'll stay away from them." She took her friend's arm and pulled her to the table, for Violett's stomach had been rumbling loudly for some time.

They ate dinner with the others and then sat in front of the fireplace. In silent agreement, they awaited Georg's return, which was long overdue. When Georg finally jumped into the hall, Angelika and Melinda were the only ones still in the seating area, and Manuel was brooding over his philosophical texts in his regular chair. When he limped over to them, conspicuously supporting one arm with the other hand, Mayla and Violett immediately rushed over toward him.

"Georg, finally! You're back!"

He smiled when he saw the concern in Mayla's expression. But he grimaced with his next step, and Melinda was immediately by his side.

"What happened?"

"I was busy chatting with a few colleagues when von Wickert and Thomsen showed up."

"Von Wickert?" Disgusted, Mayla made a face. "Of course he'd give you trouble. You did escape his custody, after all. So, who's the other one?"

"Thomsen was there in the woods with von Wickert the first time you landed in the world fold. He was also present when they flew you to my police station. Remember? He was one of the cops you suspected."

"As if I could forget! Such a rude, impertinent..."

Georg winced, unable to suppress a choked cry of pain.

"Georg!" Together with Violett, she put her arms around his back to support him.

"What malediction did they hit you with?" Melinda asked.

"They spoke too softly, so I have no idea."

"Where does it hurt? Only the arm?"

"No, my heart too."

Melinda was adamant that he lie down on a sofa. He tried to argue, but the old witch wouldn't hear it. Mayla and Violett helped him onto the couch and when Melinda pressed him down horizontally with her index finger against his chest, he tried to protest again.

"Quiet, I need to concentrate!" She ran her short fingers over his chest and arms and then nodded knowingly.

Mayla watched her grandmother hopefully. "Do you know what's wrong with him?"

"Of course. A curse I don't recognize has yet to be invented. Vola!" Shortly after, her wicker basket came flying into the castle hall and landed at her feet. While Georg's moans grew increasingly muffled, she purposefully grabbed a small bottle that had a greenish liquid sloshing back and forth inside. She pulled out the cork with a soft pop. Angelika handed her a spoon, and Melinda counted out a few drops on it and then fed it to Georg. His features immediately relaxed.

Violett pressed herself against Mayla and looked at Georg with concern. Mayla wrapped an arm encouragingly around her friend's shoulders. "He'll be fine," she whispered. Because if there was anyone who could heal everything, it was her grandmother. "What's that healing potion?"

"'This is a decoction of elderberry, elecampane,

and dandelion. The best antidote for the Debilitor curse."

"Debilitor?" Mayla recalled all the Latin words she had learned so far. "That means weakening, doesn't it?"

"Exactly. This spell makes you weaker by the minute until you can't move and are lying unconscious."

"Can you die from it?"

"It has happened before, but it takes a long time. Plus, it only happens if you don't take the healing potion in time, which everyone actually has in their medicine cabinet. It's a common spell for when you don't want to seriously hurt your opponent but want to weaken them to render them harmless. Like suspects or criminals."

"Suspects and criminals!" Georg cleared his throat and leaned on his forearms. "If I run into them again tomorrow...!"

"You'll be staying here tomorrow!" Mayla ordered. Especially since she needed her amulet key to meet Tom. As a precautionary measure, she pulled the chain with the valuable amulet over his head and put it around her neck.

"I won't give up on my mission that easily. A few of my colleagues listened and believed me. They told me the police station staff is slowly dividing into two. One group wants to finally put a stop to the hunters, while the other claims they only need to render the outcasts harmless and that will solve the problem. They couldn't say how many of them actually belong to the hunters or are just lazy and naive."

"That's good news." Artus von Donnersberg had discreetly joined them. "Perhaps once half of them recognize the need to finally put an end to the hunters' brutal rampage..."

"...then sooner or later, they will understand that we are pursuing the same goal," Manuel said, finishing the sentence. He had approached them inconspicuously, his chin nestled in the hollow between his thumb and index finger.

Von Donnersberg stroked his white sideburns. "The question remains: How do we pull it all together? Have your colleagues heard from Vincent?"

In the meantime, Georg had sat up. The potion was taking effect and he was clearly feeling better. A little color had even returned to his face and he didn't have to stifle his cries of pain. "Not yet. I told them the fold had been opened, but they wouldn't believe me. If he were free, they said, they would have heard about it by now."

"We should show them the fold," Manuel suggested, "where Vincent was held captive. When they see the abandoned place, they won't be able to deny the fact that he's free, can they?"

"That could work. I'll speak to them first thing tomorrow."

Mayla looked at him sternly. "Georg, you should first rest. You're still weak!"

Melinda sprang up from the sofa. "No, Mayla, the curse will be over by tomorrow morning. Georg should use the time. Some of his colleagues have been listening to him and we have to use the opportunity. We are running out of time and every precious minute counts."

Her grandmother said this so easily — she didn't care about him either. Georg would be going on his own, and who knew what might happen to him next?

Georg was visibly pleased with Mayla's concern and took the opportunity to stroke her hand. "I'll look out for myself. Besides, it would be an honor to see the house you were born in." He winked at her gallantly. She immediately took an unambiguous step back from him. Just because Tom wasn't here anymore, he shouldn't be getting his hopes up.

"You want to take them to where I was born?" Strangers were going to go to the house where she'd spent the only two weeks of her life with her parents? The home even she had never set foot in — since then?

She looked at the others in turn. "I'd like to see the house first. I was born there and my parents lived there before they were killed. Regardless of the fact that Vincent made it his home for decades, to me, it's sort of still... my home. I want to see if there's anything left."

"I can understand that." Georg gave her an encouraging nod.

Melinda packed up her wicker basket. "So it's agreed. Tomorrow, before we leave for our circle council, we will stop there. Now, goodnight." She left the hall, cloak billowing. Artus and Angelika followed shortly after. Manuel and his regular chair also disappeared, and Violett, Mayla, and Georg strolled through the hall to the stairs to go to their rooms.

"It's good nothing happened to you," Violett remarked. Then, since her room was in a different direction, she told them goodnight. Waving, she hurried off.

Georg and Mayla walked together through the narrow corridor that led to their rooms. "How do you rate our chances that your colleagues will fight alongside us?"

He shrugged his broad shoulders. "Things keep happening that seemed impossible before. We should remain optimistic. Until recently, I was just as gullible as they are."

"I've never seen you this insightful."

"Well now, Miss von Flammenstein! I am, after all, living here amongst you outlaws."

Laughing, they continued on their way.

"Now, please, give me the amulet key.

Tomorrow night I'll jump again — you heard your grandma. We don't have any time to waste."

Oh, dear, what could she say that wouldn't make him suspicious? She'd be needing her key the following evening. She would never risk Georg not making it back in time and missing her appointment with Tom.

Tom... Her chest tightened. He wasn't luring her into a trap, she was certain of that. Even if she didn't know what his plan was, she trusted him — regardless of his initial warning never to do that. However, he had saved her life several times. She was sure he wasn't evil and treacherous. The only question was if he realized that. Unfortunately, she didn't know how he'd escape the stigma of being the son of the most brutal wizard in contemporary history.

In any case, she had to meet him tomorrow — that's why Georg wouldn't get her amulet key.

"I made plans with my grandma for tomorrow morning, so I need it myself. I don't know when we'll be back. Maybe the von Donnersbergs can lend you theirs."

"You want to go to your former home and the Fire Circle Council, right? That should work. If you could give it to me by six o'clock that would be great."

Shoot. What could she say now?

In the meantime, they had arrived in front of Mayla's room and she put her hand on the doorknob. "To be on the safe side, you should consider an alternative. Good night, Georg."

"Good night, heiress to the mighty fire witches." He said it with such devotion and awe that it sent shivers down her spine.

Heiress to the mighty fire witches... that was her position. Every day, she grew stronger as she constantly worked to increase her knowledge. In the evenings, she studied up on Latin and books on witchcraft so that she could learn faster. But she had no idea if she was living up to her legacy.

She quickly disappeared into her room. As she had every evening before, she refrained from responding to his attempts to spend more time alone with her. Besides, the next day promised to be more than exciting and she wanted to try to get a few hours of sleep despite her agitation.

Chapter Four

The next morning, Mayla and Melinda left after breakfast. It was their first outing together and the first time they'd left Donnersberg Castle since Vincent von Eisenfels had been released. Although Mayla was more than just a little unsettled by the thought, she felt safe with her grandmother by her side. After all, she was traveling with the most powerful witch of the past centuries, and also had all those new tricks she had learned in the past few days.

Nonetheless, she wasn't about to underestimate Vincent von Eisenfels, since he'd killed her parents when they'd been about Mayla's age. Her mother Emma especially had received far better and more comprehensive training as a witch than Mayla, yet she hadn't stood a chance against him.

Georg accompanied her into the hall and winked at her, but she could read concern in his gray eyes. "Come back in one piece, okay?" He would have liked to accompany her, but as a water witch, he wasn't allowed in the Fire Witches' headquarters. Also, visiting her late parents' home was a family affair. She had to and wanted to do this without him.

"You don't have to worry about us," her grandmother replied resolutely, linking her arm with her granddaughter's. "Ready?"

"Absolutely. See you later, Georg!" She waved at him before his face, together with the gray walls, disappeared in a swirl of colors.

The next moment, they landed in a meadow in front of a little family house in the middle of a small residential area. The front door had been kicked in and the windows were shattered, with the shutters lying destroyed on the lawn. Mayla felt her grandmother stiffen next to her, as if the sight reminded her of the terrible day she'd found her daughter and son-in-law dead in the house. Mayla squeezed her hand in sympathy until she saw her grandmother's tension ease a bit.

It was depressing to see the damaged building, but she squared her shoulders and hurried forward. She had wanted to come here, at least once, and she wasn't going to back down now.

As she entered the hallway, it was as if a dark force were reaching out to her. Anger and hatred rushed at her as if Vincent's spirit were still trapped here.

She pushed the feeling aside resolutely and continued into the open living room and the kitchen space. There was an overturned white couch in the middle of the room, the covers tattered and the cushions torn. The glass side table was cracked so badly it was a miracle the glass top hadn't fallen to the floor. But there were shards all over the tiled floor, as if Vincent had smashed all the dishes.

Melinda crept past her, only a shadow of herself, and knelt near the stove and ran her hand over the pale tiles. "This is where she was lying..." Her voice was softer than it typically was, hiding a tremor that was extremely unusual for the strong woman.

Moved by a spirit of compassion, Mayla went over to her grandmother, squatted down next to her, and put an arm around her shoulders. It was easier for her since she had no memories of Emma and Markus. Of course, it was terrible that she never got to know them, but she'd had other parents, wonderful people who had raised her like their own child. Thanks to her grandma, they'd believed Mayla was theirs.

"Surely, she's resting in peace with my father." This was what she repeated to comfort herself when this tragedy weighed down on her heart.

A bitter smile crept across her grandmother's face. She clenched her hands and stared at the tiles as if she could still see her daughter lying there, her lifeless face frozen in terror. "He will pay for that! This isn't the first time I've made this promise!" She stood up calmly, as if she'd seen everything she wanted to see. Other people might not have noticed any difference, but Mayla knew that the grief kept burning unchecked inside her. "Do you still want to see your nursery or can we continue?"

Her nursery... She'd had a wonderful, lovingly furnished room under Anneliese and Peter Falk's roof. Still, she needed to have a peek at the room where her life would have begun and where she would have spent her childhood if this terrible tragedy had never happened.

"If you don't mind, I'd like to see it. You don't have to come along. Is it upstairs?"

"Of course I'll come with you. I'll show you." Melinda took her hand. It wasn't clear if she felt Mayla needed emotional support or if this was for herself. Hand in hand, the last two fire witches of the von Flammenstein family ascended the stairs to the second floor, toward the room where Mayla's life had nearly ended before it had even begun.

Mayla hesitated in the doorway. The room hadn't been ravaged but was actually meticulously clean. Apparently, Vincent hadn't spent one second of his captivity here. Had some magic prevented him from entering the room?

The walls were painted with stars and owls and the long curtains in front of the two windows were white with little pink clouds. A shelf stocked with children's books and stuffed animals sat next to a rocking chair. Had her mother sat in it with her? Had Mayla slept there on her arm while she'd watched and rocked her in the starlight?

Next to it was a plush rug and, in the center, a wooden cradle with a pink canopy. She walked slowly to the bed her parents had put her in before Vincent stole them from her forever. As she stood facing it, she remained silent, imagining herself lying there looking into her parents' beaming faces. A scent filled her nose. Was it the smell of roses or something else? It seemed oddly familiar and she could almost see her mother, her fiery red curls framing her face like flames, reaching out to her and laughing. Was it merely her imagination?

She scanned the small but cozy room. It was lovingly furnished. Every little detail, from the moon-shaped wall lamp to the rocking horse to a large white teddy bear with a red bow sitting on a dresser, testified to just how delighted her parents had been to have her. A warm feeling traveled through her and brought a smile to her face. It was nice to see all of this and it gave her some semblance of peace.

"Are you ready? Then let's go to the Fire Circle," her grandmother urged.

"I am." But, before she left the room, she hurried to the dresser and grabbed the big teddy bear. Of course, she had long since passed the age for such things, but it was still comforting to have something her parents had bought for her and given her. As she grabbed the bear, her grandmother's eyes widened.

"What do you have there?"

Frowning, she looked from Melinda to the stuffed animal. "I wanted to take him with me. It was meant for me, wasn't it?"

"I'm sure…" Her grandmother eyed the white bear with suspicion.

"What's the matter?"

"That wasn't here back then!"

"What? Who would…?"

A flash of lightning lit up the room and Mayla thought she was going blind for a moment. Swift as an arrow, her grandma whirled around in a circle and blew a ring of flames around them, causing the beam of light to bounce off the blazing fire.

"What was that?" Mayla raised her hands defensively, since it took a while before she could see anything through the blinding light.

"I knew you would come." A thin man walked in from the hallway, bending under the doorframe because of his height. Though the ring of flame protected them, the dark aura radiating from every fiber of his sinewy body threatened to fill the room. The sight of him was frightening and his near-black eyes glared at them. But the worst thing for Mayla was his resemblance to Tom. The curved, sensuous lips, the straight nose, the round shape of his eyes — but Tom didn't have the same broad, imperious chin. The man's hair was grayish, and there were silver strands covering his high forehead. He was almost as good-looking as Tom, yet he exuded a dangerous aura that made it impossible to call him handsome.

Vincent von Eisenfels raised his hands as if to show he was unarmed — which was a joke considering that those hands, along with his mind, were his most powerful weapons. But her grandmother, unperturbed, aimed her fingertips at him.

"You're no match for two von Flammensteins, Vincent, so leave it be. Or should I lock you up here again?"

"I already broke the spell around this world fold once, you little old lady, and that's why you wouldn't be able to do it again. But don't worry, I didn't come to destroy you. Not yet. I merely wanted to catch a glimpse of the woman my son lived side-by-side with and who he's told me so much about. The one you hid from me and my followers for so many years." His dark eyes stared at Mayla as if he could see inside her.

Mayla felt a sense of dread moving through her arms and then eating into her as if trying to consume her. But she thought emphatically about the ring of fire that surrounded her and her grandmother and that protected them from his spells. She pushed back the dark feeling until she felt at one with herself again. She looked at him with determination.

"Go to hell, you pathetic traitor!" Her grandma didn't blow out the ring of fire to attack Vincent but watched him warily.

Mayla had her hands at the ready, focusing on a fire spell just in case he tried to penetrate the shield. As her pulse pounded in her throat, she never took her eyes off the infamous wizard.

Had he just said Tom had told him about her? Did that mean the two had already met up? When he'd said "told me" it sounded so personal, so familiar, as if they'd spent hours together on the couch giving each other all the latest news. This question about Tom burned at the tip of her tongue, but Vincent would only tell her what he thought she was supposed to hear. If it was true, she wouldn't know until she talked to Tom in person. No, she wouldn't give him the satisfaction of falling for it!

"Normally, you're too cowardly to face two of us," her grandmother said in a scathing voice. "Get going before I make you pay for what you did to my family."

"Do you have any actions to follow your threatening words, little old lady?"

Her grandmother flushed red with anger and raised her hands menacingly, but he was already grabbing the protective amulet that hung on a chain around his neck, giving a loud and hideous laugh.

"We'll see each other again soon. See to it, little von Flammenstein, that your grandma teaches you a few things. I don't want to get too bored with you!" And with that he vanished, leaving only a faint twinkle that seemed out of place with his ominous darkness.

Mayla stared stiffly at the spot where her parents' killer had just disappeared, ready in case he came back to hurl another malediction at them. It took a while for her to stop expecting him to return. Then she looked at Melinda, who held out her hand.

"Are you okay, Grandma?"

"Of course!"

But Mayla could still see the last remains of unconcealed hatred blazing in her eyes.

"Gosh, you have good reflexes. I wasn't expecting him to make an appearance as soon as he did."

"From now on, expect an attack at any moment, Mayla. You must never let your guard down until that beast has received his just punishment. Will you make that promise to me? I couldn't bear it if something were to happen to you..."

"Don't worry, I'll be watching out like a hawk from now on." Or so she hoped. Her reflexes had never been the best — maybe it had something to do with the fact that she was extremely unathletic. But she sure wasn't going to let that wizard take her and her grandmother's lives. "Why didn't he keep attacking after you cast the protection ring?"

"I'd like to know that, too. Maybe he truly did just want to take a look at you."

"Then why did he attack us in the first place?"

Melinda blew out the flames. "Maybe he wanted to test our reflexes. Anyway, we should talk somewhere else. Come on, let's jump. And leave that damn bear here!"

Only now did she become aware of the cuddly toy that was still wedged under her arm. She dropped it, watching it fall in slow motion onto the carpet. Had Vincent used it to find out that they were going there?

"Is there some kind of...surveillance camera?"

"Yes, we must assume there was some kind of spell. In any case, your parents didn't buy it for you."

She looked incredulously at the teddy bear lying abandoned on the yellow carpet, smiling so innocently while her grandmother used the protective amulet to charm them far away.

Chapter Five

T hey didn't end up at a headquarters building with locked doors somewhere deep underground, as Mayla had imagined, but rather in the middle of a gloomy pine forest. Not a single ray of sunshine penetrated the thick, densely needled branches.

Her grandmother took a deep breath — it was impossible to judge whether she was breathing a sigh of relief or the forest air did her good. Then she grabbed Mayla by the shoulders, turned her to face her, and gave her a searching look. "Now you've seen him."

Mayla nodded, gazing into the woods. She could still see the face of her parents' killer, so much like Tom's... "How could you not have seen the resemblance between him and Tom all these years?"

Her grandmother shook her head, the white

curls bouncing around her plump face. "I was just wondering that too. To be honest, I never considered it as a possibility — I think that was the reason why. Let that be a lesson to you, Mayla. Don't trust Tom for now. We have to be careful. His father knows you were together. Maybe Vincent was lying and Tom actually didn't tell him about you, but we can't take any chances. Who knows what's been happening recently?"

"But you said to trust my instincts and..."

"Mayla, it's too dangerous. We don't know anything about Tom's history. We cannot rule out the possibility they were working together and that he actually did talk about you."

Mayla shook her head resolutely. "I don't believe that. I'm sure Vincent thought he could fool me with the information he learned from his stupid crow that was following me everywhere. Tom would never..."

"Enough. Our top priority is protecting the opposition and preserving the witch order. There is no time for romance!"

She looked at her grandmother in disbelief. "What happened to the laid-back, confident woman who told me to go with my instincts? Is it because you saw Vincent?"

"I told you, the game has changed completely! We're a team, all of us at Donnersberg Castle. Going it alone would mean putting each other in danger. Don't do anything that we haven't discussed beforehand with the group." Her grand-mother looked her up and down skeptically. "Since when are you such an ardent defender of Tom? Has he been in touch with you? Did you two meet?"

"No!" Too fast, too rash. Darn it. "I haven't had any contact with him," she said, this time more calmly. However, judging by the suspicious expression on her grandma's face, it was time to change the subject! "Where are we anyway? I thought we were going to jump into the Fire Circle head-quarters."

"Which we have. Let's go."

"The headquarters is in the forest? No imposing building? No secret access with code and symbols? Where's all the magic, the fire, the charm?"

Her grandmother spread her arms as if to embrace the forest. "You can't find more magic than in nature. Think of the lessons I've taught you. Open your eyes and your heart and feel the energy of life. You must learn to take your eyes off mundane things and see magic in its pristine state."

Smiling, Mayla looked at her grandmother's handmade shoes. "Says the woman with the fancy leather boots."

A mischievous grin stole onto her grandmoth-er's wrinkled face. "Since I see the magical things, I can certainly indulge in a few worldly things. Just because I'm a wise old witch doesn't mean I've lost sight of beautiful clothes." She wrapped her red cloak around her and trudged deeper into the forest.

The ground was littered with moss. Every tree stump and every root was covered with a soft, green layer so that with every step they sunk slightly, walking as if on soft pillows.

"Where are we?"

"In Reinhardswald."

"The fairy tale forest in the middle of Germany?"

"Exactly. Where do you think all the legends and fairy tales come from? Over the centuries, people have picked up a thing or two." Her grandmother gave her a mischievous wink.

"Are the headquarters for the four circles all in one forest?"

"I can't answer that question for you because our family only has the magic of fire in their genes and we cannot enter the others. And members of each circle guard their secrets as closely as we do."

"It has something to do with the splitting of the old magic, doesn't it? Does that mean Vincent von Eisenfels can't enter the headquarters?"

"Exactly. Though his hunters who still wear our signet ring can get inside. This is a danger that we must not lose sight of at any time."

She walked next to her grandmother, deep in thought. Where were the headquarters? And all the other witches? She studied the slender trunks of the tall fir trees, looking for burrows and caves that might reveal secret entrances. As she heard the call of an owl, she looked up curiously.

Melinda eyed the animal and winked. "This is Merlin, my spirit animal."

"I know him. He warned me when the policemen ambushed us in your hiding place."

Smiling, Melinda looked up and Mayla felt the warmth and gratitude her grandmother was sharing with him.

"Do you have a spirit animal yet?"

"Yes, little Karl, the cutest little cat in the world. But he has only been with me one time. He was born less than a week ago, so he still needs his mom."

"Then it won't be long before he's with you. Spirit animals separate from their mothers much sooner, especially when their soul mates need them."

"Georg told me that. Anyway, where are the headquarters? I only see trees and bushes, lots of small firs, and cones lying around."

"Then you should learn to open your eyes to magic." Melinda stopped abruptly, raised her arms, and whispered, "Te aperi, caput ignis!"

A bright bolt of lightning shot straight through the air, dividing the forest in two. Before her eyes, the fir trees and the moss moved to either side so as to reveal a different world between the bursts of lightning.

"A fold within a fold?" Mayla whispered, not taking her eyes off it for a second.

Within the forest there appeared several buildings that all looked like witch houses from old picture books. They were crooked with smoking chimneys, peaked roofs, and rattling shutters. There were countless ovens next to the houses, some with fires blazing. The smell of freshly baked bread, which hadn't been there a moment ago, wafted over to Mayla. A woman pulled a large baking tray with a dark loaf out of the oven and poked it expertly. A crowd of witch children rushed past her through the streets toward a large building that was apparently the school. It was a one-story, cube-shaped complex made entirely of wood. A woman stood in the wide doorway and rang a bell with a stern look on her face; but the twinkle in her eyes and the children's happy laughter revealed that it must have been a pleasure to be taught by her.

Once the fold was all the way open, a complete village stood before them. It was framed not by a stilt wall but rather strange threads of glitter, reinforcing the spell that hid it not only from the common people but from so many other witches who weren't members.

"This is the Fire Circle headquarters?"

"Isn't it beautiful?" Melinda's eyes softened as it swept across the glittering gate, which was more illusion than real and blazed brightly as her grandma walked through. When Mayla didn't follow her, Melinda turned and smiled at her. "Come, Heir von Flammenstein."

Her heart pounding excitedly, Mayla stepped through the magic gate, which lit up again, and set her feet purposefully on the ground. Who would she meet now? How would people react to her arrival? And her existence?

She watched the laughing witch children who entered the school under their teacher's benevolent gaze before she studied the rustic houses and the occasional people walking along the ordinary streets.

"Who are the people who live in the houses? Fire witches, I get that, but why do they live here? Can anyone settle in this village or does it require permission from..." She frowned at her grandma. "...from you?"

"Yes, it requires permission from our family. We not only founded the circle over six hundred years ago but also this settlement. The families who have chosen to live in this place did so centuries ago."

"Is it the members of the Council that live here?"

"No, they are elected for five years and their term cannot be renewed. Back then, it was our family's best friends that we wanted by our side, who built their homes next to ours. Many descendants of those families still remain and we live close together in friendship."

"Wait, does that mean you live here too?"

Melinda pointed to one of the crooked houses that had a red front porch and a large herb garden on one side. It was a plain structure with nothing to indicate that it was the home of the head witch. "Our family has been living there for many generations."

Smiling, Mayla hurried toward it. "I'd like to see the inside. Do we have time?"

"Of course. I want to make sure everything's all right anyway." In good spirits, they headed toward the house where Merlin the owl sat atop the brick chimney. Melinda raised her hands and put them on the doorknob.

"What? You don't need a key?"

"Key? You only lose it. No, we lock our houses with a personal spell. Ours is," she leaned closer and whispered in her ear, "Te aperi, amata domus familia ignei lapidis."

"Open up, beloved witch house of the von Flammensteins," Mayla translated quickly to herself, glad yet again for how much Latin she'd learned with Georg. Sure, he hadn't wanted to take his eyes off her because he cared for her, but he'd also helped her grow stronger and more independent. He was a gentleman, a knight, a man who liked to protect women. But now it was time to have the talk with him that she had been dreading for weeks.

Even before Melinda put her hand on the handle to open the door, someone behind them tore Mayla out of her thoughts and back to the present by calling out, "Melinda?" The two turned and a blonde woman in her fifties was staring at them incredulously, wrinkling her crooked nose.

"It is you, Melinda. Finally!" She cried out, "Melinda has returned!" at the top of her voice, and countless heads poked out of the windows, staring at them in disbelief. When they recognized Melinda, their faces brightened and they disappeared, only to come rushing out of their houses straight toward them along with the blonde woman, half laughing, half crying.

"We were so worried. You were abducted, right?" She threw her arms around Melinda's neck and the head witch hugged her, smiling.

"Don't worry, I'm fine, Viola. Mayla here helped free me."

The witch looked at her with interest and wrinkled her crooked nose as if trying to learn from her scent if they were acquainted. "Mayla? I don't know you yet, but thank you from the bottom of my heart for saving the last living von Flammenstein."

Grinning, Mayla and her grandmother looked at each other as a group of ten chattering witches rushed toward them.

"The last of the von Flammenstein is no more,

my dears," Melinda announced once the others reached them and all conversation fell silent. "Mayla is my granddaughter. The von Flammenstein family has an heiress."

This statement was followed by such silence that even the sound of an owl flying past could be heard. The amazed faces of those present changed into smiles slowly, as if they could hardly believe it, and one after the other they hugged each other as well as Melinda and Mayla as if they had known each other for years.

"Mayla? You are a von Flammenstein? That means you're the daughter of..."

"...of Emma and Markus," another finished, who hugged Mayla as if she were her long-lost daughter. "Oh, how glad I am. Where have you been all these years, darling?"

"You kept her hidden away, Melinda," concluded another, whose long gray hair shone brightly in the mid-morning sun. "Why didn't you trust us and tell us about her?"

"Emilia..." Smiling sadly, Melinda took the witch's hands. "You know, someone betrayed me and my family back then. Someone I trusted told Vincent von Eisenfels about Emma's hiding place. I couldn't afford to make any mistakes with Mayla. That's why I've never mentioned to anyone that I have a granddaughter."

"You could have hidden her here at our headquarters. Everyone here is loyal."

"But you're not the only ones who frequent this village. There are too many out there who would have noticed a little girl who looked like Emma."

"I rather think she has Markus's eyes," commented another, and immediately the chattering started again.

"Markus's hair color too, but Emma's pointy nose."

"Her laugh reminds me of Emma's."

"I understand, Melinda," Emilia said, tossing her shiny silver hair over her shoulder. "Even if it makes me sad and nostalgic, I understand your decision. The main thing is that the future of our head witches and thus our circle is secure."

"Thank you, Emilia."

"Are you here to get the council in order?"

"Absolutely. Mayla wanted to see our family home first."

"Wonderful. I'll come to the council meeting. I'll wait for you at the well." With that, she turned her broad back to them and disappeared among the other witches.

Melinda put an arm around her and led her away from the happily chattering women toward the house. Excited, Mayla walked beside her, curious to see what the inside of her ancestors' house looked like.

First, they entered a narrow hallway. It was small and dark, but only at first glance, for as soon as they had crossed the threshold, the fat red candles in gold wall brackets lit up, illuminating the corridor. Four doors and a staircase branched off and Melinda pointed to one after the other. "Through there is the bathroom, there the kitchen, here's the guest room, upstairs are the bedrooms and another bathroom, and over there is the living room that I'm dying to show you before we go to the council meeting."

They passed through the doorway, which was low, as if all of the von Flammensteins had always been short people, and entered the living room. Several rock crystals hanging in front of the panes of large windows conjured up rainbow-colored light reflections in the room, which was made up of simple, extremely cozy furnishings. Two comfortable armchairs and a matching couch faced the windows that looked out onto the forest outside the world fold. Only the bright glitter of the stilt wall flickered in between, conveying a feeling of security. Books and candles were stacked on shelves and mortars and bowls stood ready on a chest of drawers.

However, what attracted Mayla's gaze most of all was a small square table that stood off to the side but still seemed to dominate the room. On it was a three-armed candlestick with a big tome lying in front of it. It was bound in leather and so thick it must have been well over a thousand pages. Had it just called to her? Could that even be?

Slowly, she walked closer, strangely drawn to

the thick book. Once she reached the table, the candles lit up without her blowing on them, casting a flickering glow on the title emblazoned in gold letters on the book's cover: "Grimoire."

Goosebumps ran down her arms as she traced the large letters reverently with her finger. "Is this an old witch book?"

Melinda stepped next to her and tenderly stroked the well-tended book cover. "Yes, this is our family spell book. It's over a thousand years old. Can you imagine that?"

"A thousand years? Which spell did you use to protect it from decay for so long?"

"The Conserva spell takes care of that. It preserves objects."

"Do you have to recast it regularly?"

"Yes. Every descendant who receives the book renews the spell. The knowledge contained in this book is too precious to risk losing it."

Mayla put out her hand to open the book. She paused for a moment, and then flipped open the cover with due care. Old German letters jumped out at her. "Grimoire of the von Flammenstein family, begun by Lore von Flammenstein in 714 AD."

"Wow, it really is over a thousand years old. Lore von Flammenstein? Is that our...first family witch?"

"So to speak. This book was started by her and she is the oldest in our family tree."

Mayla reverently turned the pages until she arrived at the first entry. Its title was: "Our Family History." How exciting. Curious, she began to read.

The von Flammenstein family is one of the oldest and most powerful witch families. Their magic dates back to ancient times.

A faint tingling spread through her fingertips as if the book's magic were making her hands itchy. "To ancient times? What does that mean?"

"The time before the covens were founded."

Lore von Flammenstein was born in 683. Who her parents were is unknown.

"If the book was started by Lore, how can her parents be unknown? She had to know who she was descended from."

Melinda pointed to the sweeping signature below the entry. It read, "Tatjana von Flammenstein."

"Remember, she was the historian in our family. Tatjana wrote this entry about our family history around a thousand years later."

"But, it's the first few pages in the book — is there a spell so we can add extra pages appear in between?"

"Yes, using the Insere spell, it's possible to insert pages and spells anywhere in the book. That way it's always well sorted."

"I see. That's convenient." She bent over the family history again and read on.

Her powers must have been outstanding, as she

was spoken of throughout the witch world. Magic grew with each generation until, by the turn of the millennium, the von Flammenstein family was known as one of the five most powerful witch families.

With the emergence of the five leading witch families, more and more wars were waged between the families. Alliances were made and broken to gain presumed supremacy. It is thanks to our ancestor Mechthild von Flammenstein that this rampage came to an end. She was the first to advocate for dividing the magic and organizing the witch world through five circles.

"So, back then there was talk about five circles. I have to admit, to some extent, I can understand von Eisenfelses' anger."

"It was a difficult situation. None of us were present at the time, but I'm sure this could have been resolved more diplomatically. We cannot comprehend our ancestors' motives. They may have been right about excluding the family. Perhaps the stories about the atrocities of Melchior von Eisenfels are true. We cannot travel back in time, so we will never know the truth."

"I'll bet if we read the von Eisenfels family books, our ancestors are portrayed as traitors."

"We must assume so... and that's the story that made Vincent von Eisenfels act so brutally against the other founding families. Unfortunately."

Mayla nodded and went back to the ornate lines.

It was under her daughter, Alrun von Flammenstein, that the covens were founded. She is the head witch of the Fire Circle.

Alrun von Flammenstein. A smile broke out on her face as she pictured a red-haired woman as short as she and her grandma, with a pointed nose and a penchant for sweets.

Since then, there have always been important witches among the von Flammensteins. It is worth mentioning Myrthe von Flammenstein, who developed countless fire spells, as well as Regina von Flammenstein, who prevented the sole heir of our family from being eliminated by the Earth Circle in the War of 1453...

"Hold on. What war was that? Why did our ancestors fight the Earth Circle?"

Melinda sighed. "The founding of the four circles did not bring the longed-for peace. On one hand, Melchior von Eisenfels and his descendants tried time and again to sow discord and win over individual coven members to their side. But there were other reasons too... typical power struggles.

"So, in the mid-fifteenth century, the biggest war to date took place. The Air Circle fought on our side, the Earth Circle on the von Eisenfelses' side, whereas the Water Circle tried to stay out of it, but then briefly joined our side. Regina von Flammenstein was the head witch at the time and her two daughters were killed in the war. Only her granddaughter was still alive, so Regina asked friends of hers to give her refuge. But someone had seen this and reported it to the Earth Circle. It must have been damned close, like with..." Melinda's expression turned serious.

"...like with me?" Mayla saw her grandmother nod. "I get it. But how fortunate that it worked then as it did now." She took her grandmother's hand. "Thank you for coming in time to save me."

"Oh, please, you are my granddaughter. There is no need to thank me. Anyway, now you have to break yourself away from our Grimoire. You can continue reading later. What do you say? Want to stay until tomorrow?"

"That's a nice idea. Then I can look around the village."

"Fabulous. Okay, let's head to the council. It's time to finally clean up our circle."

"I have one quick question. Why are you so strong?"

"Everyone in our family is powerful."

"I don't mean that. Why are you considered the most powerful witch of the past centuries? How did that come about? I mean, I have to follow in your footsteps eventually..."

Melinda smiled at her tenderly. "And I'm sure you'll do it with great dignity. Regarding your question: I feel one with the world, with nature, with all living beings. I can feel the magic pulsing... not only in me but in everything that surrounds me. I feel it in my heart. Listen, Mayla, don't just learn. Obviously, it's important to know many spells, but just as important to become one with the circle of life, the circle of magic itself."

With the wave of Melinda's hand, one of the windows opened. "Close your eyes and feel what is around you. Listen, smell, but most of all, feel what resembles the feeling of magic within you."

Mayla closed her eyes and took a deep breath. She heard children laughing and a witch swearing, smelled freshly baked bread and felt... There. Wasn't there something? She focused on the tall trees growing close to the house, hearing them rustle in the wind, the birds chirping from their branches, and again, a wispy feeling rushed toward her that resembled the energy flowing through her.

Smiling, she opened her eyes again. "I think there was something."

Melinda nodded contentedly. "You see? Always try to pay attention to this power and never forget it, and you will be a part of it and it will be a part of you."

A warm feeling flowed through Mayla. She felt that energy her grandmother was talking about and it was wonderful.

Chapter Six

When they left the house, the sun was peeking through the thick clouds and sweeping over the forest, illuminating the picturesque witch village where countless residents were going about their daily lives. Some were hurrying into the forest with baskets hanging from their arms, others were baking in their piping hot ovens, and others were busy chatting about this and that. Amidst all the crowds, crows and owls circled over the crooked roofs of the houses and cats roamed the buildings' walls.

As Mayla and Melinda strolled through the village, inhabitants kept coming up to greet Melinda and to introduce themselves to Mayla. Word that the head witch was in the village and who Mayla was had spread like wildfire. Mayla hardly had time to look around in peace because she was constantly being spoken to, hugged, and asked how she was. And best of all: she felt the people were doing this in all earnestness.

In between, she managed to look around and catch a glimpse of the settlement and the villagers who were going about their daily routines. She watched a woman her age sitting on a fallen log tying a brush broom, a man in a straw hat standing in his garden sweetly serenading the herbs, and heard a woman curse loudly as her child breathed on an apple tree and accidentally set it on fire. A familiar pang ran through her stomach as she was once again reminded that she could not have children. Once that was public knowledge, how would the people of this village react? Or her grandma? Even though she'd been saved, the von Flammenstein family would die out with her...

Setting aside the sad thought for later, she ignored the familial activities and looked straight ahead. They reached a small square that had a brick fountain in the center. It was abuzz with activity. Emilia, her long skirt almost reaching the dusty ground, stood next to it, ruffling her long silvery hair while conversing with a young girl who couldn't have been more than fifteen years old. She had her tanned arms crossed in front of her chest and when she saw them coming, she said goodbye to the girl and stepped toward them.

"The Council is assembled. I can't wait to see their faces when they see you, Melinda, and realize who Mayla is."

Mayla immediately straightened her hair and tucked a few loose strands behind her ear. "So am I."

"Have you been there since I left?" Melinda asked.

"Several times, but every week you were gone, they excluded us from their meetings more and more — and four days ago, they passed a law that only Council members could enter the circle of fire and attend meetings."

"They did what? Meetings are held outside!"

Mayla frowned in disbelief. "Outside?"

"See for yourself." Emilia pointed to a square they were walking toward that was spanned by a glittering dome similar to the magical wall surrounding the village except this dome was opaque, so nobody could see what was happening underneath. Not a sound escaped — not a scrap of conversation, not a single word.

Melinda's face darkened. Two deep vertical lines appeared between her brows as she marched toward the square, raising her hands and shouting "Rumpe!" The glittering particles immediately poured off the dome like rain, revealing six wizards. The men sat in a circle on magnificent shiny chairs with flames blazing between them, spouting colorful sparks. Was that a magic fire?

Noticing the protection around the dome had been broken, the men jumped up in anger and cursed loudly. As soon as they recognized Melinda, their protests fell silent. "Melinda?"

One of them approached her. He rubbed his thick mustache and eyed her in disbelief. "Melinda, we thought you were dead."

The head witch glared at them in turn. "How dare you exclude the members of our circle? Doesn't the first rule say that anyone interested may attend council meetings?"

"We weren't sure," the man with the mustache immediately began, trying to justify the new procedures. "We didn't know who or what was responsible for your disappearance. It was for your protection that we shared our plans for finding and rescuing you."

"Don't try my patience, Bjoern Frederiksen. You couldn't wait to get control of the Circle."

Mayla listened and watched the other men, their every move, and the uncertain glances they gave each other. There were younger and older men among them, but she guessed that none were under thirty. Almost all cringed when they saw Melinda and seemed downright afraid of her reaction. Only one watched her as if he would attack her at any moment.

"What's this outcast doing here?" he suddenly spat, pointing to Mayla's ring-less hand.

"She's not an outcast." Melinda looked at Mayla invitingly, who raised her hands and let a wind — not especially gentle — blow through the gathering.

"My name is Mayla von Flammenstein. I am the daughter of Emma and the granddaughter of Melinda and therefore not an outcast, but the future head witch of the Fire Circle."

"The daughter? But Emma didn't have a daughter at the time von Eisenfels murdered her," Bjoern Frederiksen interjected.

"Yes, she did. Mayla was in hiding until only a few weeks ago."

Watching every emotion on the Council members' faces, Melinda and Mayla approached. Behind them, Emilia hissed, "It's about time order was restored here!"

Bjoern Frederiksen seemed less than thrilled that Melinda had turned up with an heiress, but Mayla read genuine astonishment in his eyes.

The wizard who had accused her of being an outcast seemed no less surprised. Four men had stayed in the background, exchanging furtive glances. Their friendly expressions were as staged as were the smiles they wore — Mayla could tell even though she had never seen them before.

"Now we can finally hold our meetings in the open again and confidently place our fate in the hands of the von Flammenstein family," one of them intoned, starting to bow exaggeratedly.

Another remarked, "Then we should hurry you into the circle so you may receive your signet ring and we can protect you as much as possible at all times. Plus, the hunters won't think you're an outcast and harm you."

Most of all, you want to keep an eye on my comings and goings, Mayla thought.

"As a von Flammenstein, no official ritual is necessary," Melinda immediately interrupted. She stepped into the circle and with a wave, the magnificent chairs of the council members disappeared and in their place appeared several pillows on the floor, where she nimbly sat down on one. "I declare today's session open."

Mayla immediately took a seat next to her grandmother and one by one the council members settled on the cushions around the fire. Emilia settled into the second row and was followed by other villagers who eyed the council members skeptically.

Melinda pointed to the men in turn and introduced them to Mayla. The one with the mustache was Bjoern Frederiksen, the one who had cried out the moment he realized Mayla wasn't wearing a signet ring was Alexander Wolf, a blond Italian man with suntanned skin was Salvatore Russo, the one who had bowed in her direction almost mockingly was Lars Willems, Manuel Brenner was a somewhat plump wizard, and Marc Jones, an Englishman, was the only one wearing a tie.

"Nice to meet you." Mayla nodded to one after the other, watching them intently. Marc Jones eyed her openly as if measuring her powers and inner strength. Undaunted, Mayla looked him in the eyes. Luckily, her grandma was with her on her first day at the headquarters. The deep connection she felt gave her the strength to face the critical looks boldly even if she didn't yet know if her powers were worthy of a von Flammenstein. For the first time in days, she felt like eating a chocolate. Darn it, why had she left without an emergency ration?

Lars Willems was the only one who gave her a friendly smile, but his eyes had something devious about them. She smiled back reservedly. She would watch him more closely in the near future! Who was the one in league with von Eisenfels? Did Tom know the answer?

She was planning to meet him that night — hopefully nothing would come up. She and her grandmother were going to spend the night there, so the problem of Georg wanting to borrow her amulet key had resolved itself. She was planning to pretend she was tired shortly before ten and retire to her room. Her heart was pounding excitedly as she thought of the upcoming encounter when her grandmother cleared her throat, which brought her back to the Fire Circle.

"I think there are many subjects that we must discuss, but we must postpone them until later. Vincent von Eisenfels has broken out of the hidden world fold and is on the loose again. Apparently, he or one of his ancestors founded their own forbidden circle years ago and its members are the hunters. They pose a major threat to public order, which is why we need to consider how to deal with the situation. Some of them are also members of our circle, so theoretically, they could be sitting among us, eavesdropping unnoticed. Suggestions?"

Again, Mayla watched the council members, whose faces showed no surprise. Were they all on Vincent von Eisenfels's side? But that couldn't be.

The villagers who were in the back rows looked at one another in horror. Emilia immediately spoke up. "No wonder there have been more missing witches lately. He must be behind it! If he is free, are we still safe in our village?"

"Don't worry, I'll refresh the spell with Mayla today. Normally, you should be safe from him here, but don't forget that every member of the Fire Circle can enter our headquarters, so the shield won't keep them out."

"I'm in favor of dismissing the council members first," Emilia asserted, her silver tresses sparkling along with her gray eyes. "In your absence, they have excelled in abusing the office and foolishly leading our circle. Their behavior has ruined their chances."

"I agree!" an older gentleman called out next to her.

"I'd give them one more chance to show us what they're made of," another commented. "It was an exceptional situation."

Mayla and Melinda exchanged glances. Once the council members were deposed, it would be more difficult to determine who was working for them and who was against them. Simply because they were power-hungry didn't necessarily mean they had sided with von Eisenfels. Still, it was necessary for them to trust the members of the council. That was the only way for them to guide the Fire Circle through the coming crisis. Consequently, it was inevitable that they'd be removed from office.

As if Melinda could read her mind, she gave her a prompt nod and Mayla spoke. Before the council leaders left their posts, she had to try to get some more information from them. "I'd like to know why the Council did what it did. How do you justify expelling the other members?"

The six men looked at each other warily. Bjoern Frederiksen spoke first, holding out his palms to them with seeming innocence.

"I didn't know where you were, Melinda. Nobody could tell us anything about your whereabouts. Every week, concerns grew that you were not only missing but dead. Since the magic stone was in your possession, we had no way of verifying you were still alive. And I didn't know anything about you, Mayla. I feared traitors among us, which was why I thought it wiser to discuss our next steps only among us council members."

"Were you even searching for my grandma?"

"We appointed and sent a squad of eight people to search for you," Manuel Brenner immediately chimed in, "but they returned without success."

None of the others added anything else.

"It's an extraordinary situation." Melinda ran her hands through her white curls and shook them. "Nevertheless, I must take the complaints against you seriously. I am beyond disturbed that you have excluded the other Fire Witches from your meetings. Therefore, I hereby relieve you of your office. However, due to the unusual circumstances that have prevailed over the past few weeks, I will refrain from investigating and release you without shame or disgrace. Does everyone present agree?"

"Yes!" Emilia's voice stood out among the chorus of others, supported by additional nods.

The council members exchanged a questioning look. No one responded with a word of dissent. Without comment, they withdrew completely as a group, as if the session was no longer their concern.

"I hope no one is so naive as to trust them," a younger man whispered to another, who nodded in agreement as the deposed council members made their way toward the gate to leave the village as one. Mayla watched them in alarm. The fact that none of them stayed at the headquarters was extremely suspicious.

"So, dear ones," Melinda said, waving the people from the back rows towards the fire. "Feel free to come closer. Since it would be too dangerous to call a meeting of all fire witches at this special time, I am appointing six of those present to serve on the council, but they will voluntarily step down from office when the next election can be held. Does everyone agree?"

An unintelligible murmur was followed by a yes that was not unanimous, but quite loud. Melinda rose from her cushion and waved her right hand, causing the fire in the center to grow brighter and brighter until it was almost white. "I appoint Emilia Richter, Constanze Zubrican, Gregor Rogalski, Olaf Hendriksen, Anna Jones, and Luca Martinez as provisional council members." The flames turned purple at each mention. "Does anyone object to any of them?"

Those present shook their heads and Melinda raised her arms. "Then I hereby declare it settled and ask the new council members to step forward."

The six rose from their seats and moved closer to the fire, where they gathered around the council seat cushions. The flames of the fire turned white once more before calming down and returning to their normal orange-yellow hues. The sparkle in the flames, however, did not go away.

Mayla peered curiously at the new council members, who at first glance seemed to inspire confidence. Hopefully her grandma had made a good choice and they were indeed loyal.

"I selected you because you have often

defended individual members or the circle as a whole through fair and courageous behavior. Congratulations," Melinda stated, providing an explanation for her choices.

Loud clapping echoed across the square and Melinda and the new leaders settled onto the cushions.

"Is there anything you want to talk about?" the head witch asked, looking around invitingly.

"Is it true that von Eisenfels is at large?" murmured Anna Jones, one of the council members, casting a concerned glance over her shoulder as if afraid she might see him behind her. At the same time, she picked at her nails, which were painted red.

"Yes, unfortunately, I can confirm that. I was held captive and they tried to steal my magic, so the spell around the world fold weakened, giving Vincent and his followers the opportunity to break it on the full moon and escape."

Gregor Rogalski, also one of the new council members, cleared his throat audibly. He was an elderly gentleman, probably in his eighties. His walking stick lay on the ground beside him. "And his followers are members of his circle? Is it truly the hunters, as you have feared for years?"

"We must assume so."

"Are you one hundred percent certain the outcasts have nothing to do with the hunters anymore?" Gregor asked.

"They've never had anything to do with each other," Mayla pointed out, which her grandmother then confirmed.

Gregor glanced at the others present, one after the other. "Then I agree with the suggestion you made in February, Melinda. The former members of the Fire Circle who are currently living as exiles should be welcomed back to our village. I am in favor of discussing it again."

"No, simply because they don't have anything to do with the hunters doesn't mean they won't still reject our rules!" someone in the second row snapped.

"They don't reject the witch order," Mayla immediately exclaimed. "They're all about stopping Vincent and his unlawful coven. They suspect traitors in the ranks of the police, in the circle councils, almost everywhere. By removing the signet ring, they consciously evaded the control of their circles and thus the councils. Otherwise, their moves would be tracked and the hunters would be immediately informed of every meeting."

"Melinda told us years ago that most of them left their covens voluntarily or had their rings taken from them illegally," Emilia recalled, patting the long skirt under which she had crossed her legs. "I also agree. To take on Vincent, we must overcome old prejudices and work together."

"Vincent is unstoppable," called out a pale woman sitting so far in the back that Mayla had to crane her neck to find her. "He killed my parents and my brother. Nobody is safe from him."

"Do you believe he'll remain quiet now that he has his circle? Let's say we were to acknowledge it. What do you think would happen?" Luca Martinez, also a new council member, suggested.

Emilia stared at him in disbelief. "Acknowledge it? The family has brought nothing but ruin to the world!"

"Simply because a few members of the family have been cruel, doesn't mean the rest of the family is like that," Mayla pointed out. "We cannot condemn an entire family simply because one member acted terribly!"

"You don't know them!" the pale woman cried out, her voice breaking. "Don't make the mistake of trusting any of them."

"Show me a von Eisenfels who doesn't care about power, who hasn't murdered anyone, and we can talk about it. Until then..." Emilia replied, as if that were the end of the discussion.

Tom...

Mayla peered at her grandma and could tell she was busy deliberating. A quick side glance was enough to let Mayla know she was thinking the same thing. Perhaps Tom could ring in peace by taking over the coven as head witch? Would her grandma dare to continue trusting him? Would she defend and support him in front of the others? But then again, it stood to reason that

Vincent von Eisenfels would never agree to such a solution.

As renewed discussions on the subject broke out, Melinda raised her hands reassuringly. "As long as we haven't met a peaceful von Eisenfels, we'll have to postpone this decision. I'm going to send my owl to notify all fire witches of the new council members. The next session will be held at the new moon!" With that, the fire in the circle went out and the people formed groups to continue discussing the new situation.

Melinda lifted her head and Mayla followed her gaze until she saw Merlin circling above them. She thought she could feel her grandmother and her spirit animal communicating with each other when the owl flapped its wings vigorously and flew away.

"How does Merlin spread your message? He can't speak or write."

"He watched and listened to our meeting. He will send those images to every spirit animal of all the fire witches and they will pass it on to their witches."

"Hold on. That's how Vincent could have communicated with others from his prison, right?"

"Actually, it only works for head witches to the members of their coven. It is part of the togetherness that we constantly carry with us through the signet rings. But since there appears to have been a Fifth Circle before he was captured, it might be possible. It would be one explanation."

"And now that you're informing all fire witches, Vincent von Eisenfels will soon know the old council members have been replaced."

"We must assume so. But I consider the new council members to be absolutely loyal witches with integrity. It was important that the leadership of our circle not be in the hands of our adversaries."

"I agree. But I think it's even more important that we meet with the other covens, with the head witches and the council members. We need to get an overview of who is on our side."

"You're absolutely right. We need a safe, neutral place where we can talk to each other undisturbed. Though once Vincent finds out about the meeting, we'll all be in grave danger. I doubt old Alessia and her descendants would be willing to leave the Water Circle headquarters."

Mayla frowned. "How and where could we meet without von Eisenfels finding out, dang it?"

"It has to be spontaneous, just in case he hears about it, so he won't be able to trap us. Now the question remains where we could hold such a meeting..." Melinda twisted one of her curls around her finger until an insightful expression appeared on her face. "We will create a world fold and only tell those invited. That way no uninvited guests can appear."

"But even in the councils there are spies.

They'd pass it on to Vincent in a heartbeat." Mayla toyed thoughtfully with the heart on her necklace. "One possibility would be to only meet the founding families first — and the current head witch of the Earth Circle. Who is that anyway? Surely not old Bertha?"

"That would also be a possibility. And I think that might work. Maybe Alessia will agree to it. Incidentally, the current Earth Circle head witch is Phylis Drimakou."

"A Greek?"

Melinda nodded.

"And how was she chosen? The founding family, de Rochat, has been wiped out."

"Even at your age, it becomes clear which women have particularly strong abilities."

"Only women?"

"Witch energy is a different matter than muscles. Magic is a primal feminine power and the older women are, the more powerful they become. Therefore, the heads are always the oldest living women of the founding families. So, you won't become head witch until I bite the brushwood..."

"...which hopefully won't be for quite a while!"

"Don't worry, dear, I'm certain to live to over a hundred and twenty thanks to my healthy herbal brews. By the way, you should start drinking them too."

Mayla would grimace in disgust when she saw the brownish-green goo on the table that her grandmother drank every day before breakfast. She had tasted it twice already and wanted to spit it out immediately. Just a few extra years weren't worth it to her . "So, how did the procedure for choosing the head witch in the Earth Circle work?" she asked, hoping to change the subject from the ghastly drink.

"Once the head witch dies, the five strongest witches are invited by the Council and through a ritual, the most powerful of them is chosen and made head witch."

"Awesome. My friend Heike would be amazed if I told her about that..."

Her grandmother looked at her thoughtfully. Something was on her mind, Mayla could tell. "Better stay away from your friend for now. Only until Vincent and the hunters are no longer such a threat. Keep in mind, it's for her safety."

"Don't worry, I would never put her in danger — nor am I planning on seeing her anytime soon. Though I'm sure she's worried again because she hasn't heard from me in so long. Even so, I won't contact her until Vincent has been... dealt with. So, how do we let the other head witches and their families know about our meeting? Will we let our spirit animals transmit the images?"

"That won't work since they aren't members of our coven. I suggest we use a Nuntia spell that our spirit animals deliver to their companions."

Mayla clapped her hands. "Great! I'll finally

learn how to cast it. This is so important. I've read all about it but never used it. One more question. If the spirit animals of two warring witches meet, would they hurt each other or fight?"

Melinda shook her head. "Never. Unlike us, animals understand we are basically one. Magic connects us no matter what circle we belong to and what goals we pursue. The animals wouldn't hurt each other, set a trap, or anything of the sort."

"Good. I don't want to put little Karl in danger when he does things like that for me. Do we perform the Nuntia spell in the house?"

"Let's perform it in the forest so I can also gather some fresh herbs and give you your daily lesson in herbal magic."

Mayla rolled her eyes furtively. "Agreed." She wasn't all that interested in plants, but she grudgingly admitted to herself that she'd have to learn the basics sooner or later.

While she knew the fundamentals of witchcraft by heart and couldn't wait to learn more hands-on spells, she rarely consulted the herbal book. Although it was no less lovingly designed than *Witchcraft 101* and richly illustrated with depictions of plants, Mayla's eyes struggled to stay open almost every time she opened it up. Everyone had their preferences and anything plant-related wasn't her cup of tea. Maybe the vivid lessons in the forest would turn out more exciting than poring over those pages, even though she had a hard time imagining it...

Chapter Seven

With a spring in their step, the two women hurried to the magical gate that led out of the witch village. It lit up again as they walked under it and Mayla thought she felt something tingle inside her, but maybe it had just been her imagination.

"Before we enter the forest, we need to increase the security around our headquarters. I haven't been here for a long time and Vincent is free again — these are more than dangerous times! Come back under the archway and take my hand. Together we need less power."

"Wonderful, another new spell!" She stepped back under the glittering gate, which was translucent and flickered as if it were on fire, and clasped her grandma's hands.

"The spell is called 'Tuta caput ignis in omne tempus,' meaning 'eternally protect our Fire Circle

Headquarters.' At the same time, visualize that this glittering, sparkling stilt wall and gate are encompassing the entire village. Merge with the magic that lies hidden around us and your magic will grow stronger."

Mayla closed her eyes with concentration and relaxed her shoulders. She heard her grandma take a breath and, as if someone had silently counted to three, they began to say the incantation at the same time.

"Tuta caput ignis in omne tempus!"

Mayla opened her eyes, curious. The stilt wall lit up. For a moment, it appeared as if it formed an impenetrable shield, then went back to glittering and sparkling, as did the gate.

Mayla stared in amazement at the shield around the witch village and felt remarkably exhausted, which was why she could have really gone for a nap right about then. It must have been a powerful spell. "Why can't we use the ring of fire to protect the village? Then we wouldn't need to expend so much energy, right?"

"Because it only works short term and it is tied to our presence. However, whether we are in the village or not, the spell we just cast lasts for several months."

"When we got here I still saw the glitter around the village. Was the protection so weak that we had to repeat it?"

"It was about time. Besides, the world out there

has grown more dangerous. And of course, as the head witch's successor, you need to know how it works. All right, let's not waste any time. Let's go to the forest. I know a secluded place where there are plenty of medicinal herbs and we can cast the Nuntia spell unobserved."

Mayla began walking, exhausted. "Are you as beat as I am?"

"No, as a witch, age is an advantage." Melinda gave her a mischievous wink. Smiling, Mayla trudged through the forest next to her.

"Now the villagers are better protected and Vincent can't get in, right?"

"Exactly. It is important to repeat the protective spell regularly. If it hadn't been for that annoying incident in the south of England, I would have done it long ago."

Annoying incident? Mayla couldn't help but grin. "You mean being imprisoned by the von Eisenfelses?"

"Imprisoned." Melinda grunted indignantly. "It wasn't all that bad. So, Mayla, remember, you have to renew this spell at least once a year, preferably at the full moon, otherwise, the witches at our head-quarters won't be as safe as they need to be."

"Luckily, the traitors didn't tell anyone the shield was weakening because Vincent could have forced his way in long ago."

"Since this knowledge is only reserved for the

founding families, I had to show it to you. You won't find that spell, nor anything about how often it should be renewed or when it was last spoken, in any book. So, remind me in a year, at the latest. It is of vital importance."

"Well, I haven't experienced any memory lapses yet!" With a wink, she nudged her grandmother's side. "Don't worry, you're simply..."

"Don't you dare say I'm old, Mayla von Flammenstein! You make it sound like my time is up! A von Flammenstein matures to the end and grows more vital with each passing year. You'll see."

Mayla chuckled and walked on. "That sounds wonderful. I saw the glittering wall grow stronger. Why doesn't the shield work longer?"

"A normal fold will keep the protection working for years, but this is the Fire Circle headquarters. In this place there lies a greater potential for magic and the fold is located on a powerful energy point of the earth."

"Powerful energy point?" Heike had often talked about that too — and how often had she smiled inwardly at her friend?

"They exist worldwide and each one is used by witches, be it for headquarters, hiding places, residences, or rituals."

"How exciting." She would look into it once the danger from Vincent was over. She thought optimistically about the future that awaited her and consciously pushed away the thought that all her dreams were on shaky ground.

The scent of pine needles was hanging in the air, a few birds were chirping in the treetops, and then a twig snapped and they saw a deer in the distance dashing away.

Mayla hesitated. "A deer? I've seen a few birds, but never any big creatures. Does that mean animals that are not spirit animals can also enter the world folds?"

"Some, yes."

"So does that mean that animals disappear before ordinary human eyes?"

"Strangely, it only works for world folds that are in the forest anyway."

"Seriously? So, because we are in Rein-hardswald, animals can enter the world fold where the headquarters are hidden? Why is that?"

"They can enter the forest, but only spirit animals can get into the witch village itself. I think it's because the forest is full of magic anyway and the line between a fold and the human world isn't as defined as it is in the city. The laws of magic cannot necessarily be explained. Magic and reason are often at odds, so it's important to observe and study magic without trying to fully understand it."

"Fortunately, you're not giving me complicated explanations like with hidden world folds." She laughed. "I see a clearing ahead. Are we going to cast the Nuntia spell there?"

"Let's go a little deeper into the forest. Do you know the necessary spell?"

"Yes, I came across it in *Witchcraft 101*, but I never used it."

At the mention of the book, Melinda clapped her hands. "Did you know that I wrote the book for you?"

"To be honest, I was wondering about that..."

Her grandma nodded. "I was so happy when Angelika told me that you bought the books straight away. Like they called to you."

"Maybe they actually did... So, you wrote them for me?"

"Yes. For years, I've wondered what the circumstances would be like when your powers awoke, which would have happened with my death at the latest. While I never planned on keeping you in the dark for so long, even the best witch can be killed by an unpredictable spell sooner than planned."

"I've never seen you this modest..."

"Pride comes before the fall. I wrote the books so I wouldn't set you loose on the witch world without any guidance. They contain the essentials, and so does the herb book." She winked and raised her index finger.

"I'll learn the herbal spells too, but for now, it's all about the Nuntia spell. I've always wanted to try it. So, if I remember correctly, you need an object to wrap the message in, but first you have to make a video of yourself. To be honest, I still don't understand how it's supposed to work without a camera."

"Camera... video... you and your man-made gimmicks! As always, everything stands and falls with your concentration. First, you recite the incantation, then you speak the message into your hands, for other witches it's the wand, and then you project the... recording, to make it easier for you to understand, onto the object. Understand?"

"We'll find out in a moment."

"There's another clearing ahead. First, we will use the Obsurdesce spell. This means nobody passing by can understand anything we say."

"I remember hearing about that at the police station, which has one cast on it. I remember when I was watching the guard with... Tom, I couldn't hear anything they were discussing inside. I thought the spell was limited to buildings."

"Remember this, Mayla: Magic knows no boundaries."

"Wonderful. Let me cast the spell, I could use the practice. And it's easier to remember when I do it myself."

"Go ahead. Your powers should have recovered by now. Do you know how the Obsurdesce spell works?"

Mayla tapped her lip with her finger. "I read about that too in *Witchcraft 101*. It was somewhere in the middle. Well, I have to visualize the room that is to be acoustically sealed off. Since we're not in a room, I suppose I'll have to map out an area with my eyes and visualize it, right?"

Her grandmother nodded happily. "Exactly."

"Okay." Spinning slowly, she mapped out an area about twenty by twenty feet in her head, then closed her eyes, and thought, *Obsurdesce!* She opened her eyes excitedly. Nothing had changed. She didn't see a shimmering wall like with the Tutare spell and she still heard the animals in the forest. "I guess it didn't work."

"There's only one way to test that." Melinda took a few steps away and yelled, "Say something!"

Mayla spread her arms impatiently. "If I can understand you, you can hear me too!"

Melinda didn't respond, and after a moment, came back smiling contentedly. "I didn't hear anything, but I noticed the incredulous frown on your forehead. Now, let's get straight to the Nuntia spell."

"It worked? Fantastic!" Mayla stooped eagerly for a pinecone, anxious to learn the next spell. Once she mastered the Nuntia spell, she could send personal messages to Tom — if that was what she wanted to do... She held a pinecone under her grandma's nose. "Can we use this?"

"Naturally. We'll need two more, one for each circle leader." She bent down and picked up two more cones. "It's best if we speak the message together, but you cast the spell. So, after you recite the Nuntia incantation, say 'Incipe' before we start recording and 'Desine' when we're finished. Then, you pass the recording on to the cones by saying the Nuntia spell again. Ready?"

"So, transfer the recording to the cones with my hands? I'll do my best! Ready." With great concentration, she imagined herself speaking a message that was recorded like a memory and then thought, *Nuntia!* She stood next to her grandmother and nodded to her. "Incipe!"

Her grandmother immediately turned to the imaginary listeners and clasped her hands in front of her skirt.

"My dear witch sisters and witch brothers, I come to you today with good and bad news. First, the good." She looked at Mayla, who cleared her throat. Introducing herself to an absent audience felt strange. Mayla sighted a young fir tree barely two meters tall and focused her attention on it. She had to talk to someone, after all.

"Hello everyone, my name is Mayla von Flammenstein. I am the daughter of Emma von Flammenstein and her husband Markus and therefore the heir to the Fire Circle. I look forward to meeting you personally!"

"You heard right," Melinda immediately confirmed, "this is my granddaughter. And we urgently need to meet in person. Vincent von Eisenfels has escaped from the hidden world fold and together, we must discuss how to deal with the situation. For this purpose, I'm going to create a world fold later on that only we head witches know about, so we're absolutely safe. We'll be expecting you tonight at seven o'clock."

At seven? Hopefully the conversation wouldn't last too long and make her miss her meeting with Tom!

"We're going to secure the fold so only the founding families, and of course you, Phylis, can jump there. See you then!" Melinda nodded to her.

"Desine!" A smoking sphere the size of an orange formed in front of them and Mayla instinctively picked it up. It felt warm but also so fleeting, as if it could disappear before their eyes at any moment. Focused, she imagined the ball penetrating the three pine cones. "Did it work?"

"I hope so!"

"Hold on, shouldn't we convey a different message to Andrew Montgomery, the head of the Air Circle? After all, he already knows me."

"Oh, that'll take too much time. We'll leave it at that."

"All right. So now we call our spirit animals to deliver the messages?"

"Exactly." Melinda was already closing her eyes and Mayla did the same.

Little Karl. How she looked forward to seeing him again. Beaming, she thought of the sweet black cat and the next moment, she heard his high-pitched squeaking, which could hardly be considered meowing. She saw the tip of his tail sticking out between individual ferns until he sprang out and ran straight toward her, meowing loudly.

"There you are, sweetheart." She bent down and took him in her hand. She stroked his velvety soft fur tenderly and they remained with her forehead on his for a moment before Melinda cleared her throat, interrupted them.

"How cute. So, you are little Karl? I've heard a lot about you."

Little Karl squeaked and started to purr, and Mayla hugged him again. Out of the corner of her eye, she spotted Merlin the owl sitting on her grandmother's shoulder. He looked at Mayla with her big yellow eyes and hooted softly.

"I already know you." Mayla smiled at the nocturnal animal. "You warned me when I was in my grandma's hideout. Thank you."

Again, the owl hooted softly. Melinda held out two of the cones, which the raptor grasped with one of his claws, and then appeared to mentally communicate the addressees. Mayla waited until the owl brushed his head against Melinda's cheek, spread his wings, and flew away.

"To whom should little Karl deliver the message?"

"I figured he'd take it to Phylis. Can you tell him that?"

Mayla stroked her little cat's head. She didn't

know Phylis and didn't have any idea what the earth witch looked like, but in her mind she said to him, "The message is for Phylis Drimakou, head witch of the Earth Circle. Can you deliver it to her or her spirit animal, please? It's important."

Little Karl kneaded her hand and took the cone in his little mouth. It looked funny because the cone was almost as big as the young tomcat. But when Mayla carefully lowered him to the ground, he ran off as if the cone weighed nothing.

"Take care, little darling," Mayla called after him, even though she didn't know if he understood. To be on the safe side, she sent him cautionary thoughts that were similar to those a mother sends to her little one going off on their own for the first time. Little Karl responded with a warm feeling of confidence and love, and instantly he was gone. "He's still so small. Isn't it reckless to have him run errands for me without his mama?"

"You have to stop thinking of him as an ordinary animal. Even though he's very young, he has powers we don't understand, and he instinctively uses them correctly. Nothing will happen to him."

"Let's hope so, by goodness!" She felt responsible for him, but her grandmother had emphasized several times that the spirit animals were superior in terms of wisdom and powers to the witches and wizards. She probably should have faith.

"Now, let's get to the herbs." Melinda bent down and pointed to a few stalks and leaves.

With a tired expression, Mayla eyed the numerous plants her grandmother was stroking tenderly. This time, she couldn't avoid the herbal lesson. Sighing inwardly, she sat down next to her grandmother and listened, however difficult it might have been, as she told her about the plants and their properties.

"Stinging nettles are important plants. They are looked down upon, but their healing powers are enormous. If someone has been hit by a curse that threatens to burn them, they are always a good home remedy. You don't even have to brew a potion with them."

"So how can I use their powers?"

"Think about it."

"I could use the leaves. Would I place them on the affected areas?"

"Remember, with burns, you are supposed to soothe them."

"So, I rub them over the spot."

"Exactly. If you rub them between your fingers beforehand, you increase their powers. And whenever you use herbs directly without a potion..."

"...I use the Sana spell."

"Very good. Let's get to the lady's mantle. Can you spot it?"

Mayla searched the forest floor and spotted the circular leaves, slightly frayed at the edges. "There."

"Correct. Lady's mantle helps with many female matters, both during childbirth and to relieve menstrual problems. Just drink it as a tea. Does this plant have other useful properties?"

"The dewdrops that form on the leaves in the morning are a powerful ingredient in many potions."

"Exactly. You should regularly walk through the forest in the morning and collect a few vials full so you always have enough on hand. Now put your fingers on the leaves and feel their magic."

Mayla did as she'd been told with her eyes closed when suddenly a crow flew toward them, squawking loudly. Mayla immediately jumped up. "Is that Vincent von Eisenfels?" Alarmed, she pointed at the black bird that was heading straight for her with something in its beak.

"I have no idea. Stay alert."

The two quickly rose and watched the bird as it dropped a drinking goblet in front of them into the soft moss and immediately disappeared again. Mayla directly bent down and pointed to an engraving. "It looks like it's from Artus and Angelika."

Her grandmother nodded and snatched the goblet from her hand. Even as she raised it to her lips, she whispered, "Aperi!"

Immediately, the vessel floated into the air, spun in a circle, and became translucent. At the same time, a figure became visible, growing bigger and bigger until Violett was standing in front of them. Her pale face even whiter than usual, she gasped, "Melinda, come to the castle immediately!" The next moment, the apparition disappeared along with the goblet.

Mayla and Melinda looked at each other and without hesitation, grabbed their amulet keys and thought, *Perduce nos in arcem!*

Chapter Eight

"Here!" they heard Violett's desperate voice coming from the hall even before they landed in the entrance hall. As soon as their shoes touched the ground, they immediately ran, then came to a halt. Anna was standing by the sofa, sweaty and with deep cuts on her arms and face, then started staggering towards them.

"Help!"

Manuel was lying on the couch, twitching. With a pained face, he held his side and wriggled back and forth. Around him stood Violett, Eduardo, and von Donnersberg.

Immediately, Mayla and Melinda were with them. "What happened? Where's Susana?"

"They were on to us," Anna gasped. "There were so many, we didn't stand a chance. Susana distracted them so I could get Manuel to safety. She should be back any moment."

As if on cue, the well-read Spaniard rushed in from the hall and hugged Anna. "Everything okay?"

Anna nodded and pointed to Manuel, who was about to lose consciousness. He was burning up. "I don't know what curse they used, but his strength is fading by the minute."

Melinda raised her arms and got Manuel to float horizontally in the air so she could look at him from all sides before she landed him softly back on the sofa. He groaned and she bent over him, feeling his pulse, his torso, his neck, and his hands — just like a doctor would. Frowning, she pointed her fingertips at his chest, which was heaving frantically. "It's not a known curse. What have they done to you?"

Artus and Eduardo stepped back and waited anxiously with Mayla, Violett, Anna, and Susana. Silently, they stood and watched as Melinda began to help with nimble fingers.

Suddenly, Manuel's head fell limp to the side as he lost consciousness. His forehead was glistening with sweat although goosebumps had formed on his arms. Melinda danced her fingers faster and faster across his chest, murmuring one spell after another, but none of them seemed to help. "Vola!" her voice sounded through the hall and a little later, a wicker basket soared in and landed elegantly on the stone floor next to her.

With practiced fingers, she pulled out one tincture after another, circling the vials over his chest until she paused. She quickly uncorked one of the bottles, ran her little finger along the inside of the neck, and then held her finger under Manuel's nose, but he showed no reaction. She repeated the process with three more potions, but he didn't respond to any.

Georg and John came sprinting into the hall, their expressions of horror immediately visible. In a whisper, Anna again summarized what had happened while everyone followed Melinda's hand movements with anxious looks on their faces.

"My God, he's going to be okay, isn't he?" Mayla whispered, hugging herself.

"Don't worry. So far, Melinda has always gotten everyone back on their feet," Violett affirmed, but a deep worry line had formed on her forehead as well.

Suddenly, Melinda closed her eyes, took a deep breath, and put her hands on his chest. Her palms began to glow while her face paled and her body shook. She trembled more and more violently while she kept her hands on Manuel's chest, but he wouldn't regain consciousness.

"Grandma?" Mayla wanted to go to her, but Georg and Artus held her back.

"Let her be. Melinda needs quiet."

"But she is losing too much power. Don't you see how she's shaking?"

Melinda almost faltered, but she clenched her teeth and kept herself upright. Mayla saw a bright glow emanating from her that spread over Manuel, but it didn't penetrate him. Her grandmother's hands trembled even more.

Suddenly, Angelika was next to her. Where had she come from all of a sudden? She put her hands on her shoulders and whispered, "That's enough, Melinda. It is too late."

Too late?

Melinda's shoulders sagged as she dropped her hands in exhaustion and looked at Manuel with infinite sadness. His panting subsided and suddenly, his chest stopped rising and falling and remained still.

Silence spread throughout the castle hall. All eyes were on the motionless maverick whose face would never again beam over a philosophical writing or whose hands would never again hold a pen to set his thoughts to paper. His chair was gone, as if it knew it was no longer needed. Manuel was dead, murdered by the hunters with a malediction that not even Melinda von Flammenstein could heal.

Angelika took his hands and folded them across his chest, stroked his black-grey hair once, and put her hand on his cheek.

Mayla swallowed and took Violett's hand. Her friend began to tremble violently and covered her mouth with her right hand, her eyes wide.

"It can't be... I thought your grandma could heal anyone!"

"I could no longer help him..." Melinda turned to them, her face worn and her voice infinitely sad, almost stunned. Even she didn't seem to understand what had just happened, what curse was capable of rendering her powerful knowledge useless.

The afternoon passed in deep sadness. Hardly anyone said more than was necessary. Everyone was shocked at how powerful the spell must have been if Melinda von Flammenstein could not heal him.

"Could the hunters have used an old, forgotten curse?" Angelika pondered quietly.

"I can't explain it any other way." Melinda was noticeably weak. She hardly spoke a word and was deep in thought. Mayla could see that she had gone beyond her limits. She badly needed to rest to regain her strength, but Mayla knew she should never suggest such a thing to her grandmother. Somehow, she had to help her, relieve her, so that Melinda wouldn't think that all the responsibility was on her shoulders alone.

"Maybe we should look through your old book, Angelika, that you showed me to break the Exsugo spell. Do you remember that old curse that drained my grandma of her powers? Maybe in the book we'll find some of those maledictions that the hunters have been shooting lately. That way we can prepare and maybe brew a few potions or something."

Angelika nodded. "Good idea. I'll take care of it."

"I'll help you," Anna murmured. It was the first time she had spoken since Manuel's death. Von Donnersberg immediately took advantage of her rediscovered voice. He asked her and Susana for a detailed description of what had happened that afternoon. They were told over and over again what had occurred and he kept asking until he'd heard every last detail.

"We jumped to Elm Town together even though we had two amulet keys. Yesterday, we watched the hunters hand out leaflets and give speeches in the market square. It was about how oppressed the populace apparently is under the dominance of the four circles, how arbitrary the head witches rule, and how little control the councils can exercise. The best example is allegedly the Fire Circle, in which Melinda dismissed the council members without consultation and entrusted six other people with the office on her own."

Alarmed, Mayla listened. "'That just happened

this morning. If they found out so quickly, one of the council members might have been a hunter himself."

Melinda's eyes narrowed to slits. "Or any of the others present."

"They're trying to stir up dissent against the established order," Pierre mused aloud. "Merde! Manuel was my friend! They'll pay for this!"

"Mine too." Violett's chin dropped almost to her chest and she whispered, barely audibly, "He was the one who brought me to you when I was alone and abandoned after my parents were killed by the hunters. He found me and told me about you."

Mayla took her in her arms and Violett remained in her embrace, sobbing. Her friend had never told her about this and Mayla stroked her red hair sympathetically. How many of them had lost their families to the von Eisenfelses and the hunters?

"Were Vincent or Tom anywhere in the marketplace among the hunters?" von Donnersberg asked.

Anna and Susana shook their heads and the Spaniard continued, "We did see Marianna — but only after Manuel was hit. She must have spotted us and exposed us. The others' faces were unfamiliar to me, they couldn't have known us, but they were definitely hunters. All in all, maybe twenty."

"What happened after you arrived, before

Manuel was hit and you spotted Marianna?" Mayla asked.

Anna wiped away a tear from under her eye with her knuckle. "We looked around carefully. Since none of the hunters seemed familiar to us, we felt safe and mingled unobtrusively with the audience. The speaker claimed that Melinda is preparing for sole rule even though power is shared among all witches and wizards. Someone next to us asked how they came up with that since Melinda had been abducted by the outcasts led by the outlaw Tom Carlos and his gang. That's when Manuel revealed to him that the men who were distributing the leaflets and making the big speeches were in fact the hunters who had abducted and murdered numerous witches." Anna's voice broke and Susana took her hand under the table.

"They're distorting the facts," von Donnersberg remarked.

"They've done that from the start," Melinda pointed out. "But, until recently, no one believed them. So, what has changed in the last few weeks?"

"Since your disappearance, the number of witches being abducted and murdered has risen sharply. There have even been a few newspaper articles about these women and men being deprived of their powers. People are probably scared."

"Let me guess," Melinda began, glaring. "Tom

and the outcasts were named as having been responsible."

"No," Mayla interjected. "The article I read clearly blamed the hunters. But they said Tom was their leader." She would never forget the newspaper account of herself as the confused witch.

Pierre clasped his hands in front of his chest. "Still, why are people suddenly listening to the hunters and saying we're the criminals?"

"We were portrayed as the criminals from the start," Angelika interjected. "That hasn't changed. However, until recently, they lumped us together with the hunters."

"People in Elm Town were definitely confused, but some listened with interest." Susana shook her head, her large earrings swinging around her neck. "I don't know how many of those present believed the hunters."

Anna clenched her hands. "Anyway, none of us are safe now! Marianna gave our names and descriptions. She might even pass them on to the police. In any case, Vincent knows who makes up the opposition. We must prepare our families, protect them, maybe even bring them here. Obviously, we should also warn all other members who do not belong to the Inner Circle that they are in as much danger!"

Tired, Melinda rubbed her closed eyes. "We have to act faster. We should seek out everyone who has ever expressed criticism and join forces.

Build a network so that Vincent cannot divide us. Only together do we stand a chance against him."

"Luckily, we have you on our side," Susana said. "You are the strongest witch of the past centuries, after all."

Melinda gave a tired smile, but she finally seemed to have overcome the shock of discovering for the first time that her strength was not enough. Mayla watched her regaining energy minute by minute. Her grandmother slowly patted the Spaniard's hand.

"We'll work it out, my dear. So, anyone who knows someone who is not yet a member of the opposition and could possibly be on our side, go see them and try to open their eyes. Also, go to your families and warn them of possible attacks. We must not leave them unprepared."

Georg banged his fist on the table with determination, causing it to rumble. "I'll go back to my colleagues. John will accompany me — we already discussed it. I'll find some supporters, I'm sure of that. It would be good if I could borrow your amulet key again, Mayla."

Her heart started beating faster. "Unfortunately, I need it myself. I still have plans with my grandma tonight."

He peered at her curiously. She was almost certain he had figured out she had a meeting with Tom on her agenda, but that was nonsense, of course. If witches could read minds, someone would have told her by now, right?

"We'll lend you our amulet key," von Donnersberg said, coming to her aide unexpectedly. Georg thanked him.

"You want to go to the police?" Anna peered doubtfully at John. "You aren't wearing a signet ring — we wouldn't want them lock you up and for us to end up having to get you out of one of the jails."

"Jesus, they wouldn't get me." The Englishman folded his muscular arms across his chest demonstratively, but the unassailable confidence had vanished in the face of Manuel's death.

Georg held his hands, free of any signet ring, under Anna's nose. "Since I've become an outcast too — even if it went down a bit differently — they won't hurt him."

Susana tapped the table angrily with her fingernail and Georg frowned at her. "You might think it was different for us, but like you, the ring was ripped off my finger by the police."

Georg looked at her, dumbfounded. "I'm sorry, what?"

"It happened two years ago. I was going to a Fire Circle meeting and was walking around Kassel beforehand. I watched three men in an alley charm a woman to make her powerless. I immediately ran and broke the spell, allowing the innocent lady to escape. Then, before I knew it, a police officer appeared behind me. I wanted to explain to him what I had witnessed, but he was one of the hunters. He ripped my signet ring off my finger and laughed. Then I was an outlaw and they could do whatever they wanted to me. Luckily, I had a protective amulet with me. Before they could harm me, I jumped, and from then on, I've been an outcast."

Stunned, Georg shook his head. "Didn't you go to the police to explain?"

"Of course I did, but the cop who took the ring from me was stationed at the same precinct and had already written a report on me."

"What?" Mayla stared at her wide-eyed. How many of those present had the same experience? And how many people were out there who had never been part of the opposition? No wonder Tom had warned her about the police so many times and didn't trust Georg. "How did the policeman know your name?"

"Our names are linked to our signet rings."

Georg stroked his close-cropped beard. "That's so hard to believe. What happened next, Susana?"

"One of the police officers at the station pretended to lock me up but instead took me out through a side passage. He knew about his colleagues' unfair methods and no longer wanted to stand idly by. I managed to escape, but as I found out later, he was jailed so as to silence him. I was thinking about where to go when I happened to see

Melinda in Ulmen City. I immediately told her everything and she brought me to the opposition."

Melinda smiled at her encouragingly. "I remember that day well."

"Luckily, you found your way to us unscathed," Angelika said emphatically .

Mayla looked at Anna, who pressed her lips together. "So then what happened to you? How did you end up at Donnersberg Castle?"

Her eyes hardened. "Like Susana, I had help, only it wasn't from a nice policeman at the station. When it got really bad, Tom helped me get out of there and brought me here."

No wonder she was so suspicious and defended Tom vehemently.

"What terrible experiences. Sorry, I didn't mean to remind you." She smiled at Anna, who unexpectedly put her hand on hers.

"It happened a long time ago and I'm glad I ended up here and found the truth."

Meanwhile, Georg sighed. "As you know, I too have been fighting an inner struggle for a long time. For a while now, I've realized that black-and-white thinking is outdated and the outcasts need to be decriminalized. Whatever Susana's story might sound like and whatever impression it must give, not all cops are bad. Many of my colleagues were just as stunned as I was when I spoke to them. Sure, some knew about some colleagues' lawless activities and looked the other way. But you will see, a large part of my staff will stand by our side. They are ready to listen to you and will believe what you say."

"That would be great. We've been in hiding long enough." Von Donnersberg stroked his stately cloak patiently. "Let's hope the days of calling us outcasts come to an end."

Chapter Nine

Manuel's death and the silence that accompanied it weighed heavily on spirits. They decided to lay out their murdered friend in one of the rooms for the time being so that anyone who wanted to could say goodbye to him in peace. Thomas Winkler, who was finally feeling better, offered to pass the news on to the family. Manuel's parents or siblings were the ones to decide on the manner of burial.

While Angelika decorated the room with flowers and Violett washed Manuel and made up the bed, Melinda and Mayla said goodbye. It wasn't long now before the start of their meeting with the heads of the four circles, and Melinda wanted to make a detour first.

"We need to talk to Bertha. I'm sure she will join the opposition too. After all, she has been hosting guests in her hotel for decades, no matter the history that led her to it."

Mayla could picture the hunchbacked old woman standing in front of her. "Good idea. Bertha took me in my first night as a witch and told me a few things about the circles over breakfast. She was one of the first to give me some answers. I look forward to finally seeing her again."

"Then let's not waste any time."

After a quick bite to eat, the two jumped to the world fold that Mayla had stumbled into on her first day as a witch and landed in Bertha's hotel.

It was early evening and they had less than an hour before they'd be leaving for their meeting with the head witches. Melinda still hadn't created a fold where they could meet, so they kept an eye on the time.

Bertha shuffled toward them at once, her thick snow-white hair tied in a tight bun at the back of her head and her hands on a stick. "Hello, you two mighty fire witches. I was wondering when you were finally going to come see me." Her whiskey voice remained husky and her dark brown, almost black eyes lit up as she waved her hand toward a secluded seating area. The armchairs were in an alcove in the entrance hall across from the breakfast room and stairs, so no guests would be able to walk right past them.

"Thank you, Bertha. I couldn't have come sooner or I would have." Melinda hugged the old witch and it was obvious that the two had been friends for decades. Because of the old woman's strong hunchbacked posture, the two were about the same height, and when Mayla saw them side by side, she wondered how powerful old Bertha was. Ever since her grandmother had suggested she be attentive to all the magic around her, Mayla had been trying to notice it and Bertha emanated enormously strong powers.

Smiling, she gave Bertha her hand. "I'm glad to be here too. It was kind of you to take me in back then even though you couldn't have known who I was."

"It goes without saying, dear." A sly grin crossed her thin lips. "I heard you narrowly escaped death, Melinda?"

Her grandma waved it aside emphatically. "Anyway, today is the first day I'm back on the road again. That's why I'm only coming to visit you now. How are you doing?"

"Oh, I can't complain. The family is getting on my nerves, but I'm sure we'll work it out." Bertha winked at Mayla conspiratorially. "So, where has your journey taken you today so far?" she asked, turning back to Melinda.

"We were at the headquarters. I had to make sure everything was in order and cleaned up the council. I am confident I can guide our circle of new council members safely through these trying times."

Bertha watched her with interest as if waiting for Melinda to reveal more. But when she just remained silent, and Bertha didn't ask any more questions. Instead, she turned to Mayla. "You still don't have a signet ring." Again, a statement, not a question — the old woman hadn't changed.

"No, but you don't mind, do you?"

Bertha didn't reply, but she looked back and forth between her and Melinda with interest. "Why are you two here?"

Mayla took her heart-shaped pendant between her fingers and let it slide back and forth on the chain. Bertha watched the gesture out of the corner of her eye as Melinda spoke. Her eyes widened for a moment and while she listened to Melinda, she continued watching Mayla.

"Bertha, did you hear that Vincent von Eisen-fels escaped the hidden fold?"

"I heard a rumor. So, is it true?"

"I'm afraid so. But that's not all. Apparently, he founded his own coven, which the hunters belong to, years ago. That's why we're on the road. Everyone who wants to maintain our order must stick together now. You are one of the most powerful witches I know — even if you like to hide it from others."

"Oh..." Bertha waved her wizened hand, her dark eyes still on Mayla's chain.

"No, no, the time has come to put our cards on the table. I was surprised that you didn't accept the invitation to the Earth Circle headquarters to run for head witch. But I realize that your powers must have strengthened tremendously over the last few years. I feel it. We could really use you on our side!"

"On your side?" The old woman laughed. "I'm too old to fight."

"What about your family?" Mayla interrupted, taking her hand off the chain. "Wouldn't you like to leave a world where your children and grandchildren can be safe?"

"Oh, they don't care."

"Where do they actually live? Also here in the fold? Then they will have to care about the whole thing soon."

"They emigrated." Bertha waved her hand. Apparently, that was the end of the matter for her.

Melinda clasped her little hands together. The gesture made her look calm, but her impatient expression was there for everyone to see. "Bertha, we've been friends for so long. You were by my side when Emma died and helped me through my pain."

Bertha looked away from Mayla and watched Melinda warily. "And even though we've been friends for so long, you never told me Emma had a daughter..."

"You won't make me feel guilty for that. Someone I trusted back then betrayed me and Emma. I couldn't take any chances with Mayla."

"And yet Vincent was trapped in the fold."

"You know as well as I do that he has powerful supporters, all of which we haven't uncovered."

Bertha nodded with understanding and looked again at Mayla, who was playing with her pendant. "Honey, now that Vincent is free and there appears to be a metal circle, you'd better take that jewelry off. You wouldn't be the first to be strangled by her own necklace, all thanks to a von Eisenfels."

Listening, Mayla sat up and put her hands on the jewelry. "But my mother gave it to me. It provides me with strength and protects me."

"Your mother?" Bertha tilted her head slightly and peered at her so intently, a shudder ran down her spine. She had the feeling that the old woman could see into her inner being and quickly averted her eyes.

"Not from Emma, I didn't know her at all, but from Anneliese, my foster mother. The woman I was staying with."

Bertha nodded sympathetically. "Still, I wouldn't risk it. You're still at the top of Vincent's list — don't forget that, dear."

With her eyes closed, Mayla cupped the golden heart. She remembered it like it was yesterday. At the time, she had been fifteen years old and Florian, who was two grades ahead of her, had turned her down. Utterly devastated, she had confided in a friend who had laughed uncomprehendingly and called Mayla a stupid naive child.

That statement hurt her more than being rejected by the handsome athlete.

Her mother had overheard it all and comforted her. "My darling," she had said, "There are some who call kind, genuine people naive simply because they know there is good in us. They're trying to admonish us so we'll be as cynical and suspicious as they are. But I think it takes great strength to keep your heart pure, despite bad experiences, and continue to believe in the good." She had taken off her gold chain with the heart-shaped pendant and put it around Mayla's neck, and she hadn't taken off the piece of jewelry for a day since then. "Of course, it is important to learn from mistakes and to act wisely. Promise me, sweetheart, that you will always use your wits, but don't lose faith. Listen to your heart."

Mayla looked up questioningly at her grandmother, who nodded in confirmation.

"Bertha is right. I didn't even notice the chain. Otherwise, I would have told you sooner. Vincent is a master of metal like we are of fire."

"What about the chain for the amulet key?"

"The amulet keys are part of ancient magic as are the chains used to wear them around the neck."

"I understand. So, I guess I have no choice." She sighed. Another step that further removed her from her former life... Since it was essential, she unclasped it and let the necklace and pendant slip into her cupped hand. She wistfully put it in her trouser pocket, which unfortunately had no closure. She put her hand protectively over the fabric around the chain so that it didn't fall out. She really needed a good place to hide the necklace until this whole madness was over.

"So, Bertha, think about my words in peace. I'd like you by my side to defeat that wretched von Eisenfels once and for all."

The old woman's eyes seemed to glow even darker. "I'll think about it, but don't expect to see me by your side. I'm too old and this whole thing is none of my business. In addition, my family invited me to their home. I'm supposed to spend the summer with them. I'm considering closing the hotel for a few weeks."

Mayla clasped her hands in her lap. "What about the future of the people here? You could go visit your family later when..."

"When what?" She peered questioningly at Mayla while Melinda leaned back and waited.

Mayla clenched her hands and looked resolutely at Bertha. "When we have defeated Vincent."

"Will you?" Bertha looked at her searchingly, but shook her head before her gaze made Mayla too uncomfortable. "My family is gone and all I'm committed to is this hotel. Neutrality has always been my top priority, you know that. That's why people come to me. Everyone is welcome here, no matter where they come from."

They couldn't persuade the old woman and time was running out. "We still have a lot to do. It's a pity we couldn't convince you to fight for the good with us. Should you change your mind, let me know." Melinda and Bertha hugged each other for a long time and said goodbye to each other.

Melinda grabbed Mayla's hand. "We'll jump to a secret place. Hold on tight, I'll take you with me." In the next moment, the hotel's wooden walls and furniture whirled around them in a mixture of brown shades. They lifted off the ground and a strong green mixed into the colors until they landed on soft ground.

Chapter Ten

They landed in a dense forest where not a soul was to be found. A few steps ahead was a tranquil clearing where tall forest flowers provided splashes of pink.

"They look nice. What are these flowers?"

"Dwarf orchids. I like to collect them for stomach or intestinal problem potions. But now we must hurry and create a world fold before the coven leaders jump."

Mayla surveyed the idyllic clearing until something occurred to her. "How do they know what spell to use to get here?"

"They'll just say, 'Perduce me ad colloquium cum Melindae,' or 'take me to the meeting with Melinda.'"

"I see." She stepped into the meadow. "This is where we're going to create the fold, isn't it?"

"Exactly. It's best if we do it together again. That way, we conserve energy and you learn."

"Wonderful. Count me in. But wait, there was nothing about that in the Basics book."

"It would have been too conspicuous if I had written it in there since only members of the founding families can use the spell anyway."

"And the von Eisenfels..."

"Correct."

"It's a good thing my magic was released before you resigned. Why did you wait so long? I mean when I was small, okay, but I could have been initiated and trained, at the latest, when I was ten or fifteen, maybe twenty."

"I struggled with the question a lot, believe me. I postponed it for a long time because you were happy and I didn't want to tear you out of your familiar surroundings... Especially not as a child. I didn't want to see your sad face when I told you your real parents were dead. And then you were studying and so happy at the same time and not much later, you met that stupid Henning. Excuse me, darling, but what were you thinking choosing him, huh?"

"Now don't change the subject. Remember, you promised never to interfere in my choice of men. Besides, we're not together anymore."

"Which, strangely, was not initiated by you..."

"Gosh, I was happy. We had a wonderful

couple of years together and I thought he was the man of my life, who I wanted to..."

"Who you wanted to what?"

Who I wanted to start a family with, Mayla thought, but she didn't voice it. She didn't want to see her grandmother's face when she found out the real reason for their breakup. And at that moment, she understood why her grandmother had been hesitant to break the spell and tell her the truth over the years. Tenderly, she looked at Melinda and nodded to her.

"It's okay. Let's create the fold — before the meeting falls apart because we haven't finished in time."

"I'm never late finishing! So, come with me to the clearing, right in the middle." With unusually long strides, Melinda hurried ahead with Mayla following. The sun had passed its zenith hours ago, but it would be light for a few more hours, so it lit the meadow with its warm rays.

"You have to imagine the space you want to seal off. We'll take the entire clearing, understand? Visualize this clearing closing once, so it disappears, then opening again. We'll cast the spell 'Contrahe, munde' spell! Are you ready?"

Mayla tilted her head left, right, and left again, and placed her hands in Melinda's so she was facing her grandmother in the middle of the clearing. One last time, she surveyed the area that was to become a world fold and closed her eyes. In her mind, she imagined the clearing shrinking until it collapsed in a vertical beam of light and vanished. Then, the flash reappeared, opening up, and the clearing pushed the trees apart again so that it looked the same as before. Since she'd watched a hidden fold open when her grandmother had been rescued in southern England, her memories made it easier for her to focus on the creation of a new fold and visualize it.

"Ready."

"Contrahe, munde!" they cried out in unison, causing the space around the clearing to glow brightly. When Mayla opened her eyes again, she thought she could still see something like an electrical charge near the trees, but a little later, the sparks disappeared.

"Wow, did it work?"

"Of course it did."

"And we're in the middle of the fold, right?"

"Exactly."

"Phew, I am exhausted, like I ran a marathon — not that I've ever run one."

"You will recover quickly. Rest until we begin. We can only wait now anyway and keep our fingers crossed the others will come."

"Are you doubting they'll show up?"

"Andrew and Phylis will not dare refuse my invitation. Alessia, however, has been chilly towards me in recent years. We haven't seen each other since Emma's death, since she wouldn't so

much as dip as much as a big toe out of her headquarters. Although I'm still hoping she'll show up,
deep down I know she won't."

They waited a while, both growing impatient.
While Melinda paced, stomping the blades of grass
into a trail, Mayla kept rubbing her bare neck and
collarbone, missing the familiar feel of the chain
and pendant. What if she were to lose them? Again
and again, she made sure the piece of jewelry was
still in place by reaching into the pocket of her
trousers. It had never occurred to her that the chain
could be her undoing. Luckily, old Bertha had
warned her.

How much longer before the circle leaders
showed up? Glancing at her watch, she saw it was
one minute to seven. Who would be the first to
arrive? Would everyone jump simultaneously?
What would Alessia De Fonte's decision be?
Would she again refuse to help and continue to
isolate herself in her headquarters? Or had the time
come when she would grow bolder? Somehow,
Mayla could hardly imagine it after all the stories
she'd heard, but hopefully she was wrong.

As the big hand jumped to the twelve o'clock
position, two sparks of light appeared a few feet in
front of her. In the next moment, Andrew Montgomery was standing in front of them. He was still
wearing the long black cloak and his dark eyes were
extraordinarily suspicious as he swiftly blew a ring
of wind around him, from behind which he could

safely study the area. Mayla again noticed how charming he looked, but there was something dark in his eyes that she didn't like. Peering closer, she clearly saw the green in his eyes. He no longer veiled it — but his irises seemed almost black.

At the same time, an old woman materialized next to him, her white hair in stark contrast to her suntanned skin and dark eyes. The wide sleeves of her turquoise dress swung around while she used her wand to cast a mound of earth around her, which apparently also had a protective effect. This had to be Phylis Drimakou. Her brown eyes glanced around, her gaze open and friendly even though she had cast a protective ring around her.

There were no more sparkles. Was Alessia late or would she actually be a no-show?

"Welcome, Andrew and Phylis." Melinda spread her arms and smiled. "I understand you want to protect yourselves, however, we told no one but you about this meeting and this world fold was just created. I assume we are safe. Once we're complete, we can cast a ring of protection."

With a wave of her wand, Phylis lowered the earth wall. Her broad laugh radiated so much warmth that Mayla couldn't help but smile.

"How gratifying to meet the next generation of the Air and Fire Circles. I am delighted you are both doing well, Mayla and Andrew, and that we have the privilege of welcoming you among the head witches."

"Thanks. I'm happy too." Mayla looked curiously at the old woman, who, judging by her moderate wrinkles, had to be slightly younger than her grandmother. Her aura was powerful though she appeared humble and peaceful. Then Mayla turned to the heir to the air dynasty. "How are you, Andrew?"

He kept the protective circle of wind around him and stopped a few meters away from them. His facial expression was impenetrable, not revealing a thing. The wind around him actually increased the distance he was determined to keep between them. "I have no room for complaints."

"I am happy to see you again. Have you joined your circle?" Melinda tried to reach him.

He didn't say anything, but rather responded with a simple nod. "Why did you call us together? I hope you now have a plan. What are you going to do about Vincent?"

"Shall we wait a moment?" Mayla looked around questioningly. "Maybe Alessia will be here in a few minutes."

Andrew's expression darkened even more. "Certainly not. She abandoned our families a long time ago. She doesn't need to show up."

"With so much old rage, we won't be able to ally, dear Andrew," Melinda said admonishingly, her look stern.

"Maybe I don't want to. I've gotten along fine on my own for the past few years. I'll bring

Vincent down without you, no matter what the cost!"

No matter what the cost? It almost sounded as if the air heir would stop at nothing to get his revenge. "I think we can achieve more together than alone," Mayla replied, even though she suddenly felt uneasy at the thought of fighting by Andrew's side. Why was he so distant and suspicious? He had helped them free her grandma, so he trusted her and her abilities.

He lifted his chin and it seemed he was looking down on her even more. "I'm here and I'd love to hear what you have to say. But I am not willing to waste what little time we have left waiting!"

As if on cue, the air next to Mayla began to crackle and sparkle and Mayla wanted to let out a cry of joy. A moment later, a woman in her fifties was standing next to her. Her blonde hair was streaked with gray and her blue eyes twinkled as she looked at them in turn. Was this Alessia? But she was so much younger than the other two head witches...

"Good evening, my name is Gabrielle. I am the daughter of Alessia De Fonte, and the future head witch of the Water Circle." Her voice was firm and her posture confident. One by one, she looked them in the eye without fear, presumably to gauge their reactions to her presence.

Melinda, Mayla, Phylis, and Andrew stared at her in surprise — apparently nobody had really expected a member of the water founding family to appear — when Mayla caught herself and stepped toward Gabrielle. She stopped at a suitable distance. "Fantastic, Gabrielle, I'm Mayla, Melinda's heir. I'm glad you came."

"Am I right in assuming your mother isn't coming?" Melinda asked.

"That would have been a miracle!" Andrew pointed out, eyeing Gabrielle disapprovingly.

"My mother won't come." Gabrielle looked at them in turn. She was the only one who had waived a ring of protection upon arrival. "Is it true Vincent von Eisenfels is free again?"

Melinda brushed one of her white locks from her forehead. "Yes, and we'll need every available force to stop him."

"I will fight him at your side. I promise!"

"I'm so glad to hear that." Melinda smiled at her.

"What's your plan?" Andrew repeated his question, ignoring Gabrielle.

"We don't have one yet," Mayla admitted. "He started a forbidden circle. Surely you can tell us more about that, Andrew?"

Phylis and Gabrielle eyed him suspiciously. "How do you know about it?" the earth witch demanded.

"I lived among them for a while to spy on them so I could prepare my revenge. And yes, they established a fifth circle a long time ago. The metal coven. All hunters are members of it, in addition to their previous covens. They are all something like spies for their orders. And the only ones who understand that are the outcasts, which is why the hunters track them down so fiercely and the police denounce them."

"How many moles are there in the police force?" Mayla asked.

"I can't give you the exact number, but at least two or three in each station. Decades ago, they planted a few people in almost every strategic facility."

"How do the hunters communicate with each other?" Melinda asked. "They still have the signet rings of the circles on their fingers, but how does that work with the metal circle?"

"They all wear a small, nondescript amulet, barely the size of a thumb."

"And Vincent started this coven before he was captured?" Phylis asked.

"It was one generation before that. His father, as far as I'm aware, but I could be wrong."

"And is he still alive?"

"Not that I know. Anything to do with the family itself was never discussed. It was almost impossible to find out anything about the von Eisenfelses. Everything is kept under wraps."

Melinda nodded. "Distrust, even of one's own coven members. That's like Vincent — and that's the weak point in his circle!"

Andrew shook his head vehemently. "You won't be able to destroy him simply because of a lack of trust! And we must! Forever!"

"It would be enough to imprison him in a world fold again," Phylis pointed out. "He's not that young anymore. Prison for life."

Gabrielle clasped her hands in front of her. "If we all cast the spell together this time, it could work permanently."

"Lock him up? No!" Andrew looked at each of them in anger. "I won't allow that. He wiped out my entire family. He deserves nothing but death."

"First, we have to render him harmless," Mayla reminded them. "Although, if we all curse him together, it shouldn't be a problem, should it?"

"The key is doing it together," Melinda pointed out. "Together we cannot be defeated. And nobody should endanger this community by going it alone." She looked at Andrew searchingly.

Meanwhile, Mayla was trying to be as inconspicuous as possible. Would her grandmother consider her meeting with Tom tonight a solo effort? Most likely. But nothing and no one would stop her. She had to meet him, come what may.

Melinda continued, "Do any of you have any knowledge about old curses?"

While Phylis and Gabrielle shook their heads, Andrew narrowed his eyes. "Did the hunters use one?"

"Yes." Mayla told him about how Manuel had died from one.

"They're experimenting with old curses on prisoners," Andrew immediately explained, while Phylis and Gabrielle looked at Melinda in horror.

"You couldn't do anything about it?" the earth witch asked incredulously.

"No. I still don't know what spell it was. Many of the old curses have been forgotten."

"Almost all..." Phylis's mouth turned down. "How terrible that the killing should continue. And they practice these maledictions on prisoners, you say? How did they learn about the ancient magic?"

Andrew explained, "The way I understand it, Vincent and his family have many of the old books in their libraries. Once they have tested the effect, they pass excerpts on to the hunters. I, myself, never had access to any of these libraries, let alone any of the books."

Phylis ran a hand through the white, chest-length hair. "So we have no knowledge of the antidotes for these curses, right?"

Gabrielle folded her pale arms across her chest. "I'll do some research in my family's library. I might discover something. As soon as I find out anything, I'll let you know."

"My family's belongings were all destroyed." Andrew glared at Gabrielle as if she had something to do with it. "But I learned a few things during my time with the hunters. For ancient maledictions, you always need the old magic — that is, the original united form of it — as the antidote."

"Like when we freed my grandma?" Mayla asked.

"Yes, for example, but there are also potions that can be used to unite the old power. However, I don't know how they work. I only learned how to use the forgotten curses, not how to cure someone of them."

Phylis and Melinda exchanged thoughtful glances.

"Perhaps it would be beneficial if we could cast those maledictions as well," the earth witch suggested.

"They're dangerous," Melinda pointed out. "We all have only a fraction of the old magic left within us, depending on to which circle we belong. If we play with the forgotten spells, it will destroy us sooner or later since our power is no longer designed for those spells. Arrogance is the operative word."

Andrew looked at her disdainfully. "You're only saying that because you're afraid of burning your fingers. But we must fight with weapons as mighty as the fifth circle. The hunters, at least, don't seem to have had any problems with the forgotten curses so far."

Mayla, Gabrielle, Melinda, and Phylis looked at each other and none of them asked about the old maledictions. They all had a deep respect for ancient magic — something that the hunters, and possibly Vincent, lacked. Mayla too had learned enough from her grandmother not to play with it lightly.

"How can we stop von Eisenfels and his hunters?" she asked, bringing the conversation back to the subject at hand. "If his weak point is his distrust and possibly his arrogance, how can that help us?"

"What do you think about offering to recognize his coven?" Phylis mused. "That could eliminate the centuries-old potential for conflict in one fell swoop."

"Never!" Andrew's dark eyes blazed with anger. "After all his crimes, we must not reward him. He must be punished. If you don't see it that way, we're not on the same side!"

"Unless someone other than Vincent is the head of the Iron Circle." Melinda looked at each of them in turn. "Everyone here knows Tom Carlos," she added, glancing sideways at Gabrielle. "Or heard of him, right?"

Gabriella nodded.

"He has been by my side for a long time and is a member of the opposition's Inner Circle. Do you know he's Vincent's son?"

"You mean he could be the head of the Iron Circle?" Gabrielle asked.

"You must never trust a von Eisenfels!" The protective barrier of wind around Andrew whirled more violently as if he were standing in the middle of a tornado. It was a reflection of his emotions and clearly revealed how much anger he had inside. How could they manage to get through to him? "If that's your plan, I'd rather fight alone!"

Melinda raised her hands as if to break through his protection, but then lowered them again. "Andrew, we need a permanent solution. Those who only seek revenge are thinking short-term. Honestly, I don't know if we can trust him either but we have to consider all possibilities."

"I will destroy von Eisenfels — and all of his family! If you think this line deserves a reward for the atrocities they have committed over the past centuries, then you are dumber than I thought!" With those words, the hurricane vanished around him, and the next moment, he did too.

Phylis' mouth twisted in disappointment. "I can understand his bitterness, but that attitude won't do him much good. He will never be able to compete with Vincent. Von Eisenfels will kill him and in doing so, will weaken us all."

Melinda slowly shook her head. "Naturally, he believes he's invincible, but just wait until he faces Vincent. He may come to his senses in time."

"I'm also not sure that approving the fifth circle would be a solution." Gabrielle tilted her head back and gazed up at the massive canopy of oak and beech that framed the clearing. "The ones belonging to this coven have brought much evil upon us."

Mayla shook her head uncomprehendingly. "Who are these people who heedlessly follow Vincent and turn a blind eye to his brutal ways?"

"Apparently, he promises them power." Again Gabrielle stroked her plump chin, which was so pale it appeared she hardly ever left the house even at the Water Witches' headquarters in Italy. "Also, their powers are limited, and if what Andrew said is true and they're practicing forgotten spells, maybe they're hoping to gain strength by doing so."

"Power is seductive," Melinda said emphatically, "but few people realize how much responsibility comes with it."

Gabrielle nodded. "Before we start thinking about whether or not to accept the fifth circle, we need to figure out how to stop Vincent. Apparently, he has continued his rampage and we must stop it at all costs!"

"We have to set a trap for him." Mayla thoughtfully stroked her hair, which she had pinned up with a clip at the back of her head. "If we plan another meeting like this and spread the word, he might show up. But our people will be there too and then we can capture him."

"That could work."

Gabrielle shook her head. "That provides an opportunity to destroy us all. Then there will be no one left to stop him."

"Well, then, it'll be your mother's responsibility," Phylis whispered, and Gabrielle gave her a warning look.

"Don't think I don't know how cowardly she's acting! But I will not allow bad things to be said about her or any member of my family in my presence. She tried to protect us all and she succeeded."

Phylis's face darkened. "Your family, yes, but as head witch of the Water Circle, she is not only responsible for you, but the entire circle and the witch community itself."

"Phylis." Melinda put a hand on her arm. "We mustn't start blaming each other. That will tear us apart faster than Vincent could. Things happened the way they happened and I can't go back in time. But we can learn from past mistakes. We have to coordinate and pull together. If each circle fights only for itself, then the deck is stacked against us. Vincent is strong — damn strong — and that's why we should join forces against him."

Phylis nodded and shook hands with Gabrielle. "Melinda is right. I'm sorry. The past is the past. I am happy you are here to support us."

The water witch reacted with forgiveness and then looked at Mayla. "If we set a trap like that for him, we'll have to plan it carefully. Nothing can go wrong, nothing can be left to chance. It's not only about us, it's about the future of the entire witch world."

Melinda pushed up the sleeves of her dress. "Then we'd better get started right away."

Chapter Eleven

Mayla conjured up four chairs and a table from the surrounding branches and twigs, then sat at them with Phylis and Gabrielle. Meanwhile, Melinda blew an extra ring of fire around their meeting point so they were safe and could focus on planning.

Together they would create a secret world fold and hide their people in the immediate vicinity in good time. Anyone who wanted to face Vincent would probably get their chance because one thing was certain: Vincent wasn't going to show up alone either! But there were a lot of details that needed clarification. For example, how could they prevent the moles in their ranks from learning this was a trap and warning Vincent? How could they make everyone present stand side by side without erupting into other conflicts like the one between the outcasts and the police?

Planning took hours. Again and again, Mayla glanced at her delicate watch. It was already after nine-thirty and still no end in sight. Her date with Tom was in less than half an hour.

Was he already there? Was he waiting for her longingly? Did he want to win her back? Explain everything to her? Or was it a factual meeting that would be devoid of any emotion? What should she brace herself for?

It hadn't occurred to her that it was a trap, not even for a moment. But now as the meeting drew nearer, she wondered if she wasn't being gullible. Since Vincent was free again and he was his son, his father surely was watching over him. In the message he'd sent before they freed Melinda from the von Eisenfelses' manor, Tom had mentioned that he would return to the hunters. That his fate was now sealed. But was that really the case? Were there really no chances left for him? For both of them?

"Gabrielle asked if you could talk to Georg about the police officers," Melinda asked, breaking through her thoughts.

Mayla glanced up. The three witches were staring at her as if they could read her mind, as if they knew she was planning to meet Tom. She cleared her throat decisively. "Of course I can talk to him. What about?"

"Mayla, concentrate. This is very important!" her grandmother admonished.

"Sorry, it's really late. We should stop soon." She yawned exaggeratedly and stretched.

"We're far from finished here!" Melinda said emphatically, while Gabrielle repeated her question.

"I want to know if you could talk to Georg, your friend in the police force, so that he only reveals our plan to colleagues he trusts one hundred percent."

"Of course, I'll speak to him. I'd assume he'd only pass it on to those he considers friends anyway. He's now realized that there are traitors among the police and will choose wisely — I am convinced of that."

It was growing dark and Melinda turned three sticks into fat candles by blowing on them. The flickering light cast dancing shadows on the witches' faces as they continued to debate their options. An owl hooted in the distance, but it wasn't a warning call, just a nocturnal hoot.

Mayla's mind stayed focused this time, even if she kept glancing furtively at the time, and soon realized with horror that it was five past ten. Darn. Would Tom wait for her? Or would he think she was standing him up and just disappear again? She wanted to send him a Nuntia spell to make him wait. But she could not conjure it up without arousing suspicion.

The meeting lasted until just after half past ten. Extremely nervous, Mayla was the first to get up from the chair after they'd agreed on the last details and said goodbye.

"Excuse me, but I have an appointment with Georg. He's waiting for me and I'll talk to him about our plan right away."

Melinda peered at her suspiciously. "Georg isn't even at the castle."

"Yes, he is now. We made an appointment for half past ten. So, if we're done here..." She avoided meeting her grandma's eyes, and instead, turned to face Phylis and Gabrielle. Hopefully the candle-light would hide the telltale blush she felt on her cheeks.

A deep crease appeared on Melinda's forehead and her grandmother started to object, but Gabrielle waved her off. "Let her meet her friend. We've discussed everything important. I'm leaving now too. Thank you for inviting my family and I pledge from the bottom of my heart that you can count on me. Like you, I will use the next few days to research ancient magic and the curses that go with it. When they attack with such spells, we have to be able to defend ourselves. Unless one of us cancels our meeting in advance, we will meet at the Weisser Stein the day after tomorrow at 6 p.m. for further planning. Okay?"

At the Weisser Stein? Shoot, Mayla hadn't been paying attention. If she were to ask where it was, it would only make them more suspicious. It would be best if she inconspicuously asked Georg or Violett about it. But now she really had to leave.

"I am pleased we met. Take care and we'll see you in two days."

Shaking her head, Melinda placed her hand on Mayla's. Her grandmother knew she was up to something, Mayla could see it in her eyes. But that didn't matter. She had to go. Now! Immediately! Before Tom was gone. Shoot, twenty to eleven. Please, Tom, wait for me!

"See you later, Grandma." She quickly kissed her wrinkled cheek and squeezed the protective amulet in her hand. She imagined Lake Constance in front of her and the spot behind the rocks where she and Tom had landed together so many weeks ago. The place where he had told her his name and, shortly thereafter, taken her to see Tauber, the detective, for the first time. Would he still be there? She squeezed her eyes shut and thought, *Perduce me ad lacum Brigantinum!*

The flickering of the candles faded away and where she landed, it was pitch black. A strong wind immediately tugged at her hair, there was soft sand under her heels, and she heard the steady rushing of the waves. Then nothing. Shoot, Tom must have been long gone. She was over forty minutes late, after all!

Nervous, she blew a small flame on her finger. When the surroundings were illuminated by the small flickering light and a large shadow emerged from the darkness in front of her, she was startled and jumped back. The flame immediately went out again.

"Mayla..." His voice was rough as ever. Despite the darkness, she saw his form and heard his soft, familiar laugh. She had almost forgotten how tall he was. Her heart was beating so fast, she thought it might pop out as she blew a new flame onto her fingertip. As the light pushed back the shadows, his green eyes flashed and she tilted her head back to look at his face.

Tom. He had waited for her...

He was wearing his dark leather jacket and a light shirt underneath. That was all she could make out in the darkness. The eyes in his familiar, narrow face showed deep worry that possibly hadn't let him sleep much. The shadows around his eyes also testified to this. Or was it just because of the dim light? Something also simultaneously flashed in the green of his eyes that sent a pleasant shiver down her spine and made her heart beat a bit faster.

"You waited." She couldn't think of anything better to say.

"I didn't know why you weren't on time, but I was certain," he pressed his fist to his heart, "that you would come..."

For heaven's sake, she wanted to throw herself crying against his chest and sink into his arms. The shadows made his lips appear even more lustful and she recalled their kisses longingly. How wonderful it had felt, how familiar and how intoxicating. But she clenched her hands to maintain control. He mustn't know what he still triggered in her... Not until she could be certain why he wanted to meet her —when not just her heart screamed that he was good, but her mind was fully convinced of it as well.

"Why did you summon me here?"

Tom took another step toward her, but he seemed reluctant to take the last one between them. "I..." He eyed her, her face, her tousled hair, his hand twitching as if wanting to tuck the loose strands behind her ear. But he didn't. Laboriously, as if his arm were trying to resist, he lowered his hand and suddenly stood in front of her so helplessly that her heart tightened.

"Please don't think I ever betrayed you, Mayla. I know I should have told you the truth about my family, but... I haven't told anyone since I walked away from them. No one knew who I was and I was torn between living a life of absolute solitude and tranquility and helping stop my father and his allies. I kept delaying that decision, even after I had accompanied your grandmother for a long time. But then I met you..."

Her stomach was on a roller coaster as she listened to his words, not uttering a peep so as not to interrupt him.

"I didn't know who you were, believe me. But I

couldn't leave you to the hunters. Since then, I watched you and together, we found out who you are. From that moment, it was clear to me that I couldn't lead a life in the shadows. I had to help stop my father. You must believe me, Mayla. At no time have I used you or lied to you for nefarious reasons. I tried to keep my distance from you, but I couldn't. Please tell me you believe me. It's so incredibly important to me."

The corners of her mouth twitched at his disarming honesty and a smile spread across her face. Warmth flowed through her and a feeling that she thought she had lost a few days ago returned to her heart. It was hope.

"Of course I believe you, Tom!" She sighed happily and started to take the last step between them, but he moved back almost imperceptibly.

"I'm not here to whine to you. I wanted you to know that I never toyed with you and that you can trust me. I've always been serious about you, Mayla, very serious. But more importantly, I was with the hunters."

The sudden change of subject shocked her at least as much as the distance, which he had put between them with his slight movement. Tom. Why couldn't they just be together?

"You were with the hunters?" Her voice sounded strangely foreign and leaden to her ears, as if someone else had spoken and let the words out of her mouth by magic. She would rather have discussed other things with him now that he was finally with her again, tangible and approachable. She wanted to reach out and stroke those well-defined cheeks, his dark brows, even his forehead. She wanted to put her hand on his chest and feel his heart beating. But she didn't. She stayed where she was and just looked at him. "Why did you... I mean... you have something important to tell me?"

"Yes. You've already learned about the fifth circle, right?"

"Why didn't you tell us about it sooner? You must have known about it since you were born."

"I would have given myself away. And until recently, it made no difference whether the opposition knew about it or not. But things have changed. I met... him."

"You mean your father?"

He nodded. "Vincent has always been a megalomaniac and unscrupulous. But the time he was imprisoned made it worse. It's no longer enough for him to lead a fifth circle and get credit for it. He wants revenge. And he wants absolute domination. Mayla, he awakened the ancient magic."

"We realize that. Manuel is dead. He was hit by one of the forgotten curses."

"Manuel is dead?" He remained motionless for a moment, rubbing his face until he caught himself. "You need counterspells. I didn't think of that, dammit. I'll research it, but there's something that, to the best of my knowledge, might help. You must brew a potion and incorporate the ancient magic into it."

"Andrew told us about that too. How do we prepare it?"

"One member from each circle must help. You need to brew strong healing potions — your grandma will know which ones are suitable. And use metal for stirring so that our element also flows into it. It could work that way. And of course, you must make a fire on the ground, use fresh water, and let fresh air feed the flames. That's fundamental."

"Very well, I'll let my grandma know."

"Do that. Also, it's incredibly important that you tell the others that my... that Vincent has started to unify the old power within himself."

Her eyes widened. "Like the witches of old? How did he manage that?"

"Back when he started wiping out the founding families, he saved their magic. He obtained fire magic from your mother, Emma, earth power from the de Rochats, air energy from Andrew Mont-gomery's parents, and he always had the magic of iron in him. All he needs is water to reach his goal. If he accomplishes that, your grandma and all the others won't be able to stop him."

"For heaven's sake! Can he still be defeated if he already has so many powers in him?"

"It will grow harder every day. Mayla, you have to tell your grandma and the others. The family of water witches must remain at their headquarters at all costs. None of them should put themselves in danger — it's no longer just about the family itself, but about the future of all of us."

"Gabrielle... she..." Shoot! Gabrielle had just grown braver and come out of the headquarters. She shouldn't do that again!

"Alessia's daughter? What about her?"

"I met her. She was with us. I hope nothing happened to her. I have to tell my grandma about this." Darn it, how were they supposed to proceed with the plan they had hatched earlier? She turned and grabbed the amulet key — the others had to know about it immediately! — when her gaze fell on Tom again. She stood still for a moment, studying his distinctive features and green eyes.

"Mayla, I..." Abruptly, he took the last step. He approached her and in what seemed an infinitely long moment, placed his hands on her cheeks.

"Tom..."

She parted her lips longingly and stood on her tiptoes, but he stopped again. This time, though, she wasn't going to let him back away! She grabbed his head resolutely and pulled him down to her. The kiss that followed was so beautiful and complete... more beautiful than any before. It was sweet and full of promise and at the same time, the fulfillment of all her dreams and desires. She sank into the connection and momentarily forgot all the threats and worries.

When they broke apart after a little eternity, he looked at her in surprise but then chuckled softly. "So fierce, Heiress von Flammenstein?"

"I... Tom, I want you. No matter who your father is, no matter what your family name or your real name is. You are a good person, I see that and feel it. I trust you and I want you to do the same."

Smiling, he tenderly tucked a loose strand of hair behind her ear like he had just been waiting for it. "I trust you, Mayla."

With those words, her heart was freed from a tremendous weight. "Don't you want to come and tell the others yourself? Most are willing to listen and trust you."

"No, I can't. My position is too valuable. As Vincent's son, I will have access to a lot of information and I will update you on the important steps. I also need to research antidotes and ancient magic. But I'm glad we both..."

"...found each other again?"

"Yes. Especially after I heard that Vincent and you had met. He said I told him about you. Believe me, I only mentioned what was necessary to reassure him. And to gain access to the secret library."

Mayla's ears pricked up. "Access to the secret library? Does it have books on forgotten maledictions?"

"Yes. My family, especially Vincent, has gathered many of them and has been doing research for numerous years. Several writings are stored there that deal with the secret spells that are actually only reserved for the founding families. And, of course, tomes on ancient magic. I've already found out a lot, but I have to be careful. He must not grow suspicious. That's why I usually only read at night and early in the morning. Nobody would find me there at that time. And I've already discovered some interesting information."

"Tell me."

"Apparently, Vincent needs a place that was forgotten along with the old magic. A place where the combined magic worked and is sacred."

"What does that mean?"

"I don't know yet. But I need to find out if such a place exists. Well, I should head back before he grows suspicious."

An intangible fear crept around her heart and she squeezed his hand even tighter. "Will you be safe?"

"Hopefully all of us will be soon."

They kissed one last time before Mayla said goodbye to him with a heavy heart. With any luck, Vincent wouldn't harm his only son...

Chapter Twelve

When Mayla landed in the entrance hall of Donnersberg Castle, no one came to greet her. She immediately felt that the mood there was still depressed — no wonder, given that Manuel had died less than twelve hours ago. It was also quite late, meaning that many had probably retired to bed.

Before she entered the castle hall to pass on Tom's important message, she focused her thoughts on one of the boxes of chocolates in her room and thought, *Vola!* A short time later, the box flew in and landed in her hands. Overjoyed, she opened the lid and let her eyes wander over the tiny treasures. A rum praline was just the thing for a day like this. She relished the chocolate melting on her tongue and closed her eyes. She was finally feeling better and everything was settled between Tom and her. How had she been able to go without sweets for so long? Then, she braced herself before joining the others.

The amorous grin on her face disappeared when she entered the gloomy hall. Was the information about Vincent so important that she should get everyone out of bed or was it enough to divulge it in the morning? Contrary to her expectations, the Inner Circle was still assembled. On their faces were expressions of sadness, helplessness, and dwindling hope. Because of this, they appeared to be mere shadows of themselves.

"Mayla? There you are, finally." Georg jumped up and immediately approached her. When he spotted the chocolates in her hand, his gray eyes narrowed and he studied her intently. "Where have you been?"

Not spotting Melinda among those present, she paused briefly before telling them Tom's news. "I was traveling with my grandma, but that's not the issue. I have important news."

Immediately, everyone glanced up from the table and all eyes were on her. "What is it?" Von Donnersberg asked wearily.

"I've just learned that Vincent von Eisenfels is not only leading a fifth circle, he's also embracing ancient magic."

"He's doing what?" Angelika shook her head in disbelief and stared at Mayla like an impatient mother would look at her child for saying some nonsense. "Who told you that?"

She breathed in deeply. The others wouldn't believe her if she didn't cite Tom as the source. On the other hand, wouldn't they immediately disregard any information knowing it came from him? However, there was no avoiding the truth.

"I met Tom."

"You did what?" Von Donnersberg sat up angrily in his magnificent chair and lowered the mug he had been about to drink from.

An incredulous murmur made its way through the hall and all but one had something to say. It was Georg. He looked at her as if he had expected it. He stared at her hands as if he could see Mayla grasping Tom's, and then at her lips as if he also could see them kissing.

Suddenly, he turned and joined the others at the table. He didn't wait for her to come with him, didn't pull out her chair, didn't give her any support or assurances that no matter what had happened, everything would be fine. As one of many, he looked at her with a mixture of distrust and disappointment and didn't say a word.

Mayla took it all in without commenting, even if his behavior pained her. Was he under the impression she had promised him something? Subconsciously, had she given him hope? At no point had she hinted that she felt something about him other than as a good friend. The best friend she'd ever had, though he could have misinterpreted her behavior. However, clearing it up would have to wait until later.

"I just met with Tom and have a message from him."

Pierre swirled his wine glass without looking at it. "Merde! Isn't he one of the hunters now?"

"No, but he lives among them to spy on them. He's the only one who can get close to his father. And he wants to find out more about what we can do about the forgotten curses."

"Porca madonna, no matter what he says, he's a von Eisenfels!" Eduardo exclaimed.

"Let her finish!" Anna demanded. "Tom was the one who brought me to you in the first place. Without him, I would have been lost and never have joined you. He is neither evil nor does he want to destroy us all. I trust him as well as Mayla. So now, let her finally say what she has to say!"

The objections died down and Mayla summarized what Tom had explained to her. "Tom warned that once Vincent harnesses the ancient magic, he'll become unstoppable. And the only element he's missing is water."

"So all he has to do is kill a water witch to make his plan a reality?" Thomas asked.

"No," Angelika interjected. "For him to unite the old powers requires members of the founding families. Hence, Alessia and her children are in greater danger than ever."

Mayla nodded. "That's how Tom explained it to me. Now I have to tell my grandma about it as soon as possible. Maybe she knows how to stop him."

Von Donnersberg rose. "I'll send my cat to her with a message. She'll be at the Fire Circle Headquarters, right?"

"Yes, but I'm going to spend the night there anyway, so..."

"Stay here and tell me everything you found out. I'll send her a message that you'll be a little late and explain the most important things to her."

"Okay. By the way, there is a discussion about whether the fire witches who have been expelled should be welcome back at the headquarters."

"That's good news," Violet cried enthusiastically. "I really would like to attend council meetings again. It was always so exciting and I didn't miss a single one until I... well... was no longer allowed."

"I hope we can convince the remaining skeptics," Mayla pointed out. "Anyone who wants to take action against Vincent must unite and fight side by side. That's even more important now than before." Mayla looked at Georg and his hostility hurt her. Still, she took heart. The matter was important. "Georg, would it be possible for you to persuade crucial police officers to join us in fighting him? We're in the process of making a plan." Without giving too much away, she summarized what was discussed among the circle leaders. "All of us must prepare and arm ourselves. This might be our last chance."

Georg agreed tersely and remained distant. Von Donnersberg wrapped his royal cloak around himself. "I'll let Melinda know and you can talk in peace."

"Thank you." Her tongue stuck to the roof of her mouth and with a wave of her hand, the carafe poured water into her glass, which she downed in one gulp.

They talked for a while longer about ancient magic and discussed ways of setting a trap for von Eisenfels. Mayla dragged herself up to her room an hour later, exhausted. She was so tired that for a moment she'd considered sleeping in the castle. However, she wanted to talk to her grandma. Granted, Melinda must have learned the most important things from von Donnersberg's message by now, still, Mayla wanted to be with her and discuss everything in person. Besides, she was still looking forward to staying at her ancestors' home as they had planned. But first, she wanted to get some of her belongings — not only the chocolates she had collected but also her mother's crocheted blanket.

Once she closed the door, she leaned against it wearily and kicked her pumps off her feet. Drowsy, she padded toward her bed and reached for her nightgown under her pillow when she noticed a little black shadow.

"Meow, meow," little Karl squeaked.

Smiling, she sat down next to the cute kitty on the bed. "Hello, my little one. Are you sleeping with me tonight? That's so nice. But I wasn't planning on staying here. So, will you come with me to the village of the fire witches?"

Little Karl didn't curl up or stomp his paws on her lap, but instead used his black nose to nudge a fake praline that was lying in the middle of the blanket.

Maya rolled her eyes. "Another Nuntia spell? What else could be so important right now? I'm so beat, maybe I'll just check it in the morning."

Little Karl wouldn't stop mewing and kept nudging the praline with his nose until Mayla finally took it.

"Okay already, darling." She gently stroked his little head. "You did well." He purred and kneaded her blanket. "By the way, are you hungry? Do you want me to buy you cat food?"

Little Karl meowed and sent her a picture of him still being suckled by Kitty. He padded onto her thigh and tapped the chocolate in her hand now with his front paw. The message must have been urgent.

"Okay, I'll take a look." She brought the fake treat to her lips and whispered, "Aperi!" Not two seconds later, Tom was standing in front of her. Her heart leapt. Although she'd just seen him a few hours ago, the sight of him still took her breath away and longing gripped her heart. Did he miss her just as much and want to send her a goodnight message? She wouldn't have guessed that he'd be so romantic. But why did he appear so harried and keep glancing over his shoulder?

"Mayla, Vincent and the hunters know who your parents are. I mean, the ones who gave you refuge. He intends to use them to blackmail you. You must go to them immediately and get them to safety. I know they don't remember you, that's normal. All people without magical abilities forget us. So, you'll have to use a trick to get them somewhere safe. Hurry, you mustn't lose any time!" With those words he disappeared, leaving Mayla alone with the terrible message.

She sat frozen on her bed. No one from her past life remembered her. That was why her parents hadn't recognized her and her boss hadn't made a fuss about her not showing up at the ad agency. One question remained: What about Heike? Would even her loyal friend forget her over time? Or had she already? As if she had suppressed it up until now, she remembered the start of his message: her parents, Anneliese and Peter Falk, were in great danger!

She couldn't let Vincent abduct them. It wasn't their fault. All these years, they had protected Mayla, and now she had to protect them! For heaven's sake, she had to tell her grandma. Darn it, there wasn't time for that.

She shot to her feet and immediately wanted to jump with the amulet, but the protection around the castle prevented her from doing so. She could only use the amulet key in the entrance hall. She slipped on her shoes, yanked open the door, and ran. Her footsteps echoed through the castle's deserted corridors, like a menacing reminder that time was running out and at any moment it could be too late. He could not be allowed to get her parents!

She sped through the darkness without blowing a flame onto her fingertip. She knew her way around so well that the pale light of the moon shining through the narrow windows sufficed. Suddenly, two broad arms appeared out of the darkness in front of her and grabbed her waist.

"Hey, what's going on? Let me..."

It was Georg, glaring at her with his gray eyes. "Are you going to see him again? Don't you know how risky that is? You're not only putting your life in danger! He's one of..."

"Stop it, Georg, and let go of me. I have to leave immediately."

He recognized the panic in her voice and instantly, the anger disappeared from his eyes, as did the furrows in his brow. "What's going on?"

"Vincent, he knows who my parents are. He knows about Anneliese and Peter Falk."

"What? How?"

"I don't know, but I have to get them to safety

immediately. I have to lure them away, though I don't know how. Anyway, I have no time to waste!"

"Don't worry, we'll get through this together." He took her hand resolutely and together they ran down the steps into the hall. Even before they set their soles on the stone floor, Mayla grabbed her amulet and thought, *Perduce nos ad silvam prope a fragis!*

They landed at the edge of the forest not two paces from the strawberry field, over which rose a waning moon. Georg looked around for orientation. "Where are we?"

She still clearly remembered this unknown forest area, which was in the middle of the strawberry field not far from where her parents lived. It was the closest world fold she knew. "I parked my car over there. My parents' place isn't far."

"Your car? Where is it?"

Mayla pointed in the direction of the road, which was barely visible, and ran across the dark strawberry field to the gravel lot where she had parked her Mini. "There!" She pointed to the trusty vehicle that fortunately had not been towed or stolen. "But darn it, I don't have the keys with me."

"We don't need them!" He pulled out his wand and in the next moment, the driver and passenger doors flew open. "Get in!" He jumped behind the wheel and waved his wand as he put the seat further back. The engine roared to life and before Mayla had slammed the door shut, he drove off.

"Where do we have to go?"

"Left!" Mayla guided him to Nieder-Erlenbach and her parents' house. Hopefully they would make it in time. Hopefully Vincent hadn't already abducted her parents. Hopefully they could save them!

Chapter Thirteen

Mayla's thoughts were racing at least as fast as the car down the street. "What am I supposed to tell them? How can I get them out of there? It will be hard for me to tell them the truth given that they don't remember me."

"Use whatever you know about them. Just because you are no longer part of their memories doesn't mean their passions and dreams have changed. Is there anything they've always wanted to do?"

"Oh, I don't know, they were... Canada! They always wanted to go to Canada!"

"Perfect. We'll say they've won a trip and we'll send them to the airport."

"Even if they believe us, it'll be over as soon as they arrive at the airport and then they'll go back home. And since they'd be flying under their real names, Vincent or the hunters could easily track them."

"No, Mayla, we'll use a spell and give them new names with forged papers."

"Forged papers... coming from a policeman! Then they'd be breaking the law and might end up in jail! Stop, here it is!" She pointed to the familiar family home, which was completely dark. Georg braked abruptly and parked the Mini on the side of the road. They pushed the doors open at the same time and jumped out.

"What is the spell?"

"Let me do it."

While Mayla was running to the front door, Georg looked around warily. All was quiet in the idyllic village. Everyone seemed to be asleep — well, it was after midnight. That was a good thing. If the hunters showed up, no innocent people would be in the line of fire.

Mayla was ringing the doorbell when Georg came running up to her. Her hands were sweaty and shaking. "I still have no idea what to say to them."

"Improvise, Mayla, you can do it! Remember, few know them better than you do." He raised his wand and whispered, "Aperi, tesserae falsae!" Two plane tickets and a hotel voucher showed up in his hand.

"Wow, are they real?"

"The charm on them will make anyone your parents show these tickets to think they're real."

"Excellent. Now all we have to do is convince them to start the journey immediately. And how are we going to explain to them that we have to give them new names and passports?"

At that moment, the door opened and Peter Falk stood before her, wearing his striped pajamas. He peered at them suspiciously and frowned.

"Who are you and what are you doing on my doorstep at this late hour?" He couldn't suppress a yawn and covered it with his hand. "Are you from the police?"

"We... we..." Mayla was at a loss for words as she looked at the familiar lines around his eyes and the receding hairline at his temples. She would have loved to hug him, tell him everything, and then put him in the car with her mother. But before she could say anything else, Georg had raised his wand.

"Mihi crede!"

Her father blinked, and then the look of skepticism disappeared and a strangely blissful expression spread across his slightly tanned face. "You have won a trip to Canada, including air tickets and accommodations at a five-star hotel and spa. All inclusive, of course. Your flight leaves at five in the morning, so you must leave for the airport immediately."

The familiar smell from inside drifted out and

Mayla inhaled deeply. How she would have liked to go in and see her former home. But the clock was ticking. "The hotel is on Vancouver Island!" she added firmly, looking decisively at Georg, who adjusted the spell accordingly.

"Okay," Peter Falk replied, oddly stiff.

"Now go upstairs, wake your wife, get dressed, and come back down at once. You don't need any luggage. Everything is provided. We only need your passports. You have to be in your car in five minutes or the voucher will expire."

"Okay." Peter Falk turned and hurried upstairs without closing the door.

Mayla watched him sadly. This strong-willed man was behaving like a puppet. "Georg, what have you done to him?"

"Without magic, we could never have convinced him fast enough."

"But he can't enjoy his vacation that way."

"Oh, he will, believe me. It's just now that he's acting so strange. As soon as they are in the car, it'll be clear to them and they'll look forward to the journey."

"I hope so!" How long had her parents dreamed of such a trip? Sometimes they'd even talked about emigrating. But because of Mayla, they had never seriously considered it, no matter how many times she'd assured them that she didn't want to stand in the way of their dreams. It was going to be the best hiding place, far away from

Europe and Vincent von Eisenfels! And with new names, too —because of the world folds and protective amulets, distance didn't matter in the witch world. "Who knows if they'll ever come back..."

"We have no choice, Mayla. We have to hide them and as normal people, they cannot enter world folds. Nowhere would they be safe from Vincent and his hunters."

They studied the surrounding area. It was still quiet. Hopefully her parents could get away before the mob showed up.

"Peter, what's the matter with you? What kind of prize rouses one out of bed in the middle of the night?"

Fully dressed, her parents came down the stairs — or rather, her father was pulling her mother along. Anneliese resisted vigorously, but Peter Falk was so determined that she followed him anyway. Her mouth gaped when she saw Mayla and Georg.

"Who are you?"

"We came here to bring you the good news!" Mayla said quickly. How wonderful it was to finally talk to her mother again, even if she had no idea how Mayla felt about her. She smiled and looked at them, feeling happiness wash over her.

"But it's the middle of the night! We also didn't take part in any sweepstakes. What company are you from?" Suddenly, her expression changed. Had Georg already charmed her? She tilted her head and studied Mayla closely. "Do we know each other? You seem so familiar."

Excuse me? Mayla's mouth fell open and she stared at her mother, unable to say anything. Could it be?

"I don't know why, but I have a feeling we've met before. Please refresh my memory?"

"I... I am..."

While Georg was pulling out his wand to subdue her with a spell, realization crept into her blue eyes and a tender smile appeared on her face. "Mayla?" She stepped toward them in disbelief and tears welled up in Mayla's eyes.

"Mom? Do you remember?"

Georg raised his wand and Mayla could hear the spell, but she raised her hand to stop him and turned back to her mother.

Anneliese stretched out her hand in disbelief, stroked Mayla's arm, and looked her up and down. "Where have you been? What happened? It's all such a strange blur."

"You remember."

"Mayla, quick," Georg interjected.

Infinitely happy, she took her mother's hand and smiled. "Mom, I can't explain it to you now, but you're in great danger. Quick, fly to Canada with Dad. You have a new identity and you'll stay there for now. You'll be safe there."

"'To Canada? What are you talking about? What happened?"

"May I have your passports, please?" Georg asked, and Peter Falk handed them over to him complacently. Georg ran his wand over her parents even though they could see him. Anneliese's eyes widened.

"Mayla?"

"I'll explain when you get back. Now is not the time."

"No, I'm not going. If we're in danger, so are you. I cannot leave you!"

"Hello, Mayla!" called an all-too-familiar voice from the street.

Mayla turned in disbelief. It couldn't be true! "Heike?"

Without further ado, Georg raised his wand, pointed it at Anneliese, and whispered, "Mihi crede!" causing Anneliese's eyes to glaze over. "Now go to the airport with your husband and enjoy your vacation!"

"All right!" her parents replied in unison, then hurried toward the garage as Heike came panting toward them down the narrow path through the front yard. Mayla's heart ached as she watched her parents go, but it wasn't going to help matters any. The two had to get away as soon as possible. She turned her back on them resolutely and threw her arms around Heike's neck.

"Mayla, sweetie, where have you been?"

"Long story. So, what are you doing at my

parents' place at this hour? You're completely out of breath."

"You won't believe it, but I saw my tarot card reader. She told me to watch for signs. You'll need my help before long."

The garage door automatically opened and her parents backed out, passing them in their silver VW. Heike raised her hand and waved enthusiastically. However, Peter and Anneliese Falk didn't pay any attention to them and quickly drove past them without so much as a glance. Mayla watched them wistfully. Her mother had recognized her. How wonderful! So, once all this madness was over, she should visit them in Canada...

"What kind of tarot card reader?" Georg asked, looking at Heike with a frown.

A broad grin appeared on Heike's face. "So, is this him? The new man who keeps you away from me? What a piece of eye candy! Nice to meet you, I'm Heike, the best friend."

A breeze rustled through the bushes and they looked around attentively. Hunters?

Georg grabbed the wand and pointed it at Heike. "Mihi crede!"

"What? What are you doing?"

"Now go back home and forget about running into Mayla and me."

"Excuse me? Now listen up! I'm definitely not doing that. What's this supposed to mean?"

Stunned, Georg stared at Heike, who was unaffected by his magic. "She couldn't be..."

"No, she isn't — as far as I know," Mayla confirmed, no less surprised. Why didn't the spell work on her friend? Simply because she believed witches existed? Or was she also someone whose magic was blocked?

A flash of light illuminated the neighborhood and shot toward them. Mayla quickly blew a ring of fire around them, stopping the curse.

Heike's eyes widened as she stared at the dancing flames. "What is going on? It almost looks like you're doing it, Mayla."

"Damn, they're here! Quick, we must go." Georg took Mayla's hand and she quickly grabbed her friend's as well.

"Mayla, what the...?"

Another malediction shot toward them, ricocheting off her protective shield in a spray of sparks.

"Back to the car!" Georg shouted.

Mayla blew out the ring of flames so they could run to the street, and she and Heike ducked and sprinted after Georg. More curses came rushing toward them, setting fire to the bush beside them. One of the hunters must have been a fire witch. While sprinting, Mayla blew out the flames so that her parents' house and the development wouldn't fall victim to a major fire.

Heike watched each of her gestures in amazement. "Mayla, are you a witch?"

Shoot. Of course, her friend immediately understood what the source of the strange occurrences was. "Yes, Heike, and there are evil witches who want to kill us. We have to get out of here right now!"

Without asking any more questions, Heike scurried after her to the sidewalk. However, the Mini was on fire, the windows were cracked, and the tires were flat.

"Darn it, my beautiful car! Now what are we going to do?"

Several young men came running down the street toward them, which didn't leave time to fix the Mini with a spell.

"We'll take mine!" Crouching, Heike ran ahead to her red Opel, which was parked on the opposite side of the street.

Mayla and Georg glanced at each other, then hurried after her and got in. Heike was already starting the engine when Mayla sat down in front and Georg in the back. The roof was so low that had to bend down, but he didn't complain.

"Go!" he yelled. "Or should I drive?"

"You need a special touch for my car." Heike kept turning the key in the ignition and the engine rattled and rattled. She held the key and stroked the steering wheel. "Come on, my old friend, don't let us down now."

Mayla glanced back and saw the hunters brandishing their wands. Before a malediction could hit them, she blew a wall of fire behind the car, deflecting the spells.

The engine finally turned over, and the car shook. Heike released the handbrake while Mayla and Georg peered out the rear window. The hunters were closing in on them, throwing more curses that ricocheted off the wall of flames. But as they drove off, the protection died.

"You don't have to worry." Heike pointed to a tin amulet hanging on her rearview mirror. It had a semi-precious, purple stone in the middle. "I bought the amulet years ago at an esoteric fair. It keeps evil curses away. I haven't had a single accident since it's been hanging here." Heike chuckled enthusiastically.

A blindingly bright flash shot through the pane and destroyed the amulet. Mayla, Georg, and Heike ducked their heads and peered behind them.

"How can that...?" Incredulous, Heike felt the fragments of the amulet, pulled back her fingers in fright, and shook them. "Hot!"

Otherwise, they'll kill us!"

Heike did as she was told and sped down the street.

"They are getting into cars too!" Georg shouted, who was keeping watch out the rear window.

Tutare! Mayla thought, but the shield immediately died down again. "Why are the protective spells not working?"

"We're going too fast."

"We're not even going forty miles an hour!"

"Well, you better speed up soon!" He pointed to the two black cars closing in on them. They certainly had more horsepower under their hoods than Heike's rickety tin can.

"Isn't there a spell you can use to make my Opel go faster?" Heike yelled euphorically.

Mayla peered questioningly at Georg. "Is there?"

He frowned, but Mayla didn't wait. The translation for "faster" just occurred to her. She imagined them speeding down the street and whispered, "Celerius!" The Opel picked up speed but it wasn't enough, because the hunters were right up on their bumper again. Another flash came toward them and Georg yelled, "Defende!" With that, the curse was gone.

Meanwhile, Heike enthusiastically steered the Opel out of the area onto the country road. "Mayla, have you always been a witch?" she cried excitedly.

"No, just for a short time. We've got to lose them. Do you have any ideas, Georg?"

"Perhaps. I don't know why the spell didn't work on your friend and why she hasn't forgotten you, but she's human, so she can't enter our world. This is our chance!"

"I don't get it. How is that supposed to help us?"

The next malediction shot towards them and this time Mayla shouted, "Defende!" It fizzled out before hitting the car.

"Why does he use a wand and you don't?"

"Later, Heike."

A loud bang made her spin around. A curse shattered the rear window and the shards flew at Georg, who protected his face with his arms. More spells flew toward them and Mayla blocked them, but one hit the back door, tearing a hole in it as if it were nothing but paper.

"You have to drive faster!" Mayla yelled.

"The Opel and I are doing our best! Where should I go? Where will we be safe from the wizards? Why are they after you anyway?"

"It's a long story!"

The next curse hit the rearview mirror and it exploded into numerous pieces. Heike ducked but kept her foot off the brake. With her hands on the steering wheel, she kept her eyes on the road and slammed on the gas. "Use the faster spell again, Mayla."

"Celerius!"

The red Opel immediately started speeding up along the dark country road.

"We're a great team!" Heike beamed. "Fortunately, it's night. Otherwise, people would see us. It's a secret that witches exist, right? I've always known there was more! Ha, I was right. Funny,

Mayla, that you of all people never believed me. So, tell me, were you pretending?"

"No, my powers only awakened a few weeks ago — ever since then nothing has been the same!"

"That's fantastic. So, there is still a chance to awaken my magic. Do you have a tip for me?"

"Um, Heike, it's not that simple..."

"Let's clear all that up later. Turn here!" Georg interrupted, pointing at which fork in the road to take.

"What are you up to?" Mayla asked.

"There's a large world fold further on."

"World fold?" Heike perked up. "Is that what you call the world you live in?"

"There's one before Bad Vilbel?" Mayla asked, ignoring her friend's question.

"Yes, a big one. And since Heike is with us, we can theoretically drive the car over it. The hunters, however, will have to go through it. That's our chance to lose them!"

"That sounds like a fantastic plan! By the way, good choice, Mayla, I mean your new one. Much cuter than Henning." She cast an admiring glance over her shoulder and Mayla blushed bright red.

"I'm not her new guy," Georg explained.

"What? Don't tell me, Mayla, that there isn't a man involved! Well, that's disappointing." Heike took the curve vigorously, as if she were in a Formula One race. Due to the unexpected change of direction, their pursuers fell further behind.

"There's a man involved, but Georg is my... my best friend." Mayla glanced back at him and gave him an apologetic look. "The kind of good friend I've never had before and the kind every woman wants."

Georg smiled half-heartedly, though his eyes betrayed a certain melancholy. Then they were hit by another malediction and quickly ducked their heads.

Mayla raised her hands and cast the Dirumpe spell at her pursuers. Their windshields exploded, but the car drove on unimpeded. "How far is it to the fold?"

"We should see it soon."

"Why didn't my amulet work?" Heike shook her head in disbelief and shifted down to fourth gear for more speed. The Opel roared and the distance between them and their pursuers increased. The engine noise was so loud that they had to shout to be able to hear each other.

"Get down!" Georg yelled, and a curse hissed past him by a hair's breadth.

"Aaaahhh!" Heike's hands slipped off the steering wheel. The spell had hit her shoulder. Her right arm hung down motionless and she felt her shoulder with her left hand in a panic. "Help! It burns!"

Mayla grabbed the steering wheel before they ended up in the ditch. "Heike! Hold on!" Her eyes darted between the dark street and her friend, who had turned as white as a sheet. It better not be one of the forgotten curses...

Georg immediately pulled out his magic wand. "I'll fix the gas pedal with a spell, then charm her onto the back seat next to me. You must climb into the driver's seat immediately, Mayla, do you understand?"

"Will she recover? Is it one of the ancient curses?"

"Focus on driving. Just continue straight ahead! I'll see if I can help her!"

In the next moment, Heike was lifted off the seat, her legs swung out from under the steering wheel, and she floated toward the back seat. She hardly reacted, and kept pressing her hand to her shoulder, groaning repeatedly. Her eyelids flickered and she screamed again when her shoulder bumped one of the backrests. Georg immediately charmed the backrests to the sides so that her friend could fit through, and Mayla crawled into the driver's seat and floored it.

Glancing over her shoulder, she saw her beloved friend lying almost unconscious in the back seat, her head resting on Georg's lap. He was sitting crammed into the corner, running his wand over her.

"Can you help her?"

The next malediction shot inside the car. Thankfully it went up high, since Georg was having trouble ducking his head. There was barely

Jenny Swan

enough space in the back and he was too big for the tiny car.

"Concentrate on the road! I'll take care of her."

She hoped he could help Heike! What happened to a regular person hit by a witch's curse? Was there even a cure?

She was hurtling through the darkness, the two black cars close behind her, when something in front of her began to sparkle and twinkle. A spell was cast in front of them, but... wait, or was it the world fold? The glitter wavered across the street, hints of green and blue flickering in front of them. She couldn't make out any other details.

"Is that the entrance to the world fold?"

"Yes!" Georg's gray eyes lit up. "It'll work. Thanks to your friend, we'll just drive over it. Faster, Mayla, we're almost there!"

The next curse hit one of the wheels and the tire burst with a loud bang. The Opel continued driving on the rim. A blinding flash of light hit the car again. It rattled and howled, slowing down until it came to a stop, smoking.

Mayla put her hands on the steering wheel and again called out "Celerius," but the car didn't respond. "Shoot. Now what?"

Georg turned around. The black cars were speeding toward them, and they were right before the glittering wall. "Let's get out and push."

"Are you serious?"

"We have no choice. We don't have time to fix

the car and we shouldn't leave it behind, either. We still need it."

"Okay." Without further ado, she jumped out the door and saw the next malediction closing in. She took a deep breath and blew a wall of fire behind the Opel while Georg exited the car.

"Vola!" The Opel lifted off the ground, but only a little. "Quick, Mayla, go to the other side and push from there. The car flies, we can do it, but we have to keep touching Heike at all costs. Do you understand? Otherwise, we'll end up inside the fold."

Mayla darted to the other side and grabbed Heike's ankle. Her friend was turning her head from side to side as if delirious. She certainly was in terrible pain. They had to lose the hunters!

Georg looked at her across the Opel's roof. "Ready?"

"Ready."

"One, two, three." Together, they pushed the car, which moved through the air, which made it easier to make some progress. Still, it was hard and Mayla needed more strength than she expected.

"Why don't we charm it forward?"

"We could lose direct contact with your friend and end up inside the fold." Georg held Heike's hand tighter while Mayla gripped her ankle.

"Hold on, Heike, we'll help you in just a second."

The twinkling was getting closer, with the

hood already through the glitter. Mayla gritted her teeth and kept pushing. Sweat had formed on her forehead, but she didn't give up. Together, she and Georg moved the car forward until they too passed through the magic. A tingle traveled up her body, pulling her to it and calling her. She felt the magic hidden at the border, all the strength and energy flowing through the fold. In the next moment, they passed through the flickering sparkle. Then, the magic was gone and they continued to push the car down the dark road as if nothing had been there.

After a few meters, Mayla turned around excitedly. No one was behind them. The street was empty! "We made it! The hunters are in the fold!"

"Great, now we have to fix the car quickly before they come out again. I don't know the exact size of the world fold."

"How can we get the car running again?"

"First, I have to find the problem." Georg rolled under the floating Opel like a mechanic. Hopefully, the car wouldn't collapse and bury him beneath it. Her friend groaned and Mayla rushed to her.

"Heike, hold on!"

"I found it! The radiator was hit and the coolant ran out."

"Shoot. Now what?"

"I'll fix it and refill it with water."

"Where are you going to get water? It spilled all

over the street and is already seeping in. We can't conjure up provisions."

"Well, you just so happen to be in the presence of a water wizard." Pointing his wand at the damaged radiator, he whispered, "Repara!" Then, he crawled out from under the vehicle, turned his gaze to the dark water stains on the asphalt, and blew on them. First, the water hissed and evaporated, then it flew to Georg, who ran to the front, opened the hood, and removed the radiator cap. He blew again directly over the opening, liquefying the water vapor that flowed directly into the radiator as if Georg were using a funnel.

"That's just insane. Now what?"

"I'll quickly change the flat tire. Since the Opel is an older model, it should have a spare in the trunk." He opened the trunk and raised the liner. "Here it is!" He pulled it out hastily, whispered a few spells that Mayla didn't understand, and the tire was replaced in no time at all. "Now, let's get going. You sit with Heike and I'll get behind the wheel! Once we've made a few detours and are certain the hunters haven't spotted us, we'll hide somewhere and take care of your friend."

Mayla crawled into the back seat, laid Heike's head on her lap, and stroked her cold forehead. "Heike? Can you hear me?"

Her friend groaned, sounding terribly powerless.

"Hold on, Heike, I won't let you die!"

Chapter Fourteen

After driving around for a while with no sign of the hunters, they felt safe. Georg pulled the red Opel in front of an abandoned supermarket and parked. He conjured Heike out of the car and before she landed on the street, Mayla quickly took off her blouse and transformed it into a fluffy bed for her friend to rest on. Wearing only a tank top, she bent over her, pulled off her glasses, and stroked her sweaty forehead.

"Heike, can you hear me?"

Her eyelids fluttered and she moved her head, but her tongue seemed too heavy for her to speak.

Mayla started to feel overwhelmed with panic, but she suppressed it and remained calm. There was no one around who could help her friend. She had to do it herself. "What kind of curse was it?"

"She said she was on fire. So, probably the same

malediction the hunters hit you with that one time."

Mayla tugged at her friend's tunic to reveal the shoulder and discovered the skin around the joint was a fiery red. "Tom was able to save me back then. Do you know how he did it?"

Georg shrugged his broad shoulders helplessly. "He only said he was good at herbal charms — unlike me. I have no idea how he healed you."

"Shoot. I should have paid more attention when my grandmother talked to me about this topic. Now, I'm sitting here unable to help my friend because I didn't concentrate during class!" Agitated, she closed her eyes and recalled every-thing she had learned. Combustion, burning, Flamma curse. Flamma, flamma, burning... "Net-tles! Burning must be healed with burning! Quick, we have to find some."

"Stinging nettles? Are you sure?"

"Positive. My grandmother explained it to me. I know that for a fact." She stormed off, searching the adjacent patches of green for the plant. Georg looked on the other side.

"I have some!"

"Great!" Mayla ran toward him and snatched it out of his hands. She ignored the burning, small pustules spreading on her palm. Not recalling in detail what her grandmother had told her about it, she felt certain she was doing the right thing, she plucked the leaves from the stem, rubbed them between her fingers, and stroked her friend's shoulder and the fiery red ring around the joint.

"I don't remember how Tom did it, but it wasn't like this."

She ignored Georg, put her palms on Heike's shoulders, and stroked them. "Sana!" A glow spread from her hands and enveloped her friend until she relaxed. A gentle smile appeared on her pale lips and Mayla sighed with relief.

Georg wiped his brow with his forearm. "Wow, impressive. Where did you learn that?"

"My grandma told me about it — founder magic. Luckily, I remembered it in time. I won't ever complain again about spending an hour learning about herbal magic, believe me!" She looked tenderly at Heike, who was finally breathing more calmly again, and was immensely relieved that she had subdued the curse. "My dear, faithful friend... Why does she remember me? Why don't the spells work on her? She can't be a witch or we wouldn't have been able to cross over the world fold. Or, do you think her powers are suppressed, like mine were?"

Georg stroked his chin. "That's a very interesting question. I don't see any magic in her and it's not often that witches are blocked. It's also possible that a protection spell was placed on her that prevents her from being charmed."

"Protection? Who would have done that for

her? I'm not aware of her being in touch with real witches."

"She had that amulet hanging in her car."

Maya laughed. "Yes, and we saw how well that worked!"

"Maybe she has more such items and not all are useless."

"Where would she get such an item?"

Georg rubbed the back of his neck. "I have no idea." He looked more closely at Heike, the yellow-orange tunic, the brown, slightly curled hair, when his eyes spotted something twinkling around her neck. "Look, she's wearing a necklace. Take it off carefully."

Frowning, Mayla examined the piece of jewelry and then gave George an indignant look. "I don't want to do anything like that while she's unconscious. I'm her friend!"

"But if you take it from her, we can probably charm her and she won't remember the last hour."

"I'm not going to enchant her after that chase!"

"We have no other choice. No one must know witches exist — besides, she even overheard us talking about the world folds."

"She always knew witches existed anyway. She simply had no idea I was one."

"But the world folds, Mayla..."

"She can't enter them anyway — and even if she tells someone, they can't do us any harm. They can't even find the folds — not to mention the fact that Heike won't tell anyone if I ask her."

"Are you talking about me?" Heike blinked and leaned on her forearms. Then she rose to her feet and groped around on the ground. "Where are my glasses?"

"Here!" Mayla handed them to her and Heike meticulously brushed her tunic clean. She put the glasses on her nose and gave Georg a stern look. "I'm sure you won't take my amulet from me. Besides, even if you try to charm me, do you seriously think I'll ever forget any of this?" She beamed at Mayla, overjoyed. "Can I become a witch too?"

Smiling, Mayla shrugged. "Who knows, Heike? I believe anything is possible. Now tell me, where did you get that amulet that's under your tunic?"

Heike cast a skeptical look at Georg, who raised his hands defensively.

"I won't take it from you. I promise. But to explain my motives: I am a police officer at heart and therefore remain partly responsible for people not finding out about us."

Heike nodded thoughtfully. "But really, I already knew about your existence. And I bet the owner of the new occult shop is a witch too!"

Mayla laughed. "Who knows. But now we have to think about how to protect you because we have to go back to our world to..." She stopped.

Heike was all ears. "Yes...?"

"There are a few important things to take care

of that can't be put off," Georg said before Mayla could reveal any more.

"Unfortunately, we can't take you with us, Heike, and since you have been with us, magic is clinging to you."

Heike looked down at herself enthusiastically, but she couldn't see any glitter or a bright glow. "On me? That's fantastic."

With a flick of her hand, Mayla transformed the mat on the ground back into her blouse and put it on while Heike watched, wide-eyed.

"Fantastic, Mayla!"

"On one hand, it is fantastic, but there's a group of wizards who want to... harm others. We have to prevent them from noticing you. Do you have any ideas, Georg?"

"And you honestly can't take me with you?"

"Unfortunately, no. I'd love to show you my world, but as long as your powers haven't awakened, the gates will remain closed to you." Granted, Mayla's magic had only revealed itself so late because her grandma had blocked it, but she didn't want to deprive her friend of her hope that the same could happen to her. It wasn't out of the question, after all. If Mayla had learned one thing over the past few weeks, it was that almost anything was possible. And who was she to claim that Heike might not have magical abilities at some point?

Heike sighed. "A shame. I could go back to the

occult shop and ask for a more powerful protection spell."

"I don't want to take the risk that it won't be enough. So, Georg? Let's hear some ideas!"

"As far as I know, there are a few witches running shops outside the world folds. The magic there isn't conspicuous since the hunters know where it comes from. And usually they are not outcasts, which is why the hunters leave them alone. Maybe we could hide you with one of those witches until the situation is resolved."

"That's a good idea. Maybe the woman in the occult shop is indeed a witch and sold you this powerful amulet. The broken talisman in the car, is that from her too?"

"No, no, as I said, I bought it years ago at a fair."

"Then it can't be ruled out. The store might be a good hiding place for you." Mayla glanced at her watch. "But it won't open for at least seven hours. It's one o'clock in the morning."

"We could kill time at my apartment," Heike suggested.

Georg shook his head. "The hunters saw your license plate and they have police contacts. They'll be watching the apartment by now."

Heike peered at her curiously. "What do these men you call hunters want from you, Mayla?"

Drat. Her friend was too intuitive. "What makes you think that this is about me?"

"You sent your parents away. Now they must

not catch me. They planned on blackmailing you by taking your parents hostage, right? And now my life is at stake." The theory didn't seem to bother her at all. Amused, she watched Mayla as if it were all a game.

Georg gave her a warning look, but why mislead her friend? Heike should be aware of the seriousness of the situation. "Yes, Heike, it's about me, among other things. That's all I can tell you."

Her friend's eyes widened ecstatically. "I wouldn't tell anyone, I swear!"

"Of course, I trust you. But first I need to see how the other witches will react to you knowing who I am. Baby steps, all right?"

"I'll find out — when my powers awaken at the very latest." Satisfied, Heike folded her hands in her lap. Apparently, she had the patience to wait forever for that day, just as long it came at some point.

Grinning, Mayla shook her head. That Heike. "So, now we need a solution. I also could use a few hours of sleep or I won't be useful tomorrow."

A faint squeaking rang out a bright "meow." Little Karl tiptoed out from behind the red Opel and jumped toward them.

"Little Karl?" Mayla spread her arms and the little cat hopped first onto her lap and then into her hand. They remained forehead to forehead for a moment as she sent him a thought of the love she felt for him and he meowed brightly again.

Heike deliberately stretched out her left hand to him and patiently let him sniff her fingertips until he determined they were harmless and began to purr. He happily stretched his little head toward her and Heike gently stroked it. "How adorable! Such a sweet cutie. He won over my heart immediately. But wait a minute, does he belong to you, Mayla? When did you get a cat?"

"Only recently." But her mind was elsewhere as little Karl sent her pictures of a hut in the forest. She knew this simple dwelling and had often walked by it with her parents when she was a child. It wasn't far away. Little Karl meowed again and gave her the feeling that they would be safe there for the night.

"Thanks, my darling. That's a wonderful idea."

"I'm sorry, what? Tell me, as a witch, can you talk to cats?!"

"Kind of. Little Karl showed me a place where we'll be out of harm's way tonight. Come! Let's leave at once."

Georg brushed the dust off his jeans. "Okay, if little Karl showed you the place, we can hide there. Where is it?"

"It's a hut in a small grove nearby. We can conjure up beds and take turns sleeping for a few hours."

"That sounds fantastic." Heike tenderly stroked little Karl's head and the cat began to stomp. "Thanks for the tip. You did well, little man. Oh, I would take you home with me right away. If you ever want a vacation, Mayla, I'll be happy to take care of him."

Little Karl gave Mayla a feeling of warmth and she knew it was meant for her friend.

"Thanks, that's nice of you. By the way, he likes you."

"Yes? What an honor!"

"You can go back to Kitty, darling. Have a good rest and send her our greetings." She kissed little Karl on the forehead, who meowed.

"Come on," Georg urged. "Or there'll be nothing left of the night and we might as well stay right here in the parking lot."

"He seems even more impatient than you, Mayla."

They laughed and as little Karl disappeared, they got back into the red Opel and made their way to the simple wooden house.

Chapter Fifteen

They had no trouble finding the secluded hut and parked the Opel in front of it. They camouflaged it with leaves so the twinkling wouldn't illuminate the forest and lead the hunters to their trail before they entered the hut. Mayla conjured beds out of twigs that wouldn't collapse under her weight and savored the feeling that coursed through her veins. Ever since her grandmother had introduced her to the magic connection, every spell became easier for her and she'd finally come to believe that one day she would be able to become a worthy successor to her powerful ancestors.

Georg insisted on doing the night shift alone. Ever the gentleman, he left the conjured beds to Heike and Mayla and sat down on a chair next to the window so that he had a good view of the area. He didn't believe they were in any danger, but he still wanted to keep watch. They deliberately chose not to place a protective spell around the hut since the magic would give away their presence.

Contrary to Mayla's expectations, Heike didn't bombard her with questions. The curse and the late hour had taken their toll and her friend sank in exhaustion onto the bed to then fall asleep instantly.

Mayla didn't keep Georg company, for she also was exhausted and in urgent need of rest. If she failed to catch up on sleep, she wouldn't be in top form the next day, which she couldn't afford. There was a lot to do, but she didn't have the strength to think about it. She sank into the pillows and with her next breath fell into a deep sleep.

After a quiet night, they got on the road shortly after eight with growling stomachs. Once again, Mayla regretted that witches couldn't conjure up food and the fact that she had forgotten her chocolates because she'd been so scared. She didn't know herself to be so careless.

Heike remembered that the occult shop opened at nine o'clock, and they didn't want to waste any time. Before they got back in the car, Mayla turned the Opel black and swapped the numbers and letters on the license plate. Using illusion magic, Georg made the scratches and holes disappear.

"So, now there's magic on the car too. Doesn't

that make it easier for the hunters to find us?" Heike asked curiously.

Mayla nodded. "Yep, but we won't be the only ones using magic outside the world folds at this hour. Besides, we'll make it quick. Leaving the car as it was would be riskier. Then they would recognize it immediately. This way, we have a better chance of getting to the shop undetected. Now, let's go!"

"So, your world is called world folds, is that right..."

Behind Heike, Georg gave Mayla a warning look as they left the hut. Mayla nodded knowingly and shrugged. Of course, theoretically, her friend already knew too much, but even if she told others about it, they would certainly react the same way Mayla had all those years before. Just to be safe, she reminded her friend that everything that happened last night had to stay between them.

The drive was uneventful and no hunters crossed their path, so they entered the small corner shop at the Frankfurt Hauptwache unscathed at nine o'clock sharp. The ringing of the doorbell announced their arrival and they were immediately greeted by the smell of joss sticks and incense. Dream catchers and wind chimes adorned the walls, small table fountains and singing bowls crowded the shelves, and scattered between tarot cards and dream interpretation books were vast amounts of crystals and semi-precious stones.

Chains of amethyst and rose quartz dangled from a filigree metal stand shaped like a tree of life, and small figurines of angels stood nearby.

There was a woman behind the counter, which had another metal stand with amulets and necklaces with pendants. She had brown hair and light blue, knowing eyes that were directed at the newcomers. She was willowy and tall, and her posture was as straight as if she had taken countless ballet lessons.

"Thank you for visiting my shop. Make yourself at home! My name is Nadine."

For the first time, Mayla saw magic dancing around a human. Streaks and sparks were moving through the air around her, and she knew immediately that she was dealing with a true witch. Could Nadine see it in her and Georg too? Or was it Mayla's ability as a founding family member?

"Thanks, my name is Mayla. This is Georg and you probably already know Heike."

"One of my favorite customers!" Nadine gave Heike a hearty smile that didn't seem forced at all. A radiance emanated from the woman that transcended her magic. "What brings you to me?"

"We bumped into a couple of hunters while trying to escape," said Georg, who didn't seem to doubt that Nadine had recognized their magic and was therefore laying their cards out on the table. So he'd also understood that Nadine was a witch, and it wasn't just Mayla who could see it. "Heike has traces of our magic and we want to prevent her from being abducted in her apartment. However, we can't take her with us because we have to go back."

Heike shrugged her shoulders. "May I stay here until the situation becomes less dangerous? I'm happy to help with the day-to-day business. I have some wonderful ideas on how to use a few little marketing tricks to attract more customers to your lovely shop."

Mayla couldn't help but smile and judging from Nadine's look, the owner had no objection to Heike's presence. With a loving wink, she waved Heike closer.

"It would be my pleasure. You're welcome to stay with me until the situation has calmed down. That's one of the reasons I came to this side of the world. There are quite a few who need a good hiding place."

"So why don't your customers forget you?" Mayla asked.

"As long as I stay and don't enter a world fold, the magic won't work and everyone can remember me."

"You remain here? Why?"

"I enjoy people like your friend who are fond of witchcraft." She looked over at Heike, who was rummaging through the shelves curiously. "Just because she and other interested parties weren't born with magic doesn't preclude them from being able to use a spell or two."

Hearing this, Heike immediately perked up. "'That's fantastic. I'd love to quit my job right now and start here!" However, all of a sudden, her smile faded and she clapped her hands against her cheeks in shock. "One thing I didn't consider. Kasimir, Moor, Mikesch, Pauline, and Astrid. What if those nasty scoundrels do something to them?"

"Your cats? We'll find a solution," Nadine reassured her immediately.

Heike looked at her gratefully. "Any chance you also have an idea on how we can help my Kasimir? Vets say I should put him to sleep."

Nadine stroked her back. "I'll see what I can do. You should eat something now. I'll take care of your cats during breakfast." She turned to Mayla and Georg and nodded to them. "You can leave now. Your friend is safe with me."

"Thank you so much." Relieved but heavy-hearted, Mayla said goodbye to Heike and left the shop. How nice it had been to talk openly with her friend about some of the things that had happened to her over the past few weeks. And how wonderful that Heike hadn't forgotten her. And who knew, once Vincent von Eisenfels was stopped, maybe her friend might somehow continue to be a part of her life.

Mayla and Georg took the quickest route to the world fold at the police station in their enchanted Opel and parked the car. Then, Mayla jumped with Georg back to Donnersberg Castle with the protective amulet. They parted ways in the entrance hall.

"I'm going to jump now to the Fire Circle head-quarters. I need to talk to my grandma about Vincent." Along the way, she charmed a vanilla truffle from one of the boxes in her room and popped it into her mouth indulgently. The choco-late calmed her nerves and limbs and she sighed with contentment.

"As soon as I get the amulet key from Artus," Georg explained, "I'll set about developing coopera-tion with the police. Take care, Mayla."

She looked at him uncertainly. "Thank you for helping me tonight even though..."

"...even though you're not in love with me?"

She cocked her head and looked at him steadily. "You're the best friend I've ever had. And no, I'm not in love with you, but you're still dear to me. I'm incredibly fond of you and I understand if you need some alone time."

He looked at her wistfully. "Away from you? I couldn't stand it." He stroked her cheek gently, then smiled. "You never led me on and it wasn't right for me to be so offended. Forgive a stupid love-drunk oaf. I should have realized long ago that your heart only beats for one man. See you later."

He turned his back to her and hurried into the castle hall. Would he remain her friend? Did he even want that if a relationship was out of the question? She really liked him a lot and enjoyed spending time with him. But he didn't make her feel the way Tom did and never had. Rather, it was the feeling she'd have for a brother — at least that's how she imagined love between siblings to be.

"See you later," she whispered after him, then grabbed the amulet key and thought, *Perduce me in caput ignis.* The dull gray of the stones and the gleaming silver of the knightly armor blurred as green and brown joined in and Mayla landed in the middle of the forest. With her stomach rumbling, she marched over the moss and needles that littered the ground until she reached the spot where she would open the headquarters. Hopefully, her grandma had the ingredients for a proper breakfast at home!

Raising her hands, she focused on the village and cried out, "Te aperi, caput ignis!" The ancient fir trees were pushed aside and before her eyes, the idyllic witch village surrounded by the glittering wall appeared. Smiling, she stepped through the glittering gate, which flared, and then walked down the path to her ancestral home.

Some people met her and greeted her kindly or

just nodded. The residents now knew her and were clearly pleased that she was back. It was a nice feeling, though it entailed a certain melancholy. How would fire witches react if they learned that Mayla would end the line of von Flammensteins? She'd pushed the thought— the fact that she couldn't have children — aside for a few weeks, but ever since seeing the hopeful faces of these people, she felt the pain inside her like she did after the doctor's first diagnosis.

Dwelling on such sad thoughts was not useful. She had come to terms with it, sad though it may have been, but it was what it was. These people would simply have to do the same.

She stroked her hair and picked lint from her blouse, which distracted her from her uneasiness, and headed for her family's quaint home. She took a deep breath and thought of her grandma and her ancestors who had lived in this house for so many years. How nice it would be to live in this place with her grandma, to spend some time there until she knew where she wanted to settle down and what she was going to do with her life as a fire witch.

Should she knock? Or just walk in? Without further ado, she raised her hand and was already saying the spell when a deafening banging sound resounded throughout the village. She crouched down instinctively and covered her ears. Still squatting, she turned and froze.

Smoke rose from the village entrance. The old firs swayed restlessly to and fro even though there was no wind. What was going on over there?

The fog cleared and she stared out until she could finally see something. A large shadow loomed, growing larger and larger until the smoke cleared to reveal its full magnitude.

Unable to say a word, she stared at the village entrance — or rather, where it had been. A hole gaped in the magic wall where the gate had once stood. And none other than Vincent von Eisenfels was stepping through it.

Chapter Sixteen

Mayla shouted to give the alarm, but her grandmother and all the other witches, including the teacher and the schoolchildren, were already rushing outside. Each of them paused for a moment when they saw who had broken into their village. Melinda, however, didn't hesitate to take in a deep breath, and Mayla joined in. Together, they blew a ring of fire around the children and the school building. The teacher immediately directed her charges back inside.

Alongside Vincent, a vast crowd of hunters poured into the village. This included all the former council members Melinda had ousted the day before. Everyone in the village held their breath.

"My dear Fire Witches," Vincent's cold voice began, ringing through the settlement. "The days of head witches and covens are coming to an end and each of you is welcome by my side. Become part of my invincible power and enter the only true circle. That of ancient magic reunited!"

"Get out of my circle!" Melinda raised her hands and threw a spell at him, but Vincent simply raised his left hand and the curse bounced off it. Melinda didn't give up that easily. And as if the malediction had released all the others from their state of shock, a fight broke out between the villagers and the hunters, and also between Vincent and Melinda. Mayla, too, raised her hands resolutely. All the spells she had learned and all the magic rushed out of her to fight alongside her grandmother and all the people she had only met yesterday.

Sparks hissed through the crowd. There were screams and the first houses caught ablaze. Mayla blew out the flames to prevent an inferno, but someone behind her threw a curse at her neck. She saw it out of the corner of her eye and quickly blew a ring of flames to deflect it. When she turned to find out who had tried to take her out from behind, she was standing face-to-face with Marianna Lauber.

The hunter wrapped a strand of her long black hair around her finger and looked at her haughtily. "Well, have you learned anything in the meantime or will this be quick and easy?"

"You're welcome to find out for yourself!"

Mayla quickly blew out the ring of flames and hurled an explosive spell at Marianna. But she easily blocked it and retaliated with a curse that made Mayla's renewed protection shake.

Mayla gritted her teeth and imagined the wand in Marianna's hands getting hotter and hotter.

"Ouch, don't burn me!" But Marianna just laughed and gripped her wand even tighter. "You won't get anywhere with childish tricks like that!" She raised her wand and threw a curse, which Mayla deflected. Her arms shook in the process. Why was Marianna so strong? Were those forgotten spells? Ancient magic? Were the members of the new circle about to unite the old powers?

She fought on bitterly. She managed to look briefly at her grandmother, who was fighting a duel with Vincent. Melinda cast one spell after the next at him, but he easily blocked them all. Yet, when he conjured a curse and a flash of light thundered against her grandmother's shield, she saw her grandmother's hands tremble.

The next malediction that hurtled toward Mayla made her look back at Marianna, who was suddenly making the earth tremble beneath her. Shoot, an earth witch. What could she do about it? The earth shook and cracked beneath her. She had to jump to the side and could do nothing but watch as a rift worked its way through the village, growing deeper and wider. The others jumped aside in horror, and Mayla grew alarmed when she noticed the direction the crack was moving. It was heading beneath the protective ring of flames, which couldn't do anything to check its progress, for the school.

Mayla poured all her anger into a bolt of lightning that she summoned from the sky. Quickly, she brought it down on Marianna and the witch fell to the ground under its force. She groaned and hardly moved, so Mayla was finally safe from another attack. Straightaway, she dashed between the other villagers, who were being pushed back by the hunters, but she couldn't pay attention to that now. She had to save the children! Rushing headlong towards the school, she blew out the ring of fire to keep the building intact. But the rift was faster than she was. It was already eating its way into the foundation of the school building, lifting it off the ground. The school slipped sideways toward the abyss. Darn it. How could she save the little ones?

A completely absurd idea popped into her head. But she had to try. If anyone could do it, she could. She was a von Flammenstein, after all, and her powers were greater than most.

"Vola!" she roared, imagining the school building flying a few feet into the air. But the crack in the earth was pulling it down and it could disappear at any second. As hard as it was, Mayla took her eyes off the deep gaping crack and the sinking school building and closed her eyes. Highly focused, she blocked out all ambient noise and in her mind she saw the school floating through the air. She sensed the magic — that of the trees, plants, animals, and the other witches — around her. The energy pulsed through her veins as she tried again. It had to work. It just had to! "Vola!"

Slowly, she opened her eyes and laughed with relief when she saw her spell working. Her hands were shaking and with all her strength, she managed to hold the building up. Now all she had to do was levitate it to the side to keep the kids safe. She gritted her teeth and mobilized all her energy again when the house finally floated a little to the side. Using tiny little steps, she charmed it away from the abyss.

A jolt like an electric shock to her back sent her to the ground. At the same time, the school crashed to the ground and remained teetering on the edge. Slowly, it tilted sideways toward the chasm. Mayla had to save the children, but she instinctively felt the next curse hissing toward her. She turned quickly and blew a wall of fire even though her back hurt like hell and she could hardly move. Three hunters stood behind her, casting maledictions at the wall of fire, but their curses couldn't penetrate it.

Mayla immediately turned back to the school building and ran toward it. It rocked on the edge of the abyss. She heard the children screaming. Where the heck was the teacher? "Commove!" she yelled, imagining the school being pulled back onto solid ground. With infinitesimal movements, the building slid away from the crevasse that had already swallowed countless homes. Finally, the school was safe and Mayla ran to check on the children.

"Are you okay?" she yelled out before even pulling open the door. No students answered.

Filled with a horrible fear, she yanked the door wide open and looked into the building. The tables and chairs were all piled chaotically along the wall that sloped toward the abyss. In front of and in between, the children were crying and moaning, but so quietly that Mayla hadn't heard them from outside.

"Come on, quick, get out of here!"

The children were in shock, so hardly anyone moved. Without further ado, Mayla ran to them and took two of them by the hand, but the others still wouldn't move.

"I'm Mayla, Melinda's granddaughter. I'm here to help you. Come with me, I'll take you to safety!" Finally, a taller girl with two blonde pigtails stood and took the two smallest by the hands. An older boy rode on the back of another, whose legs were scraped, and who had managed to emerge from his state of shock. One after the other, the children pushed toward Mayla, each trying to reach for her with their small hands. She made sure that nobody went alone and that the two youngest ones were with her. Together, they hurried to the door.

"Where's your teacher?"

The boy pointed outside. "She's fighting!"

Mayla looked to where he was pointing and gulped. A fierce battle was still raging behind her. Where would the children be safe? Where should she hide them from the hunters and especially from Vincent?

"Come with me!" She nodded to the left and together they ran from the deep rift in the earth and the fighting until they were near the fir forest and thus near the glittering wall. But the wall no longer existed. The protection around the world fold was broken, allowing her to run unhindered into the forest with the children.

"Go, go!" Mayla stopped and guided the children from the village between the trees until the last ones were out of the line of fire, and then she brought up the rear. However, a curse strayed toward them, whizzing a hair's breadth past a little boy.

"Don't be afraid!" Mayla insisted, even though she was shaking inside. How could she protect the children without drawing too much attention to them?

Finally, it occurred to her that she had to create a world fold and seal it with a spell. The children would be protected in it! *Contrahe, munde!* she thought, imagining the area where the children were standing folding together and disappearing and unfolding again. She drew a circle of protection in her mind and whispered, "Tuta mundum liberorum!"

Glitter surrounded the children and stretched over them like a protective dome.

Mayla breathed a sigh of relief. "Now you're invisible. Stay under the protection of the dome until the fighting is over!"

"But my mommy!" a girl cried out, and Mayla ran to her. She crouched in front of the little girl, whose tears left tracks on her dusty face. She stroked her arms sympathetically.

"Don't be afraid. Your mom is a strong woman. I'm going to help her and the others to drive away the bad people. Okay?"

The little girl nodded, but then she fell against Mayla and pressed herself against her. She wrapped her short arms around Mayla's neck and held on to her. As if only realizing now what she was doing, she abruptly let go and looked at Mayla sadly.

Mayla tenderly stroked her back. The little girl was sniffling noisily. "What's your name?"

"Juna."

"Juna, did you learn anything about herbal magic at school?"

The little one nodded.

"Then I'm sure you know how to use pine needles to heal the little boy's scrapes, don't you?"

Juna nodded eagerly and immediately set about collecting the needles.

Mayla smiled encouragingly at the children. "Not long now and you'll be reunited with your parents. Have faith!" Then, she turned and sealed the shield behind her so that nothing could happen to the children.

How long did had this all taken? What had happened in the meantime? She dashed back to the village and surveyed what was going on there.

The hunters were definitely in the majority and were pushing the fire witches closer to the chasm that had torn through the settlement. Every house was damaged by the earthquake and the fissure, with many no longer standing. Innumerable lifeless bodies lay on the ground. But from amidst the fighters, her grandmother spotted Mayla. She and Vincent were fighting a fierce duel, with lightning crashing down on him from the sky, but he fended everything off rather calmly.

Shoot. They were outnumbered. They needed assistance. With her eyes closed, Mayla turned her thoughts to little Karl and immediately thought, *Don't come here, sweetheart, just give word at Donnersberg Castle that we need help or the new circle will destroy us!* She also sent him pictures of the devastation.

A high-pitched meow wandered through her thoughts and she knew the kitten had understood her. Hopefully their people would come even though they had not been welcome at this head-quarters as outcasts for some time.

Ready to fight, Mayla raised her hands and attacked the hunters from the side. At the same time, she ran to her people so as not to unwittingly lead the hunters to the children and the hidden fold. Better safe than sorry, and she wanted to be sure the fighting didn't take place too close to them.

As she threw spell after spell at the attackers, sweat trickled down her forehead and pasted strands of hair to her face. She brushed them aside with the back of her hand and cast one Dirumpe spell after another to blow up anything near the hunters. Using the Dearma spell, she managed to disarm a few enemies and kept blowing flames at the attackers, pushing them back. Still, they were vastly outnumbered by Vincent and his men.

In the midst of all this, Melinda was still fighting a witch duel with Vincent, with neither one penetrating the other's protection nor succeeding in a disarming or producing a fatal blow. They threw their hands in the air, sparks of light flashing between them with seemingly no end in sight.

Another group of attackers rushed the village. How much longer would the fire witches hold out?

Screams erupted and more curses flew as a familiar face finally appeared from behind the hunters. Violett. And next to her stood Angelika, Eduardo, Anna, Thomas, and the other members of the Inner Circle. All but Artus had come to stand by their side. In addition, she spotted a few outcasts who had returned to Donnersberg Castle in the evening.

The fighters were attacked from two sides and although they still outnumbered them, their opponents huddled in the middle. Even Vincent took a few steps back and stopped. He scanned the dead lying on the ground and laughed. A shiver ran down Mayla's back.

"Nowhere are you safe from me! I'll be back. And little by little, I will destroy all who stand in my way!" With that, he grasped his amulet key and vanished along with his hunters, as if his spell encompassed all his coven members.

Exhausted, some villagers fell to their knees while others looked around in horror. The settlement was completely destroyed. Fires burned in several corners and none of the houses looked as they did before. Many were broken in two, walls had collapsed, and all windows were shattered. The deep chasm that cut through the center of the headquarters had dragged countless buildings and objects with it. From afar, Mayla couldn't make out if there were people among them.

She ran to her grandmother, who was standing among the outcasts.

"Are you okay?" she called out to her.

Melinda merely nodded and ran her hands

through her white curls. She appeared exhausted. The fight hadn't left her unscathed.

"What happened?" Angelika asked, looking around in bewilderment. "How were they able to enter?"

"They've grown stronger." Melinda shook her head in disbelief. "They fight using ancient magic. Still, I don't understand why Vincent himself is growing more and more powerful." Wearily, she stroked her forehead when a determined expression appeared on her face and she looked around. "Look who came to our rescue!" she called out to the surviving villagers, who kept a wary distance from the outcasts.

"Where are our children?" a woman screamed, pointing to where the school had stood and where the teacher lay lifeless on the scorched earth.

"Don't worry," Mayla explained immediately. "I took them to safety. Maybe they shouldn't see all the dead."

"We must clean up!" a man shouted.

"No, we have to get to safety first. Us, and especially the children!" another replied.

"But we're no longer safe here..." a young woman wailed sadly.

"All of you are welcome in our castle!" Angelika announced.

"Thank you, dear Angelika. That's a good idea!" Smiling, Melinda took her long-time friend's hand. "'Those who want to come to the castle, pack your things within thirty minutes and come to the entrance to the village."

"What about the dead?"

"We'll lay them out side by side and come back as soon as we can," insisted Emilia, who, with the support of other council members, immediately put her words into action.

"Where are the children?" The woman who had asked earlier approached Mayla again, followed by other worried mothers and fathers who hurried closer.

"I'll take you to them."

They hustled across the devastated ground and climbed over broken house walls and fallen fence posts until they reached the forest and the place where the children were waiting for their parents. They couldn't be seen, but Mayla knew exactly where the hidden world fold was. She released the protection shield around the fold and immediately the children ran out. Overjoyed, the families hugged each other and everyone thanked Mayla heartily. Luckily, she had managed to save the children. Satisfied, she watched the exchanges of hugs and kisses before returning to her grandma and Violett.

"By the way, where's Georg?" she asked her friend.

"He's with the police." Violett glanced around. "It's good that you called us, Mayla. What terrible destruction they caused to our beautiful head-quarters."

"We'll rebuild it all when the time comes," Melinda pointed out. "It's not the first time we've had to rebuild, and we'll get through it."

Together, with her grandmother, they retrieved a few things from the destroyed house including the thick grimoire and other old books before jumping to Donnersberg Castle. No one stayed behind — none declined the invitation. And so, for the first time in over thirty years, the Circle members and the outcasts shook hands.

Chapter Seventeen

At the castle, Angelika assigned rooms to the homeless fire witches. It was nice to see how the distrust toward her was diminishing, little by little.

Meanwhile, Mayla went to the castle hall with her grandmother and the other members of the Inner Circle. "Where is Artus anyway?"

Apparently nobody knew.

Susana sat down next to her at the table and touched a purple discoloration running down her arm. "How did Vincent manage to break into our headquarters? Granted, the hunters who are still members of the Fire Circle can enter, but he shouldn't have been able to gain entrance to the magic gate, let alone see the village fold."

"I can't explain it either," Melinda moaned. Not knowing made her appear even more tired. She had emerged from the fight with Vincent unscathed, but Mayla could see the duel had used up a lot of her energy. "Mayla and I renewed the protection just yesterday. Vincent can't be that strong already."

Exhausted, Mayla sat down at the table. "Could it have something to do with him starting to incorporate the ancient magic?"

Melinda whirled around to look at her, eyes wide. "He what? Why don't I know about that?"

Mayla perked up. "I just found out yesterday and Artus said he'd let you know right away. So, you didn't get his message?"

Melinda knit her white eyebrows. "No, I didn't hear from him." She looked up searchingly. "Where is he?"

Violett shrugged her bony shoulders. "He hasn't been around since this morning. Nobody has seen him."

"Tell me, Mayla! Who gave you this information?" Melinda asked, still looking around suspiciously.

"I met Tom. He told me." Mayla expected to get an earful, but her grandmother did not seem at all surprised.

"What exactly did he tell you?"

"That his father doesn't just want revenge but also plans on uniting the old magic with his metal circle. When he killed my mother Emma and almost all of the Montgomerys and the de Rochats as well, he gathered their powers and absorbed them. All he needs now is the power of the water witches to completely bring the old magic together."

"So that's why he was so strong. And Emma's energy allowed him to infiltrate our headquarters." Melinda closed her eyes and exhaled deeply. "To hell with that cursed von Eisenfels! Why didn't you rush to me as soon as you found out about this? For heaven's sake, Mayla! What were you thinking?"

"I was going to, but then I got another message from Tom."

"Another?" Melinda and the others looked at her in surprise.

"Why didn't you tell us about it?" Violett asked.

"Because I had no time to lose. It was about von Eisenfels finding out where I grew up. He wanted to abduct my parents to use as leverage against me."

"So, you spent the whole night saving them instead of coming to me and warning me," Melinda concluded.

"Correct."

"How clever." Eduardo tapped the table with two fingers. "Tom made sure to gain your trust with the first message, only to distract you with the second."

"Excuse me? What are you implying?"

"That he fooled you!"

"No! He didn't. He was serious, he..."

"Mayla." Matthew looked at her angrily.

"Eduardo could be right. It would be one hell of a coincidence if..."

"No, he's wrong! I feel I can trust Tom." She reached for the heart-shaped pendant on her chain, but it was no longer around her neck. Her hand went to her pocket where she found the necklace, pulled it out, and ran it through her fingers. She knew how stubborn and naive she must sound to others, but she listened to her instincts and her heart, and that voice was unambiguous. "I trust him and all of you should do the same. Only through him did we receive this information. And he said he's looking for a cure so we can heal the forgotten curses in the future."

"We talked about solo runs endangering others!" Melinda proclaimed, ignoring her arguments.

"Stop, it's not my fault they were able to attack."

A deep line appeared between Melinda's white brows. "If I had known about it last night, things might have turned out differently today."

"Wait!" Anna interjected. "Artus wanted to send you his cat! That's what he said and that's why Mayla stayed with us longer. She wanted to see you immediately. Artus, however, slowed her down. All of us heard him assure her he'd take it upon himself to tell you about it. You didn't receive a message from him?"

Curious, Melinda sat up in her chair. "No, I did not."

Angelika had returned and was silently following the conversation. Now, however, she could no longer contain herself. "I don't know what you mean by that, Anna, but my husband is innocent. I have been married to him for over fifty years and if there is anyone I blindly trust, it is him."

"Then why didn't he deliver the message to Melinda as promised?" Anna asked.

"He didn't spend last night in his bed. I don't know where he went last night, but I'd put my hand in the fire for him!"

An embarrassed silence followed until Anna spoke again. "Either Artus or Tom... Neither seems to be telling the truth. Personally, I'd put my hand in the fire for Tom!"

Melinda observed Angelika for a long time without saying a word. Mayla, however, thought she could hear her grandmother arguing with herself about the dilemma.

"I'll search for him and then everything will be cleared up!" Angelika stormed out of the hall.

Eduardo watched her, shaking his head. "I can understand where she's coming from, but we have to consider everyone."

"Let her find him. In the meantime, we'll think about what to do next." Melinda waved and countless coffee pots and cups appeared on the table and Mayla conjured up her boxes of chocolates.

Gradually, the fire witches whose village had been destroyed entered the castle hall and joined the others at the long table. When Georg entered the hall, Mayla immediately ran to meet him.

"What's going on here?"

"Vincent and his followers raided the Fire Circle headquarters and destroyed it. Everyone there was in great danger."

Georg's features dropped. "He what?"

She quickly told him what had transpired.

"He was able to enter the headquarters? Heck, then the witches have no place to hide from him. We must warn the De Fonte family. He must not capture them."

"No, I'm sure they're safe in their place. He hasn't murdered any of them and robbed them of their powers, so technically, he cannot enter their headquarters. He still lacks the water power to fully unite the ancient magic."

"Then it's a good thing that Alessia and her children have been hiding for so long." He stroked his lips, pondering. "We have to stop him at all costs. Just how?"

Violett stepped up to them and smiled at him. "Hello, Georg. Were you successful?" She blushed slightly when he looked at her.

"Yes, there are some who are not . A few police officers no longer want to pursue the matter of the missing witches, even though it's so urgent. They pretend they want to stop von Eisenfels, but in reality, they just sit around and do nothing. Many of my colleagues are becoming skeptical. They are willing to hear you out."

"That's wonderful." Violett beamed and for a moment, it looked like she wanted to throw her arms around his neck. But she held back and hugged Mayla instead. "Honestly, I hate life as an outcast. How I would like to be an active member of the Fire Circle again, attending meetings, strolling through the cities, and meeting old friends. Going around without a signet ring makes it increasingly harder every year."

"This is our chance!" Mayla smiled at her encouragingly and turned back to Georg. "So, how did you leave things with them?"

"I wanted to speak to Melinda, Angelika, and Artus about how we could have a meeting on neutral ground so that everyone is comfortable and sensible words can be exchanged."

"Oddly enough, Artus has disappeared. He didn't deliver the message to my grandma last night like he promised. And according to Angelika, he didn't spend the night in his bed."

He stroked his copper-red beard thoughtfully. "That's strange. And because of Tom's message, you didn't go to your grandmother in person either. That looks like a..."

"Georg, I can already guess what you want to say. But I trust Tom."

"I know you do, but I hope you trust me too. So feel free to let me finish."

She smiled. "I'm all ears."

Georg crossed his arms in front of his chest. "Someone wants us to stop trusting Tom."

Violett's eyes grew round. "Vincent! He knows he was with us. Maybe your parents were merely a red herring."

"But the hunters showed up! You can confirm that, Georg. Who knows what they would have done to my parents or to Heike!"

"Yeah, they kept us on the run for most of the night and then we stayed in hiding, so you couldn't see your grandma. That's quite a coincidence, don't you think?"

Mayla nodded thoughtfully. "Both of you could be right. Vincent doesn't want us to trust Tom. So he must have found out that Tom was seeing me. Meaning, he's in great danger!" Her eyes widened with concern.

Georg shook his head. "Not necessarily. Maybe Vincent just wants to be on the safe side in case Tom reveals anything Vincent is planning."

Violett put her hand on her arm. "Tom can take care of himself."

Mayla sighed. How she would like to have him safely by her side. Suddenly, she remembered something. "So, why didn't Artus deliver the message?"

"We absolutely must find that out." Georg rolled up the sleeves of his shirt and scanned the castle with his policeman's eyes. "I'll search for him too. See you later." He trudged up the stairs with determined steps and shortly afterward, he disappeared out of sight. Violett watched him, unable to hide her yearning expression.

Mayla registered it with a smile. "You like him, don't you?"

Violett turned bright red. "No, it's just... he's really nice."

Mayla took her friend's hand and their bracelets jingled together. "He and I are only friends."

Violett looked at her with uncertainty in her pretty gray eyes. "Does he know that too?"

Mayla nodded, causing a wide grin to spread across her friend's face.

"Good to know." Violett winked at her with flushed cheeks before they went back into the hall. They headed for Mayla's grandmother, who was busy planning and deliberating with the others.

"We must warn Alessia!" a fire witch shouted. "She's no longer safe at her headquarters. Everything depends on Vincent not getting his hands on her and her family."

"No, on the contrary, Alessia has to stay put!" Melinda insisted.

Mayla agreed. "I bet he raided the Fire Circle to unsettle everyone and to lure her and her family out into the open."

"Does he know we are here?" another woman

from the village asked. "Are our children safe from him?"

"I put a shield around the castle," Melinda pointed out.

"So, he was able to break the protective barrier around our village!"

"The protection around the circle keeps all at bay who are not fire witches. It didn't work on him because he has fire magic within him. The protective shield around the castle, however, isn't only to keep members of other circles from entering it. This protection is directed at any intruder, no matter what power they carry. Let's hope it's enough to keep him out." Melinda motioned to Mayla and Violett to come with her. "Come on, we have to go to the library. I need your help."

"Let me get a few more chocolates!" Mayla conjured up a box. On the way to the library, between a fine chocolate and a rum ball, she went ahead and shared what Tom had confided in her. Mayla explained in detail what Tom had told her. She also told them about the healing potion and how to prepare it.

Her grandmother nodded in understanding. "I know what he means. I can brew such a healing potion with Anna, John, and Pierre. I'll take care of it right away. But first, I'll show you what you two are going to start with."

Melinda led the two into the library, where several old books were stacked on a worktable in one corner. "I've gathered every book I have. We must skim them all as quickly as possible. If you find anything about ancient magic or forgotten curses, let me know immediately. Understood?"

Violett's eyes brightened at the old works that could not be found in any public library. "We'll start right away."

While Mayla and Violett bent over the texts, Melinda rushed off to brew a healing potion. It wasn't long before she returned. Together, the three studied the ancient knowledge. Mayla was letting one praline after another fly into her mouth — after all, she had some catching up to do — when she suddenly jumped up.

"Ha! I have something! In *Rosalind von Flammenstein's, Ancient Knowledge*. Let me read it to you.

Ever since the Circles were founded, there has been a fear that someone might attempt to reunite the ancient magic in order to usurp the witch world. Many people claim that this is impossible. However, there are enough practitioners of black magic who don't shy away from even the most abominable experiments. It's always safe to assume that one day someone might succeed."

Violett's eyes lit up. "Great, that's what we were looking for. Read on."

"As long as the magic stones remain separated, this union does not apply to the entire witch world, but only the one who casts the spell."

Maya looked up. "The magic stones... at least Vincent doesn't have them."

Melinda nodded. "I hid ours."

"Didn't Artus take possession of ours?" Mayla exclaimed.

Melinda immediately shook her head. "I took it back long ago. Don't worry, the stone is safe. There's no need for concern. But have you come across anything that tells us how to stop the one who has the ancient magic within them?" Curious, Melinda also bent over the book in front of Mayla and scanned the yellowed pages.

"*Should someone succeed in uniting the ancient magic within themselves, only the combined power of the mighty Circle families can stop them.*"

"The combined power." Violett looked at Melinda. "So, from each circle, a member of the founding family must be involved?"

"Presumably so. We might even succeed. The two of us, Mayla, Phylis..."

"But Phylis isn't a member of a founding family," Violett pointed out.

"But she's the strongest earth witch I know. In the broadest sense, she too could be described as a member of a powerful circle family. We have to try. Plus Gabrielle, Tom, and Andrew."

Mayla paled. "I hope Andrew hasn't already gone off on his own to stop Vincent."

Melinda looked at her determinedly. "We have to meet him and tell him what we found out. I hope he's still with us after his hasty departure yesterday."

Mayla toyed with the chain in her trouser pocket. "I'll take care of that! I have an idea about how to get him to finally work with us."

"Fine, but return to the castle as soon as you can. It's dangerous out there..." A worried look crossed Melinda's face, so Mayla smiled confidently at her grandmother.

"Don't worry! I know what I have to do."

Chapter Eighteen

After jumping to the Black Forest and creating an additional world fold there, Mayla prepared two Nuntia spells that she had little Karl deliver to the recipients. Hopefully her plan would work. Despite all the events of the past few weeks, she was still a confirmed optimist at heart, which was why she rubbed her hands in anticipation.

As time ticked by and no one showed up, she grew nervous, pacing back and forth, rubbing her arms over and over again. Would her plan work?

Finally, she saw the sparkle she'd been waiting for appear next to a small fir tree. Then Andrew materialized before her and immediately blew a protective ring of wind around himself as she grinned steadily at him.

"Andrew, I'm so glad you came."

His gaze was cold and dismissive. He peered

suspiciously around the deserted woodland, where nothing could be seen but conifers, saplings, moss, and ferns. "What do you want?"

"We figured out a way to stop Vincent together."

"I thought I made myself clear. I'll take care of him on my own!"

"You won't succeed. He has begun to unite the old power within himself. Listen, Andrew, we need you. Only with members of the powerful Circle families standing side by side can we stop him."

"And by members of all the Circle families, you probably mean Tom too... or should I say Valerius?"

"Him too, yes, and..."

"I will never stand beside a von Eisenfels." His jaw clenched and Mayla thought he was going to disappear, but he paused.

"Please, Andrew. I can see why you're having a hard time trusting him and all of us, but there's no other way we can stop Vincent."

"You don't have any idea about me and my life!" he yelled, but Mayla didn't flinch.

"My parents were killed too. Nevertheless, I know that we only have a chance with Tom. We must join together."

"I'll never join anyone again!"

"That's not nice to hear," a man said.

Andrew spun around, startled, and his eyes widened for a moment as he beheld Cesaro Aguilera in front of him.

Mayla smiled at the paunchy Spaniard. "I'm glad you came. Thank you, Cesaro."

Andrew narrowed his dark, blazing eyes. "You arranged this?"

"I thought it was time for a talk!"

"You..."

"Andrew, please." Cesaro walked up to him and held out his hands. Despite the whirlwind, he continued to approach him. What would happen if his hands touched the shield? Would he be thrown back? Would he sustain life-threatening injuries? However, Cesaro kept smiling and walking toward Andrew. His fingertips would touch the twister raging around Andrew at any moment. Before he made contact, the wind died down and hissed away through the fir branches. Cesaro took Andrew's hands and smiled at him.

"Gracias a Dios that I finally see you again..." Although Cesaro barely reached his shoulders, he hugged him as only a father could his son. And Andrew allowed it. But then he straightened up and stepped back from Cesaro.

"Stay away from me! You know how dangerous I am," Andrew shouted, sounding desperate.

"You are not dangerous. What happened then was an accident. It could have happened to anyone."

"But it happened to me and it's my fault Sofia is dead!"

"No, that was a mistake."

"Yes, I practiced secretly with your grimoire even though you told me not to. I spoke the spell that killed her."

Tears welled up in Mayla's eyes at the desperation in Andrew's voice.

"You lost your beloved wife because you were good and took me in. I condemned you to a life of solitude — and how did I thank you? By killing one of you!"

Cesaro smiled sadly. "You were young and unaware of your abilities. We should never have stopped you from testing your strong powers. Then you would have known how to control them. I asked you repeatedly to hide your abilities. So, it's my fault, Andrew. I should have supported you more."

"You always supported me, Papa."

"Then why did you walk away?"

"How could I ever forgive myself for what I did to Mama? Evil lurks inside me. Everyone around me is in danger."

"Andrew, that's not true. You're a good boy, a good man. Look at you! You are trying to stop the one who has brought untold evil upon us. Though you have lived among the hunters for so long, I see that your heart is still pure. I know you were pretending, that you never took part in the killing and tormenting the hunters did."

"How do you know...?"

"Do you think I gave up my most important job

of protecting you simply because you left me? I never left you, my son. I've always tried to have your back."

Andrew was silent and looked sadly at Cesaro. "How can I ever forgive myself..."

"I forgave you long ago, and Sofia," he said, gesturing up at the sky, "I'm certain she did too. She loved you like her own son. She wouldn't have wanted this because of an accident — because that was what it was, an accident, it wasn't done on purpose! She wouldn't have wanted it to tear us apart."

Andrew took a deep breath.

"Forgive yourself, my boy, and please, forgive me too."

Abruptly, Andrew wrapped his arms around Cesaro. "There is nothing to forgive!"

While the two spoke, Mayla quietly withdrew. She didn't want to disturb the two under any circumstances. It was the only way she could persuade Andrew to stand by her side. She didn't know what had happened back then with the Aguileras, but she suspected that a meeting between the two could set things right. And even if they didn't succeed in stopping Vincent, at least the two of them were reunited.

Cesaro looked up and nodded to Mayla. She waved, clutched the amulet key, and jumped back to the castle. There was a lot to do.

Before joining the others in the castle hall, she

crept into the kitchen and made herself a sand-wich. Her stomach was growling so loudly it was unbearable. After the snack, she felt her strength return and she hurried to the others in the castle hall in good spirits.

Melinda, Violett, the other members of the Inner Circle, and the residents of the destroyed witch village were still arguing.

"Has Artus made an appearance yet?" she asked Violett, who only shook her head.

"Georg and Angelika have been searching for him for hours, so far without success."

"Artus as a traitor, hard to imagine," Anna reflected, which immediately ignited a heated debate again. They discussed it for a while until Georg and Angelika came back into the castle hall.

"Have you found my husband anywhere?" the lady of the castle asked, unusually nervous.

Violett gave her a doubtful look. "No, so you still haven't found him either?"

Georg shook his head. "No, nothing. There's no trace of him."

"He's a traitor!" cried out a witch from the village who had been listening in silence for a while.

"I won't allow such comments!" Angelika looked at him sternly. "Don't forget who's giving you shelter!"

The others grumbled and murmured, but no one spoke up.

"Artus?" a thin female voice drifted in from the castle hall. "Artus? Are you there?"

Pale as chalk, Melinda and Angelika rushed into the hall, closely followed by Mayla, Violett, and a few others. Standing there was an old woman with shoulder-length gray hair that swept around her head in great waves. Her eyes were watery and the look in her light-blue eyes was frightened. Still, she'd positioned herself like a mother hen in front of a lanky man whose light-blond hair was streaked with gray and a woman Mayla knew. It was Gabrielle De Fonte. At that moment, it dawned on her.

Alessia De Fonte and her only offspring...

"Alessia, what on earth are you doing here?" Melinda exclaimed angrily. At the same time, she looked around warily as if she feared an immediate attack by the hunters or Vincent himself.

Shoulders hunched, the head witch looked around the hall as if an enemy might leap out from behind any of the suits of armor. She gave Mayla, Violett, and the others skeptical looks before focusing on Melinda. "Artus sent us a message. The Fire Circle was attacked and we are no longer safe from Vincent. He said I should come with Gabrielle and Francesco."

"What?" Angelika stared at her in disbelief. "When did he send you the message? And how?"

"Less than an hour ago! I received a Nuntia spell."

Mayla and Violett looked at each other, speechless.

Angelika rubbed her forehead. "How can that...?"

"Artus told you to come here?" Mayla looked at Gabrielle in horror. "But that isn't right. Vincent only needs your power to unite the old magic. You should have stayed at your headquarters."

"We had planned to. I wouldn't shoo my children from their safe nest to get eaten by lions simply because Artus sent us the message, but we were attacked by our own people."

"Excuse me?" Mayla peered wide-eyed at Gabrielle and her brother. "Who are you talking about?"

Francesco held back while Gabrielle snapped, "Our own people. The members of the Water Circle. They also heard about the attack on the Fire Circle and accused us — not without justification — of inaction. They yelled that this is the only reason it has come this far."

Alessia gasped for air. There was horror in her doll-like eyes. "I have to protect my children. That is my primary duty!"

"First, come in," Violett prompted her, pointing to the hall with her hand.

"No, you cannot stay." Melinda shook her head vehemently. "He expects you to come here to take shelter with us. I'm sure his people incited the water witches to make such a mess of your headquarters and drive you out. We need another hiding place."

Gabrielle clenched her hands into fists. "I'm tired of hiding! I'll help you and..."

"No, if he catches you, it's over. Then, he'll be unstoppable," Melinda warned. "He already has combined the earth, fire, and air power. He already possesses metal. If he murders one of you and robs you of your energy, it will become almost impossible to do anything against him."

"I'm telling you, my child, we have to hide!" Alessia laid her wrinkled hand on Gabrielle's. Despite being the oldest living witch in the family, she lacked the vitality of the other old women. Her face was pale and wrinkled, her skin sagging and withered. If Mayla didn't know any better, she would have bet it was a perfectly normal woman and not a witch, let alone the head witch of the Water Circle.

"Alessia De Fonte?" Georg came into the hall. "I thought I recognized your voice. What are you doing here?" He was followed by John and Eduardo, who appeared equally shocked to see the family. They immediately positioned themselves protectively around her as if they were her bodyguards and as if the head witch and her adult children were unable to protect themselves.

A rumble echoed throughout the castle, shaking it to its very foundation. Plaster trickled from the ceiling and a suit of armor tipped sideways, landing with a clatter on the stone floor. Mayla and Violett looked at each other questioningly while Alessia's light-blue eyes widened in shock.

"He's coming..."

Chapter Nineteen

"We need somewhere else safe to hide you!" Melinda brooded. "Do you want to go to my house where I hid for a few weeks?"

Georg stroked his red beard. "No, the hunters know that one since police officers were there. It's too obvious! Do you want to go to my place?"

"All opposition members' residences are not good." Mayla peered questioningly at Violett. "I would suggest my home in the human world, but the hunters know that too."

"We'll take her to Bertha!" Eduardo suggested. "She accommodates everyone, no questions asked. Besides, the hotel is in a neutral zone. He would never expect us to hide the De Fontes in such an unsecured place."

"Didn't she plan on closing it so she could visit her relatives?" Mayla asked.

More thunder rang out over the castle. Silently, they gazed at the ceiling as if they could see the horror drawing nearer. They heard shouts and a commotion in the hall.

"There is no other alternative!" Melinda nodded. "We have to take you away right now. I'd like to accompany you, but he's counting on that. You can't even be near me."

"I'll take them," Violett suggested.

"I'll go too," Eduardo confirmed. "Together we can do it!"

Gabrielle looked determinedly at Mayla and Melinda. "I would like to fight by your side. Believe me, this is the last time you will have to do without my help. I swear to you on my family's behalf!"

Mayla hugged her goodbye.

"Come!" Alessia held out her trembling hands to her children. "Let's not waste another minute."

"Good luck," Mayla called after them, and Violett disappeared with a wink along with Eduardo, Alessia, Francesco, and Gabrielle.

"I'd love to go with them!" Mayla glanced down at her hands. "But even that would probably be too obvious."

"That it would." Georg put his hands on his hips. "We'll defend the castle and the people here."

"But how can we stop him? Maybe we should have kept Gabrielle here and called Phylis, Andrew, and Tom after all."

More thunder shook the walls, announcing the imminent arrival of their enemies.

Melinda shook her head. "As long as Vincent hasn't fully mastered the magic, we might be able to stop him without her. He mustn't catch Gabrielle. It would be foolish to keep them here. Hurry, we need to prepare!"

They rushed back into the castle hall, where everyone had formed a circle with their backs to each other, their wands drawn, and the children in the center.

"We have to get the little ones away," Melinda demanded.

"We should hide them in a fold!" Mayla suggested. "I'll take care of it." She ran over to them, waving the children along. The little ones already knew her. After saying goodbye to their parents, they followed Mayla without any hesitation. Only two little girls started to cry and clung to their mothers.

Mayla stroked one of them comfortingly on her brown shock of hair and glanced at her mother. "It would be better if the children weren't left to their own devices anyway. We don't know what's going to happen."

"You're absolutely right. Did you hear, Malea, I'm coming with you. Mommy is going to stay with you." The little girl clutched her mother's neck as if still afraid someone might pull her away. The mother of the other crying child also came along.

Together with Georg, Mayla guided the crowd
to the exit of the hall. The next clap of thunder
shook the paintings from the walls, their heavy
wooden frames crashing to the floor. They darted
around the pictures as fast as they could with the
children. Many of the little ones were scared and
kept looking up at the ceiling.

Georg winked at one of the boys, who seemed
so scared it was heartbreaking. "It's going to be a
wonderful adventure. You'll see."

The little boy nodded bravely and ran on with
his friends.

When she arrived in the foyer, Mayla glanced
around uncertainly. "Where shall we hide you?
Maybe in the vaulted cellar?"

"And what if the castle collapses?" Georg asked
in a whisper.

"Then we'll take them to the library."

They rushed through the dark corridors up to
the large reading room. In no time at all, Mayla had
cast a world fold in the middle of the bookshelves,
giving it extra protection so that no curse could
penetrate it and nobody would discover the children. The little ones were unusually quiet, none
speaking a word. They stood close together like
penguins and peered around anxiously. Mayla
would have liked to hug them one by one, but they
had to sell it as a game to the children so that they
wouldn't be afraid.

"So, you'll stay up here all by yourself in the

library and..." She looked questioningly at the two mothers, who quickly introduced themselves as Helen and Franziska. "And Franziska and Helen will tell you some wonderful stories. It's going to be a wonderful adventure, okay?"

"Stories?" The children's eyes lit up and they sat on the floor in a circle around the two mothers. Helen and Franziska immediately started talking about a clumsy bear and his cheeky little friend the squirrel. The children laughed and were hanging on the storytellers' every word, spellbound. Still, Mayla found it difficult to break away from them.

Georg gently pulled her away. "Come on, Mayla, we're needed downstairs."

"You're right." She closed the fold so that no one could see it and left the library with Georg. "I hope it's enough, given the power Vincent has amassed."

"You did your best. Now it's up to all of us to stop him and his followers." He took her hand and squeezed it, and when Mayla looked up, she saw him grinning as usual. Relieved, she smiled back at him and took a deep breath. Finally, they could be just good friends.

A loud crash resounded through the castle and instinctively, they squatted on the stone floor. Shouts rang out and loud cries mixed with strange voices echoed throughout the castle. Mayla and Georg stared at each other in shock.

"'They are here."

Together, they ran down the narrow passage to

the stairs. However, the first hunters were already advancing on them. Curses flew and Mayla swiftly blew a wall of fire so that the spells ricocheted off of it. But the attackers didn't let up, firing one male-diction after another so that Mayla couldn't break the shield, let alone attack the intruders.

"We have to get downstairs to help the others! How do we get past them?"

"Patience, Mayla. They'll leave us alone soon." Wand raised, he stood ready beside her. She had met him so many weeks ago and now here they were alongside each other in their last stand. Was this the last stand? Would the future of the witch world be decided here and now, at Donnersberg Castle?

Screams rose from below.

"We can't wait, Georg, we have to risk it. Get ready," she whispered to him. "One, two, three!" She blew out the flames and immediately a beam of yellow-white light shot out of his wand at the attackers, but they swiftly conjured a shield in front of them.

"Now, let's see what I've learned." Mayla raised her hands and sent a lightning bolt at the hunters, shattering their protection. She then cast another knock-out spell, causing her opponents to fall to the ground, where they remained motionless.

"Wow, Mayla." Georg looked at her as if he were seeing her for the first time.

"Let's go!"

They charged the stairs, but more attackers hurled curses at them. "Defende!" Mayla and Georg shouted in unison, and the approaching maledictions disintegrated in thin air.

"Dirumpe!" Georg yelled, causing a pillar to break. The rocks fell on the hunters. When the attackers turned to protect themselves, the distraction was enough for Mayla to fire another knock-out spell at the wizards, causing two of them to fall to their knees and remain motionless. The others, however, threw a curse at her that missed Mayla by a hair. It slammed behind her into a door, which squeaked open. Mayla involuntarily followed the malediction with her eyes and glanced briefly around the room when her mouth fell open.

Someone was lying in the middle of the small room on the wooden floor. All she could see was a motionless hand and arm, but the royal cloak was unmistakable.

Before she could run, an attack spell hit her hand and she cursed. In a flash, she blew a wall of flames in front of them. "Come here, Georg. Look at this!"

His gaze darted to the room for a moment. "No, we have to..." But then he fell silent. With his mouth open, he stepped into the room next to Mayla and finally got a glimpse of the man lying on the floor.

It was Artus von Donnersberg.

They quickly bent down to him and Mayla felt a weak pulse. "What did they do to him?"

"Rather, the question is: Who did this to him?" Georg jumped up and searched the room, but it was uninhabited. The bed wasn't rumpled and there weren't any clothes in the closet or chest of drawers. There were no books on the bedside table and no trash in the wastebasket by the door. Not a single clue could be found as to who had immobilized the lord of the castle and confined him.

"Goodness, how long has he been here? Someone must have prevented him from passing the message on to my grandma!" Mayla's eyes widened in shock. "There's another mole in the Inner Circle!"

"You're right. That must be it. And that someone was at the castle earlier to manipulate Artus with a spell so he'd send a message to Alessia to come here."

"Georg, who could it have been?"

He patted Artus down, looking for any clues that might tell them more, but nothing could be found. He pointed his wand at the unconscious lord of the castle. "Indicia!" Nothing happened and Georg stroked his beard. "The person responsible definitely did a thorough job covering their tracks."

Mayla held her hands over von Donnersberg and whispered, "Sana!" Still, the lord of the castle didn't move.

Georg shook his head. "He needs a healing

potion. His pulse is weak but steady. We'll have to leave him for now and deal with him later. At least he's safe in this room."

"I'm sure the hunters saw we were in here!" As if in confirmation, they heard the attackers' curses hiss through the air, which sent pictures crashing down from the walls and broke glass lampshades on the stone floor.

"We'll seal the door with a spell and try to get downstairs. Then we'll let Angelika know."

"All right." Suddenly, Mayla stopped and looked up. "Do you smell that?"

Georg shook his head. "What do you think?"

"Peppermint! It smells of peppermint!"

"So?"

"Artus never smelled like that — and I know because I have a darn good nose. I only know of one person who that smell follows like a shadow."

He listened. "Who?"

"Eduardo."

"Eduardo? You mean to say that... he...?"

"I bet that's it." Mayla slapped her forehead, aghast. "Along with Violett, he accompanied Alessia, Francesco, and Gabrielle to Bertha's hotel! We must go after them immediately and warn them!"

"Damn, you're right. Now I smell it too. But the defenses around the castle are still intact enough that we can only jump from the hall."

"Then we have to get there at once!" Mayla

grabbed his hand and pulled him along. They ran into the corridor, closed the door, and sealed it. Then they turned back to the hunters, who were still hurling curses at the wall of flames. Mayla smothered them and the battle continued. More and more attackers advanced on them. Darn it, how did they enter the hall? Was Vincent already there? Was he fighting her grandma? If Eduardo had let Vincent know where the water witches were, it was over. Every second counted!

Determined to move on, Mayla blew a sea of flames at the attackers, who backed away in terror, some even jumping over the banisters to escape.

When she stopped, Georg cast countless spells on those remaining so that they began to make progress again. They fought doggedly against the hunters, who fell one after the other, and he and Mayla continued down the stairs. They used magic to clear the way until they were finally in the hall.

"We have to tell the others!" Mayla exclaimed.

"No, we have no time to waste. Besides, who knows if we'd even make it to them." Flashes of light hissed through the air and Mayla and Georg ducked to avoid being hit.

"Shoot, you're right." She held out her hand, grasped the amulet key, and thought, *Perduce nos in domum Berthae!* and together they jumped straight to Bertha's hotel.

Everything was dark. No guests were in the reception room or going up the stairs. No voices could be heard. The hotel must have been already closed.

"Violett?" Mayla blew a flame onto her finger-tip. The flickering light illuminated the dark wooden furniture and cast a long glow across the floorboards. Mayla slowly turned in a circle. Nobody was around. "Why did Violett and the De Fontes leave it dark?"

"I'm sure they didn't want people on the street to notice that someone was in the hotel since Bertha isn't here. Lux!" A small flame appeared on Georg's wand, which, together with Mayla's, cast flickering light through the deserted hotel. "Stay behind me."

"But I..."

"Never forget, he wants you dead too."

A shiver ran down her spine, but they had to warn Alessia, Gabrielle, Francesco, and Violett. "My powers are stronger than yours, so the time of hiding behind you has passed, Georg."

His eyes spoke more than a thousand words. He didn't care. He was the man, the protector, and he couldn't allow her to take the lead.

Mayla smiled half-heartedly. "We'll do this together, okay?"

"Fine. Maybe they're still in hiding and Eduardo hasn't contacted Vincent yet."

"I hope so."

They crept into the deserted room where just weeks ago, Mayla had enjoyed having breakfast while talking to old Bertha. "Fortunately, Bertha has gone to see her relatives."

"It would be horrible if she and other hotel guests were in the line of fire."

They moved on and quietly left the room before heading for the stairs. "Let's continue looking upstairs."

She nodded. Hands raised, she crept up the steps beside him. Everything was dark here, too, with all the doors locked and the thick curtains drawn in front of every window. "Where did they go?"

"I'd like to know that, too." Georg raised his wand so that the glow of the flame reached higher, but there was still no one to be seen.

"I'll use the Seeking charm to find them!" Mayla focused on her friend and thought, *Quaere Violettam!* A fine glitter emanated from her fingertips, then spun in a circle and flew down the stairs behind them. Immediately, they rushed after the sparkle. It spiraled through the air, wafting down the steps and whizzing around corners until it lingered in the middle of the breakfast room. However, there was nothing to see. The glitter spun circles in the air and disappeared.

Georg frowned. "How can that be?"

Tilting her head, Mayla stared at the spot. Nothing out of the ordinary stood out to her, but then she had an idea. "Perhaps there is a world fold here. Even if the room doesn't appear any smaller than usual..." She looked around, undecided.

"A fold? That would explain it. But who created it? Do you think Vincent was here already and forced Gabrielle or one of the others to form one?"

"Vincent can do it just as easily as can Tom. He's probably already here." She looked up, startled. "If Eduardo was spying on us, then he told Vincent I was seeing Tom."

Georg nodded. "Which is why the hunters were sent to your parents' house that same night. They deliberately let Tom know about it so he could tell you. That distracted you from telling Melinda what Tom told you."

"Quite possible. Now let's not waste any more time!" A shudder ran down her shoulders as she listened to herself. Something dark was waiting in this house. Something cold and unpredictable. And it was hidden in that fold.

"I'll open it."

Georg raised his wand. "We'll do it together."

"I can do it alone! But whatever I'm about to open, be ready!"

Georg looked at her almost in awe as if only now did he understand who she was, who she was descended from, and what magic she was capable of. He took a deep breath, nodded, and watched her intently. But then he held her arm. "We must let the others know. If there's one thing I've learned as a police officer, it's that you never go into unknown worlds without telling someone."

"Okay, but how? Little Karl is still so small. Imagine if he were to get in the line of fire at the castle when he was about to deliver my message!"

"He won't, believe me. He can also communicate with other soul animals through his thoughts. But just to be sure, I'll send my owl. She can take a message spell straight to Melinda, Angelika, and the police station." He picked up a salt and pepper shaker from one of the tables and prepared the Nuntia charm. He quickly summarized what they had found and embedded the message in the salt and pepper shakers. Then he called and instructed Creola, his owl, to deliver the messages.

Mayla waited impatiently, assisting as best she could until Creola had finally flown away with the news. "Ready?"

He nodded.

She closed her eyes and focused deep inside herself. A big world was hidden from them, She felt it. She took a deep breath and steadied herself for the spell.

"Te aperi, munde contracte!"

A rift went straight through the air, dividing the breakfast room in two. The chairs and tables were pushed to the sides, but no extension of space appeared, zip. The ground broke open and in between, a new world opened up. As it appeared

before them in its full size, they stood as if
paralyzed.

Chapter Twenty

Before them was a forest so big that Bertha's hotel was no longer visible. From the old floorboards of the breakfast room where they were standing extended a leafy forest floor covered in needles. It was a gloomy mixed forest that opened up in front of them and it was difficult to take it all in. Further away, they discovered an elevation — a hill. They couldn't even guess what was there because the mighty trees were blocking their view.

They were greeted by the scent of damp earth and pine needles. Georg instinctively took Mayla's hand before looking at her in disbelief. "I had no idea there was such a large hidden world fold in that fold so close to the police station. It must be ancient."

"Like from a time long forgotten..."

"It will be far older than the village itself, at

least older than this building. How did Vincent know it was here?"

"You can soon ask him in person." She took a deep breath and boldly took a step onto the leaf-covered ground. Georg held her back.

"We should wait for reinforcements."

"Every second we sit idly by increases the chance he'll kill Alessia, Gabrielle, or Francesco and consume their powers. And Violett might be in mortal danger too! We must not wait! We must act now!"

Georg nodded, then squared his shoulders and hurried along with her. Side by side, they crept toward the hill because they were both certain that it was there that they would find the answers to their questions as well as Alessia, Gabrielle, Francesco, Violett, and Eduardo.

It was eerily silent. There was not a single owl screech to be heard, no leaf rustled, and no birds were singing. Mayla glanced around warily. "I can't hear anything, not even mice or bunnies. Nothing rustles but our footsteps."

"Strange. Incredibly strange."

A dark sense of foreboding crept up Mayla's back. Was someone watching them? She turned around quickly, but there was no one there. Involuntarily, she hunched her shoulders as her gaze wandered through the deserted forest.

A black cat's tail appeared at her feet among the ferns and Mayla's heart almost stopped.

"Little Karl? What are you doing here? You must not..."

However, it wasn't her young spirit animal that came out from under the big leaves but Kitty. She meowed loudly, desperately, and Mayla immediately bent down to her.

"What is it? Is Tom in danger?"

Kitty mewed even louder, more plaintively, and before Mayla could pick her up, she ran off. Only her tail could be seen sticking out between the ferns. Without pausing, Mayla ran after her.

"Wait!" Georg followed. "We must be careful!"

"No, something is wrong. I can feel it, even though she's not my spirit animal. I know her and I trust her. Quick, Georg, come on!"

The plaintive meow died away, but the sound of her paws rustling through the leaves allowed them to follow her. Kitty was running so fast that they kept losing sight of her. But when they stood still, they could hear her steps and discovered the tip of her tail. They followed her until they came to the bottom of the hill, which Kitty bounded up swiftly. They stopped in awe, pausing briefly to look up the hill. They had been right. It was up there. The place where they would find what they were searching for.

The hill was densely overgrown with countless linden trees so that they couldn't see any further. Or who awaited them, for that matter...

They hurried after Kitty. They were only a few

paces from the crest when Georg grabbed Mayla's arm and pointed his finger through the linden trees to something at the top of the hill.

Before them loomed the ruins of a gray building. It was shaped like a cathedral, but only its side walls were still standing. There was no glass in the large windows, which tapered toward the top and had frames that were entirely undamaged. But it was as if they revealed a glimpse of a bygone era. The ancient era of magic.

Sparks danced around the forgotten stones and a dense fog surrounded the old walls, which because of the surrounding linden trees appeared to be in twilight. What time was it anyway? Time seemed to be standing still.

"What kind of structure is that?"

Georg looked at it abjectly. "I haven't the faintest idea... But I'm fairly certain Alessia and Violett didn't come here on their own accord."

Kitty came running again and meowed. Immediately, she hurried past the side of the building. Mayla and Georg exchanged a quick glance before following her past dense bushes at a safe distance from the ruins. Suddenly, Mayla stopped and pointed at a shadow stretched out on the ground between the bushes in front of them. Someone was lying there. They quietly crept closer until Mayla saw carrot-red hair.

"Violett!" She rushed to her friend, closely

followed by Georg. Simultaneously, they sank onto the cold ground and bent over her.

"Violett? Can you hear me?"

Georg felt for a pulse. "She's still alive."

Immediately, Mayla spread her hands over her. "Sana!" But the spell didn't work, and her friend didn't regain consciousness. Her forehead was covered in cold sweat and her pulse weakened. "Georg, you have to take her to someone who can help her."

"Your grandma is busy. Who else can take care of an outcast woman?" He ran his hands through his hair until a determined expression filled his face. "I'll take her to the hospital. They have to help her."

"Maybe it was a forgotten curse. Andrew said that in order to counter it, you have to brew potions that reunite the old magic. Tom explained it to me too. If a witch from each coven helps prepare it and they brew a powerful healing potion, it can cure many of the forgotten curses. Hopefully, one of the doctors knows."

Georg was already taking Violett in his arms, worriedly eyeing her fluttering eyelids. "We have no time to lose. Come!"

"No, you have to go without me."

"Mayla, you must be crazy! You can't fight Vincent alone!"

"Georg, have faith!" She smiled at him, although she herself broke out in a cold sweat at the thought of going on without him. But what choice did she have? There wasn't anybody but her to stop Vincent. She had to save Alessia and her children, had to prevent him from absorbing her magic and harming Tom. Or at least keep Vincent from killing Tom and the water witches until reinforcements arrived. "The fold is still open. Everyone you let know will come and help me. But Violett needs you now. Please, she mustn't die!"

Georg looked at the pale Violett in his arms. Mayla thought she saw something like tenderness in his eyes and nodded. "As soon as I know she's in good hands, I'll be back!"

"Hurry up, every minute counts."

She watched him run back down the hill and through the forest with mixed emotions. Violett's long red strands of hair fluttered over his arm, his footsteps crackled through the deserted forest, and she heard him whisper, "Hold on, Violett, hold on."

In less than two minutes, nothing more could be seen or heard from either of them. Mayla turned resolutely and saw Kitty sitting directly in front of her on the forest floor. She mewed plaintively again, jumped up, and ran around the crumbling cathedral.

Mayla knew something terrible was waiting for her there, something horrible. Something powerful and frightening was in the air and she felt strong energies all around her. However, Tom needed her help and the De Fontes were definitely around there somewhere too. Where was Vincent? Why hadn't he shown himself yet? Since she sensed his dark presence, he also must have sensed her presence, right?

She ducked her head and crept around the ruins as quietly as she could after Kitty. The fog stood still as if protecting something inside the derelict building. When she reached the back, she saw a gaping hole in the wall she could use to enter.

Kitty stopped and mewed heartbreakingly, pointing inside with her wet nose.

"You can't enter? Why?" Mayla tried to peer into the ruins, but the dense fog prevented it. She stopped. What could she expect to see inside the walls? Was Tom being held captive there? Possibly even Alessia, Gabrielle, and Francesco?

She raised her hands boldly, mentally preparing to blow a protective ring of fire around her, and walked slowly toward the opening. Again and again, she looked around to the sides, ears pricked, alert — with nobody there to watch her back.

Kitty stayed behind the bushes and watched her go. Her yellow eyes sparkled between the leaves as she sat there silently.

Where was Tom? Why had Kitty called her? What was Vincent doing to his only son? Would he even harm him? After all, the von Eisenfels line would die out with Tom's death. That could hardly be in Vincent's interest! Why was he holding Tom and why was Kitty so agitated?

Carefully, she entered the old building — the floor was completely overgrown with grass — and then walked through the dense fog and stopped. The image that presented itself gave her such a shock that she forgot to breathe for a moment.

The interior of the cathedral, divided into three naves, was much larger than it appeared from the outside. The area was almost the size of a soccer field. While the rear section was completely shaded, the front area was well-lit. In the middle was a stone altar on which countless candles burned. Next to it was a large golden bowl blazing with white flames that, judging by the intense scent, were burning herbs. Frankincense, rosemary, and pepper. And amidst all of them was another smell unknown to her.

And there he was, standing at the altar. Vincent von Eisenfels. A gust of wind blew through the cathedral, making his long dark cloak billow. He wore a grin on his face, which was no longer quite so pale, and which was also framed by black-gray strands. In his dark eyes she read the certainty that nothing and nobody could stop him.

Next to him were three large cages. In each, Francesco, Alessia, and Gabrielle were lying unconscious on the ground, with a glow drifting from them toward the bars. She recognized the spell being used. A similar image had been burned into her memory forever because her grandmother had been confined to such a cage. Vincent had already caught the De Fontes and was about to use the Exsugo spell to drain them of their powers.

Mayla raised her hands to summon a powerful bolt of lightning when he clucked his tongue arrogantly.

"Think carefully before attacking me, foolish von Flammenstein, because as soon as you do that, your little friend will have nothing to laugh about." He waved casually with a hand, and at that a lanky character she knew all too well stepped out of the shadows. It was Eduardo. He was not in chains or in any apparent restraints. Actually, he was the second traitor they had been searching for. However, it wasn't his appearance or this realization that almost knocked Mayla off her feet — no. Eduardo raised his arms and in his long, thin hands he held a small ball of black fur.

Little Karl.

The moment Mayla saw him, she was filled with the little tomcat's feelings. Fear and worry. His heart was beating incredibly fast and Mayla felt the cold, claw-like hand holding his neck so tightly he couldn't escape.

"Why didn't you call me?" Mayla asked little Karl mentally.

Images and feelings filled her. He didn't want to endanger her, realizing he would be used as leverage against her. That's why the loyal kitten hadn't connected with her, why he'd closed off his feelings to her. And she hadn't grown suspicious because she'd been scared for him, too, and hadn't made mental contact with him before since she'd been distracted and hadn't put out feelers to him for a while so as not to unintentionally lure him to her.

Oh, little Karl, don't be afraid!

There was no sign of Tom, but Kitty mewed ruefully somewhere outside the cathedral. For whatever reason she could not enter, and she was tormented by great fear for her child. The mother cat had brought Mayla here to save little Karl.

What could she do? How could she release little Karl from Eduardo's grasp? Should she hurl a bolt of lightning at him? However, as soon as she did, Vincent would hit her with a curse and most certainly put her in a cage to steal her powers. Thinking feverishly, she knew one thing: somehow she had to get Vincent talking, to distract him, to buy time!

"Isn't it beneath you to torment a kitten?" she roared at him, doing her best to free her voice of whatever fear this man and his power caused her.

"Little Karl, I'll save you, hold on," she mentally communicated to her spirit animal at the same time, hoping to encourage him. He shouldn't feel her worry. The little cat needed to feel secure. She would set him free somehow. She just had to succeed!

Vincent laughed. Did he suspect she was buying time?

She stared contemptuously at Eduardo. "And you, traitor, don't you have any respect for the old magic? Don't you understand that spirit animals use it and the consequences you'll reap by threatening one of them? The combined power lies hidden in nature and all animals. Do you truly think you'll grow stronger if you still don't understand the basics of magic?"

Eduardo, however, didn't react but kept glancing respectfully at Vincent so as not to miss a nod or other commanding gesture. Like a lap dog. No spine or will!

Vincent von Eisenfels laughed and the deep, malicious sound echoed unabated between the walls of the cathedral ruins. "It seems you don't understand how the old powers work!"

Finally, he had taken the bait. "What don't I get? How do you think old magic works?"

"Animals are far too weak and stupid. They are ignorant of the force with which they move and the energy they use. Only those who are worthy of the old magic can unite it within themselves. Only those who are strong enough and don't shy away from anything, who show courage and an iron will, will be able to bring them together. And who better to show iron will than the von Eisenfels family! Before long, you'll be able to see my newfound power yourself... provided you're still alive."

The glow around the De Fonteses was already fading. How long would they last? Her grandma had withstood the Exsugo spell for weeks. But she was an extraordinary witch and it hadn't been Vincent himself who had cast the spell.

Keep talking, she had to stall until a solution presented itself or reinforcements arrived. "But magic has nothing to do with power. Magic lives in everything, in plants, in nature, and also in animals, no matter if they are spirit animals or not."

"Magic lives in those who are able to use it! And since you're the only one who has shown up here, far too nice and naive to use true spells that enhance your powers, you'll soon be a side note in history." He raised his hands, ready to take her out with one curse, but he waited as if the game gave him a strange pleasure.

A strong fire crackled through her. She closed her eyes for a moment and concentrated on the power that lay in these old walls and the forgotten forest. She sensed Kitty's magic and little Karl's, and as Melinda had taught her, she mentally merged with that circuit of energies.

"I am Mayla von Flammenstein. I am a descendant of Melinda, the greatest witch in centuries, and of Lore von Flammenstein, one of the most powerful witches of all time!" She raised her hands defensively and braced herself to blast a mighty circle of flames around her. But she waited. Once the protection was in front of her, she couldn't save little Karl with a single spell. Once the ring of fire was in front of her, blowing it out would be noticed immediately.

Her grandmother's words came to her. "Magic knows no bounds!" As if a film were running through her mind, all the witching lessons with her grandmother by her side reeled through her head. She must have learned something. Any spell that could be useful now. However, as soon as she charmed little Karl free, Vincent would attack her and there would be no one left to save the De Fonteses or stop Vincent — and she couldn't be sure little Karl would make it out here without her. And the sweet kitten was holding up so bravely. He didn't cry and kept his fear under control, she could feel it. A deep trust fluttered from him to her and her chest tightened. There was no way she would abandon her beloved little partner.

"What good does it do you to be descended from these women when you stand utterly alone before me?"

"Anyone who feels the cycle of magic is not alone." The words had darted through Mayla's mind. She closed her eyes instinctively. Again, she sank into the feelings of the environment and immersed herself in everything surrounding her. She felt the energy of the plants, the strong old forest, the power of this ancient building that had not been created to do evil within, and she felt Kitty waiting behind the bushes a few meters from her. However, she also sensed something else. A powerful force that had nothing to do with Vincent. It was getting closer, coming straight for her, and would arrive momentarily. Was it Tom?

Have faith. Her own words flashed through her mind and without a moment's hesitation, she imagined Eduardo falling unconscious to the ground and thought, *Animo linquatur!*

As the Italian fell silently to the ground and little Karl jumped out of his arm in a flash, the force she had felt coming appeared beside her.

It was Andrew Steven Montgomery.

Vincent didn't hesitate to throw a curse at them, but Andrew immediately blew a ring of wind around them that trembled under the malediction.

"How did you know I was here?"

He briefly smiled at her and his green eyes shone strong and confident. He had pushed away the darkness within himself. "Georg called me."

"What are you doing here, you miserable snitch!" von Eisenfels yelled, throwing a curse so powerful that Andrew's protection vanished. However, Mayla had already blown a wall of fire in front of them, and his magic ricocheted off of it.

The glow around Francesco died and he sank even lower to the cage floor, limp as a sack. For heaven's sake, had all of his magic been sucked out of him?

"It's time!" a dark voice called from the shadows

behind Vincent. Who was it? Was someone with him? The voice was hoarse as if it hadn't spoken in a long time.

From the shadows emerged a tall, slender figure, draped in a billowy black cloak, their head hidden under a hood. They walked slowly toward the altar and grasped the cage in which Francesco's lifeless body lay.

Who was that? And why hadn't Mayla felt them? Because they had been standing directly behind Vincent?

Wide-eyed, she watched the procedure and cast another knock-out spell at the tall figure, but with a tiny wave of the left hand, they deflected the spell.

"Who are you?" Mayla called.

A deep laugh sounded. The figure slowly pulled the hood off and an old woman appeared. She had snow-white hair that flowed wildly around her shoulders, dark, almost black eyes, and was as tall as Vincent. Her face was heavily lined and her voice was rough and old.

"Don't you recognize me, Heir von Flammenstein?"

When she stared at the woman's face, a shock ran through her limbs.

It was old Bertha.

Chapter Twenty-One

Before her stood the woman who had harbored Mayla on her first night as a witch and who had listened in on her and Tom. She had trusted her, just as her grandmother had placed her trust in this old witch, and still did. And finally, the secret of who had betrayed Emma and her hiding place to Vincent was out.

"Bertha..."

She was the one who continued the circle, possibly even established it, and who founded the hunters during Vincent's captivity. She was the leader Andrew had mentioned but never met.

"That is the name you know me by, but my real name is Valentina Viktoria von Eisenfels."

"But why...?"

"You want a reason? Your ancestors and those of the other founding families deprived us of our deserved place. We were at least as powerful as you, if not more so. You were jealous of our power and wanted to eclipse us by founding the circles! However, this rift will end today and be done with forever. I will unite the old magic within me and the power will pass not only to me but also to my descendants, Vincent and Valerius. To all my blood relatives. Our circle members will be our followers, for they too will absorb the ancient power once I cast the last spell." With those words, she turned back to Francesco's cage. She whispered an incantation Mayla didn't understand and the energy in the bars formed a gleaming ball that she took between her old fingers.

"We have to stop her!" Mayla blew out the wall of fire and Andrew immediately hurled a wind spell at the old hag, but Vincent blocked it. He stood in front of his mother with his legs apart and turned to Mayla and Andrew.

"You can no longer defeat us."

He shot a curse at her. Mayla concentrated on the muscle that she'd felt in her heart for days and that showed her that she was growing increasingly stronger, and she sensed the cycle of magic. While Andrew protected them with a Defende spell, she summoned a bolt of lightning that smashed down on von Eisenfels. He lost his balance under the spell's power and staggered, but immediately righted himself. Gritting his teeth, Vincent conjured a bolt of lightning between his hands. Immediately, Mayla blew a wall of fire and the blindingly bright light thundered against it. Heavens, when did he learn fire spells? Was that Emma's energy?

Vincent took a deep breath and blew a hurricane at her, throwing Mayla and Andrew back as if Mayla hadn't charmed a shield for them.

"Get out! He's too strong!"

Maya turned. There was Tom. Finally. He had come and appeared unharmed. He was standing in the entrance of the cathedral, only his face showing through the dense fog.

"We still have to save Gabrielle and Alessia. And look, Bertha is about to unite the ancient magic!"

Tom sprang to them and silently cast a protective shield before his father's curse hit Mayla in the back. Then he held out his hand to Mayla and Andrew. "Only together are we strong enough."

Andrew peered at him suspiciously. "Aren't you also a von Eisenfels?"

"I can't do anything about my blood, but I can take action. Now grab my hand."

Without making any further objections, Andrew grasped his left hand and Mayla his right. With Tom in the middle, they slowly advanced toward Vincent and Bertha. The old witch had slipped the ball of energy into a metal bowl where there floated a strange, glittering, yellowish liquid. She raised her hands and aimed them at it. Sparks flew from her fingertips into the vessel and a violent wind arose, sending the mixture spinning faster and faster. Bertha whispered a spell and laughed out loud. "So now the ancient magic is immortalized in iron!" A glow in the bowl flowed toward Bertha and Vincent, turning purple as it did so. In a kind of trance, they stood still, arms raised to the sides, and eyes directed at the sky. Everything around them shone brightly as the purple glow invaded them.

"They are uniting the magic!" Mayla summoned another bolt of lightning and sent it down on Vincent and Bertha. However, a sparkling dome formed around the two, and the lightning bounced off and hissed toward a cage.

"Oh, no, Gabrielle!" Mayla attempted to leap to her, but Tom stopped her as the door of her prison suddenly burst open.

Andrew stared at the open cage door in disbelief. "How is that possible?"

Mayla, however, could no longer hold back. At the very least, while Bertha and Vincent were distracted, they had to save Gabrielle. She ran to the cage, crawled in far enough to grab Gabrielle's foot, and pulled her out of the prison. Tom was right next to her and helped her get the unconscious woman out. Andrew blew a protective wind in front of them even if it probably wouldn't do any good against the combined magic of the von Eisenfelses. Gabrielle's limp body slid over the threshold and Tom picked her up.

Mayla ran to Alessia's cage and shook the door, but it was closed. At that moment, the glow around Alessia faded completely and she too slumped down lifeless to the floor of her cage.

"Heavens! Is she dead?"

"It appears so." Tom nodded toward the exit. "Let's get out of here!"

Mayla stared at Vincent and Bertha, who were looking up at the sky with outstretched arms. The dome above them turned purple, ecstatic expressions covered their faces, and sparks flew between their fingertips. "But we have to stop them."

Tom threw Gabrielle over his shoulder. "It's too late for that, Mayla! Come!"

The three ran toward the thick fog that shielded the cathedral's entrance from the forest and charged through it to the linden trees. There was no trace of Kitty or little Karl, but Mayla would never cut ties with the little one out of fear again. She focused on her inner being and heard him meow. He was safe. Kitty had led him away. Mayla breathed a sigh of relief and ran down the hill through the linden grove with Tom and Andrew.

"Quick, let's get out of here!"

"Now how are we going to stop Vincent, damn it?" Andrew clenched his fists as he ran and then slowed. "I swore I'd avenge my parents' deaths."

"You can't do that if you're dead. We need reinforcements. Come with us!"

They stormed down the hill through the dense forest until they spotted the wooden floorboards of Bertha's hotel in the distance.

"Why did your lightning bolt open the cage door, Mayla?" Andrew gasped. "That was only fire energy! Like your grandma, we would have had to combine the ancient powers to stop the spell and break the bars."

Despite the stitch in her side, Mayla kept running. "Maybe it was enough that the three of us were holding hands."

"No, that can't be it."

"Then it must have something to do with my lightning striking the energy field under which Bertha was combining the old magic. In any case, Gabrielle needs the potion my grandma has post haste. So, let's get going! Luckily, she wasn't under the spell for so long."

"First, we have to get out of here!" Tom, with Gabrielle over his shoulder, ran through the woods until he landed loudly on the floorboards. Behind him, Mayla and Andrew stormed out of the hidden fold and ran straight into the arms of Angelika, Melinda, Anna, and Thomas, who rushed into the breakfast room.

Melinda immediately leaned over Gabrielle. "What happened?"

Mayla gasped. "Bertha is Vincent's mother. She is the head witch of the new coven, the Circle of Old Magic."

"Bertha?" All strength seemed to leave her grandmother and Mayla quickly conjured up a chair that the old witch sat on as if in a trance. "Bertha... it was her... she betrayed Emma..." A tear formed in the corner of Melinda's eye and rolled down her cheek. As it dripped off her chin, a determined expression returned to her face. Slowly, she looked at Tom. "Have you known all these years?"

He shook his head. "She disappeared before my father was arrested. I had no idea where she went and haven't seen her in over thirty years. But I have to admit, I've never laid eyes on Bertha, not once. My gut always told me to stay away from her. I don't know, maybe I suspected something. That's why I never went to her place. I should have questioned my intuition and found out who she was. I'm sorry." He put his hand on his chest.

"I'm sorry I ever trusted her!" The familiar deep frown lines appeared on Melinda's forehead and she stood up abruptly. "What happened, Mayla?"

"They had the De Fonteses in cages and drained them of their powers using the Exsugo spell. Francesco died. With his water power, they succeeded."

"What about Alessia?"

Andrew glanced back angrily. "She also died shortly afterward..."

"Damn it." Melinda looked at Gabrielle, whose face was noticeably pale, before turning to Angelika. "Can you take care of her?"

"Of course. I'll take her to Violett and Georg."

Mayla's heart leapt. "Does that mean Violett Is okay?"

Angelika's gaze darkened. "That remains to be seen. Tom, you told Mayla we need to brew a potion that combines the ancient magic. Can you tell me about that?"

"I found out more about it in the library. If I understand correctly, you must make a strong herbal potion and a witch from each coven must cast their spell once into the decoction."

"All right." Angelika enchanted Gabrielle so that she was floating next to her and took her hand. At the same time, she grasped her amulet key. She did not announce the destination of her jump.

Anna peered into the forest that stretched out before them. "It's incredible, I didn't know about this world fold. It must be hundreds of years old. What else can we do to stop the von Eisenfels?"

Mayla had an idea. "We must seal the fold! We'll call Phylis, and then we'll have enough powerful witches. It might work."

Tom shook his head. "I don't believe that. I don't know who created the fold, but it must be ancient. Even before Bertha opened her hotel, this linden tree grove was sealed off along with the cathedral. She must have known about it for a long time, which is why she bought this hotel. And since none of us created the fold, we can't seal it either."

"Shouldn't we at least try?" Mayla peered questioningly at Melinda.

"No, Tom's right. Only a fold of your own making can be closed to trap someone."

"So what are we going to do? It can't be over! We must do something about them!"

"I concur, let's keep fighting!" Andrew stood next to Mayla. "Together, we should succeed."

"Of course we keep fighting! Together with Tom, we will unite the ancient magic." Melinda nodded resolutely. "I'll call Phylis, but we're still missing water!"

"We managed to get your cage open in southern England without metal. Maybe four elements will do," Mayla mused aloud.

"Strange. Right, I hadn't even thought of that." Tom frowned.

"Or maybe metal isn't that important." Anna patted Tom's forearm. "No offense. But until recently, you didn't have a coven."

Tom shook his head. "No, that can't be it. It shouldn't work without metal. It was clearly stated in the books I've studied: while there has never been an official metal coven, the portion of ancient magic my family was given is necessary to reunite the power."

"Who was there when you freed me from the cage?" Melinda asked.

Mayla remembered exactly. "Andrew, Anna, Georg, and me. That's it!"

"But how..." Suddenly her grandmother looked up and gave Mayla a piercing look. "You and Tom were close? Beforehand?"

Mayla frowned. "We were together briefly before that, yes. What does that have to do with it?"

"Child, that's not what I mean. Did you two have sex?"

"Grandma!"

Melinda clapped her hands and a smile appeared on her face. "You don't have to answer me. Why didn't I recognize it long ago? Now I see it clearly."

"What?"

"You're pregnant! By him!" She pointed a finger at Tom and clapped her hands again.

"No, that can't be. I... Grandma, I..." Mayla felt a pang that had nothing to do with magic and a lump formed in her throat at the truth she was about to tell her grandma. "I can't have children."

Her grandma laughed. "What made you believe such nonsense?"

Mayla looked at her seriously. "A doctor diagnosed me. Weeks ago."

"A doctor? Some charlatan for human beings?"

"Yes, besides, with Henning, my boyfriend at the time, we tried unsuccessfully for months."

"Of course it didn't work. He's an ordinary human."

"What are you trying to tell me?"

"That you are incredibly fertile. A von Flammenstein who can't have children... what nonsense! Naturally, witches can only breed with wizards. Always."

Mayla's mouth fell open. Did that mean...? Heart pounding, she focused on her inner being and placed her hands on her stomach. As if she had been blind and could finally see clearly, she felt an energy within her that was hers and someone else's. Inside her belly was someone, there was... there was a... a child. Tears welled up in her eyes, the lump in her throat cleared, and her heart almost jumped out of her chest as she took a deep breath. Slowly, she looked up at Tom, who was smiling at her. "Tom, it's true. I can feel it. I... we are going to have a child."

A radiance appeared on Tom's face and he seemed so bright and pure, happier than she had seen him before. He carefully raised his hand, looked at her questioningly, and when she nodded in agreement, he put his left hand on hers on her stomach. "Mayla, I'm speechless. I don't know what to say."

Melinda smiled. "And with it, the eternal strife will end."

"What are you talking about, Grandma?"

"The heir of the von Eisenfels will be absorbed by fire magic."

"Because the man takes the woman's coven?"

"Exactly. While the child will carry the energy of both, fire magic will be the dominant power.

Thus, the lineage of the von Eisenfelses merges with the von Flammensteins and none of your descendants will ever have to grapple with this ancient conflict again."

Mayla looked at Tom. "That's good, don't you think?" How would he react to the fact that his legacy had, in a sense, gone up in smoke?

Tom, however, laughed at her happily. "This is the best thing that could have happened."

A wind arose, blowing in from the linden grove. There was a crack and trees fell to the ground. Thunder echoed and Mayla grabbed Tom's hand. He hugged her and smiled confidently at her.

"We will find a way! We have the founding power of metal, fire, wind — plus earth through Anna, and water through Thomas. We can stop them. We must try."

"Remember the spell you cast to free me?" Melinda remarked.

Mayla looked at Anna, Thomas, and Andrew. "Aer et terra, ignis et aqua..."

"...nostro iussu, foedus facite!" Anna finished the sentence.

"Good. We'll line up next to each other, join forces, and greet them with a bang! But not in this hovel that drips with betrayal and darkness. Come!" Melinda squared her narrow shoulders. She marched resolutely out the door onto the street with the others following.

Chapter Twenty-Two

The street in front of the hotel was deserted, as if the villagers knew something dangerous was happening.

"It's so quiet..." Mayla looked around the deserted city warily. "What exactly happened at Donnersberg Castle? Is the attack still raging there?"

"No, the hunters fought fiercely. But then suddenly, they stormed back into the entrance hall and jumped somewhere. We knew then that something must be going on."

"That's probably when the magic was united," Tom surmised. "The storming of the castle was a diversionary tactic that unfortunately worked well."

"Did you know about it?" Andrew asked.

"No, I was in the library looking for ways to

stop the unification of magic when Karla called me."

"So, what are our options?" Melinda asked. "Do you have a solution?"

"I didn't come across anything that would prevent it. The books just said over and over again that one should respect and be worthy of the united powers."

"Be worthy... what exactly does that mean?" Anna mused.

From the hotel, the sound of a loud bang rang out onto the street and they immediately grabbed each other's hands. Mayla stood next to Tom and felt his warmth and energy through his hands. She gazed at him and he winked at her encouragingly.

"We stay together."

She nodded and focused inwardly. Grinning, she put her other hand on her stomach. She still couldn't believe it. She actually had a child inside her... Tears were trying to well up in her eyes, but she fought them back. Before she could be completely happy, they had to stop Bertha and Vincent. The child had to have a future! Suddenly, Anna took her hand and Mayla smiled at her. "Did I tell you how glad I am that you and Thomas came?"

Anna smiled, then closed her eyes and collected herself like the others. Without anyone beginning to count, they simultaneously drew breath and began to recite the incantation.

"Aer et terra,

ignis et aqua,

nostro iussu,

foedus facite!"

The wind churned, sparks of fire sprayed over their heads, drops of water fell on them, and their feet seemed to melt into the earth. Simultaneously, the feeling of iron strength surged through them and a purple light rose above them.

At that moment, Bertha and Vincent stormed out into the street. Before they could cast a spell, Melinda summoned a bolt of lightning, Mayla concentrated and channeled her energy into the bolt, and together, they brought it down on Vincent and Bertha. The two, however, only raised their hands and a transparent, glittering dome appeared over them. The beam of light bounced off of it and thundered to the ground.

Thomas took a deep breath and blew on them. A cloud gathered in the sky, throwing down so many raindrops that they were in danger of being washed away. However, this magic also bounced off the dome and all the water drops evaporated with a loud hiss.

Anna made the earth shake, causing everything around them to tremble. At the same time, Andrew blew wind at their opponents. It was a veritable hurricane, but even that magic didn't do anything and bounced off the magical dome like they were kids attempting their first magic tricks.

Mayla looked at Tom, who was clenching his teeth. He hadn't yet cast a spell against Vincent and Bertha, as if he was reluctant to do so. It was his family, his flesh and blood, but he was different. He wasn't like them. He didn't want to belong to them, didn't want to see the brutality with which they seized power. Yet he hesitated to attack them, to fight his own family.

"Tom," she whispered. But he didn't respond. His face was paler than usual and he kept his dark on his father and grandmother. He was battling an inner struggle even though he had long since decided which side he was on. He finally gathered his strength and was about to hurl it towards his family, when something seemed to prevent him. Before Tom had a chance to throw a spell, Vincent cast a curse on Mayla.

"Tutare," they roared in unison, the curse crashing down on their shimmering purple shield. Vincent's powers were too great and the protection immediately broke. Instantly, the next malediction followed, destroying their gathering of ancient magic. The purple glow faded and they fell to the ground.

Behind them, countless hunters materialized and rushed towards them. The young men were howling and waving their wands in the air. But from the other side, police officers, Georg among them, were storming out of the station. Others from

Donnersberg Castle also joined them and immediately Mayla, Tom, and the others rose again.

"You're not alone!" shouted one of the police officers, whom Georg clapped on the shoulder in a friendly manner.

"We stand together!" Viola roared, rushing toward them with the other witches from the Fire headquarters.

Mayla and the others backed up a few steps to stand with their friends and allies while the hunters lined up behind Bertha and Vincent.

Mayla's heart beat swiftly in her chest and as she raised her hands — still unsure if she could do anything against Bertha and Vincent — she was struck by a realization.

This was the last stand.

The streets were filled with magic. Glitter rippled across the cobblestones and the houses seemed to cower off to the sides like spectators afraid of glimpsing the fighting in the arena.

The sun was setting and the shadows grew longer. Owls and crows circled overhead and cats crept along the walls of the houses. The first front door flew open and a witch in her forties with flowing long hair came out purposefully and ran to Mayla and the others, wand drawn. She was followed by a man with a full beard who furrowed his brows and ran to them with no less determination. More front doors flung open and more and more witches stormed out. They all joined Mayla and her allies, their wands raised against Vincent and Bertha.

Everyone held their breath. No one took the first step, as if they all hoped that this fight would never begin and that they would be spared its brutal end and ensuing consequences.

Bertha laughed out loud, breaking the tense silence. "No matter how many you become, we possess the ancient magic. We'll overpower you and there's nothing you can do to stop us. Accept the von Eisenfels family as the new head of the magical world and we will spare you. But if even one raises their wand against us, all of you will receive bitter punishment. Now come, Valerius, the show is over. Come to us and reveal to everyone whose heir you are."

Tom gritted his teeth and immediately Mayla grabbed his hand. "You're not one of them."

Vincent von Eisenfels turned his dark eyes on him. "I can see into your heart, Valerius, you're still wearing my watch. You too are part of the new coven and have the united old magic within you."

Mayla looked at him in shock. "That's impossible!"

"Yes, it is true." Tom reached for the watch hidden in the pocket of his leather jacket and pulled it out. Immediately, it began to glow red as if the iron it was made from was smoldering, as if forged in a fire. "I never wanted this inheritance! I've refused it since I was five."

"Then attack them!" Anna whispered. "You have the power to do it!"

"No, I don't want to use that magic to attack. It doesn't belong to me! It is overwhelming — and too powerful for me. I wasn't born with it, so I'm not worthy of it!" He unclipped the chain of the glowing pocket watch from his belt and threw it aside. It fell to the stony ground with a metallic clank.

Vincent narrowed his dark eyes and straightened to his full height. "Just because you discard the watch doesn't mean you're released from our circle. The metal has bound you to us forever!"

Mayla looked at Melinda, who seemed to be thinking the same thing she was. Taking two steps, they stood side by side, held hands, and concentrated on the watch.

Bertha seemed to guess what they were up to and raised her hands for a curse. Alarmed, Mayla and Melinda released the spell to defend themselves. But in a flash, Tom stood in front of the two and set up a powerful protective shield. He looked grimly at the woman who was his grandmother.

"I will never attack with that magic, but I will protect those I hold dear."

"They're only using you to harm us! Come here, son! Open your eyes and come to my side.

Your place has always been next to me because
nobody else will ever trust you, they'll never want
to live with you in peace."

Tom looked at his father dismissively. "No! I
trust her."

"You can't trust anyone! Many years ago, all of
them stabbed us in the back. Have you forgotten
what I taught you as a child?"

"I have not. Whatever happened back then, I'm
sure both sides were guilty. And we, those who live
today, must finally put this eternal grudge behind
us and join hands. It's over. The conflict will be
extinguished with the next generation!"

"What are you saying?" Bertha raised her arms
and gave Mayla a frantic look. She stared at her
stomach and her dark eyes widened in horror. She
had understood, saw her family's future swallowed
by another family, and cried out so loud, Mayla
wanted to cover her ears. "This child must never be
born!" There was a crackle between her hands and
purple lightning shot out between them. With all
her might she hurled a malediction at Mayla. Tom
gritted his teeth. His body trembled as he focused
all his senses on protecting them.

Mayla gently stroked his back and his hands
began to glow and the shield strengthened.
Bertha's curse bounced off it. Mayla and Melinda
didn't lose another second. They turned their
attention to the pocket watch again. The metal
grew redder and redder until the clock glowed

yellow and then white. The iron grew so hot it began to melt and spread across the street like liquid fire. It seeped into the ground between the stones, hissing loudly. Steam rose above the cobblestones, testifying to the fact that nothing remained of the watch magic.

Tom breathed heavily as if someone was squeezing his chest, then fell to his knees and clutched his heart.

"You didn't do him any favors!" Vincent held up his hands and at the same time, Mayla and Melinda blew a wall of flames in front of them. But his curse shot through as if there were no shield at all. It missed Mayla and Anna by a hair and hit the cobblestones. Startled, Mayla and Melinda glanced at each other.

"You have no more power. Even the powers of the von Flammensteins can't do anything against us."

And as if that was the cue, the fighting broke out. The hunters hurled spells at them. Their magic had also grown stronger. Their curses shot through the allies' shields as if they weren't there. The allies tried to join forces, but the hunters kept advancing, pushing back the cops and the other witches.

Tom struggled back up. Mayla helped him to his feet. "Tom..."

"Don't worry." Again, he cast a protective shield in front of them, which Bertha's curses bounced off, without effect. Did he still have the old magic even though the pocket watch was destroyed?

Melinda looked around in disbelief. "Our powers are not enough."

"Maybe when I join in it will be." Phylis came from behind them and immediately held Mayla and Melinda's hands. "I found a spell in an old book. We still need water and metal before we can stop them."

Thomas pointed to Tom, who held the shield in front of them with his hands raised. "The ancient magic is united within him. He could fight them!"

Melinda cut him off. "He respects the old power too much to use it in battle. And he's right. He wasn't born with it, so he can't use it without grievous consequences." She turned to Phylis. "How do we have to proceed?"

"It's about joining forces and awakening the old magic within this alliance. We can use this magic without hesitation since it only remains intact through our connection! It's best if the head witches unite. We can do it that way," Phylis explained.

"But Gabrielle is injured and Alessia and Francesco are dead. Who's the strongest water witch around here?" Mayla whispered and immediately looked around. They searched the crowd and found no one with powers strong enough to stop Vincent and Bertha.

Out of the corner of an eye, Mayla saw movement. A woman was fighting her way out of the hotel, supported by... Angelika! She narrowed her eyes and recognized the blonde woman who was struggling toward them. It was Gabrielle. Mayla rushed toward her with Andrew close behind.

Vincent spotted them and threw a spell at Angelika and Gabrielle, but Tom deflected it so that it crashed into a house wall. Plaster fell while Andrew and Mayla helped bring Gabrielle to Melinda and Phylis. Tom, meanwhile, positioned himself in front of them and reinforced the shield. Vincent and Bertha fired curse after curse at him, but they all shattered against Tom's barrier. Sweat formed on his forehead, but he kept up the protection.

Gabrielle blinked several times and Mayla squeezed her hand tightly. "What are you doing here? You need to recuperate!"

"Francesco and my mother are dead." She sobbed, but only once. Then she lifted her head and there was determination in her blue eyes. "I'm the only one who can help you."

Andrew looked at her doubtfully. "Aren't you too weak? Your powers, the Exsugo spell..."

Angelika shook her head. "She was only in the cage for a short time and fought the spell with all her might. She's weak, yes, but her energy hasn't been fully drained."

"Most importantly, I am now the head witch of

the Water Circle. I don't shirk my responsibilities. With my power, we can stop them."

Mayla and Andrew exchanged a quick glance, then nodded to Melinda and Phylis. "We must try!"

Gasping, Gabrielle looked up, squared her shoulders, freed herself from the others' grips, and lifted her chin. "What do I do?"

Mayla quickly explained how they could unite the old magic. Phylis nodded in confirmation. "When we mighty witches unite our powers, we shall be as strong as those two. At least, that's what it said in the book. And when we provoke them long enough, withstand them long enough, the ancient magic will destroy them, for their bodies were not made for it."

"The magic will destroy them?" Mayla looked at Tom in horror. "What about him?"

"As long as he only uses the power for defense, he should be spared."

Mayla looked at Tom with hope. Had he read about it too? Or guessed it? Was that why he used his energy only for defense?

Melinda clenched her small hands and her eyes blazed with fire. "Wonderful. Mayla, Andrew, Phylis, and Gabrielle, let's form a circle and let them get to find out a little more about us!"

Phylis shook her head. "Tom has to join us. Otherwise, we won't have the metal element!"

Melinda pointed to Mayla. "That has been resolved."

"How...?" Her eyes widened as she peered down at Mayla's belly. "How can that..."

"I'll explain later. Now let's get to work."

They took a breath and again, the long-forgotten incantation resounded through the air.

"Aer et terra,

ignis et aqua,

nostro iussu,

foedus facite!"

The purple glow formed above them, creating a dome that enveloped them. Mayla and Melinda slowly released their hands, lined up with the others, and hurried toward Bertha and Vincent.

Tom looked restlessly at Mayla. He didn't want to give up the protective shield because Bertha and Vincent could instantly hurl curses at Mayla. They wanted her dead by all means before the child inside her sapped the family's energy forever.

Melinda, however, gave him a confident nod. Mayla looked at him and with her eyes she said, "Have faith!" He took a deep breath and nodded almost imperceptibly when the shield vanished into thin air.

Bertha immediately shot a purple bolt of lightning at her, but Mayla, Melinda, Phylis, Gabrielle, and Andrew blew at it together, diverting the curse. Vincent ripped the long coat from his shoulders and threw it on the ground. He clenched his hands, the veins in his arms bulging. He focused his energy and hurled it at Mayla.

The spell, however, was also repelled by the allies.

Red in the face, Bertha simultaneously raised her hands for the next malediction with Vincent. Their faces furious, eyes wide, they repeatedly hurled curses at Mayla.

Mayla felt her strength tremble every time they blocked one of the spells, but she did not let on how much energy it took her. Her right hand was holding Andrew's and he gave her strength, as did her grandma, Phylis, and Gabrielle, to whom she was connected.

She could see that a battle was raging within Tom. He wanted to use the new power to defend them, but he couldn't — otherwise, the ancient magic might also destroy him.

As Bertha and Vincent prepared the next blow, Mayla instinctively knew her shield wouldn't last. But, with the same certainty, she recognized that this would be the spell that would overwhelm and destroy Bertha and Vincent. They had to cast that malediction. And they would throw the curse back at Mayla. Fear gripped her, but she forced herself to remain calm. She had to have faith. Perhaps she was wrong and their combined magic would be enough to ward off the spell.

Above all, Tom should not sense her insecurity. He must not know what she was thinking. At all costs, she had to prevent him from using his formidable power to fight.

Seemingly carefree, she smiled at Bertha and Vincent, which seemed to irritate them even more. They raised their hands and flashes of light erupted from their fingertips. Dark clouds gathered in the sky and cast large shadows over the road. The air crackled with tension. A crow and a cat cried out and the other spirit animals joined in. It sounded like Death's final musical composition.

Regardless, Bertha and Vincent flung their power at Mayla, causing lightning to rain down from the sky and a purple whirlwind to rage around them. Heavy raindrops pelted them and the earth shook under their feet. The amulets they wore began to glow from heat and the wind increased until dense smoke formed around the two, who were struck by the lightning. Sparks flew, the smoke thickened and thickened, and screams of terror, seemingly unified, echoed across the street so that everyone stopped fighting. The hunters watched the spectacle, just as horrified as the allies were. Everyone stood still and watched as the smoke gradually cleared and a loose black cloak and dark coat lay on the ground. Something was smoldering and glimmering next to the clothes — a small heap of ash was all that was left of Bertha and Vincent von Eisenfels.

Melinda stepped forward. "The ancient magic. It destroyed them!"

Horrified, the hunters ripped the amulets that had tied them to the von Eisenfels family from their necks. The metal landed with a clank as they tossed them into the street and ran away. Immediately, the police and the allies took pursuit.

Amidst all the commotion, Melinda, Phylis, Andrew, and Gabrielle finally looked at each other and only now saw that Mayla was lying on the ground with Tom on top of her. Neither was moving.

Chapter Twenty-Three

S inging birds woke Mayla and she stretched. Blinking wearily, she opened her eyes as memories of the confrontation with Bertha and Vincent flooded her mind. She was startled and her eyes widened. She struggled to sit up. She was in a bed on clean white sheets with her mother's crocheted blanket spread over her. What had happened?

She felt heavy and exhausted, but she laboriously lifted her legs, one after the other, over the edge of the bed and tried to get up.

"Mayla, what are you doing? You have to rest!"

She looked around, confused. Georg was sitting next to her bed. As usual, he was wearing a plaid shirt. He placed a soccer magazine on a glass side table and rose.

"Where am I? What happened? Where's Tom?"

"Calm down. You've been unconscious for several days."

"Several days? But..." The memory came back and she immediately put her hand on her stomach. Was the little one still there? She felt nothing. Panic threatened to overwhelm her, but she took a deep breath. Again, she felt inward and sensed a warm, small flame blazing inside her, which brought a soft smile to her face. "You're still with me..."

"Don't worry, nothing happened to the little mite. You will be fine soon, too."

She glanced around. Whoever's bed she was in, she had never been there before! "Where's Tom? Where are we?"

"We are in Greece, on the island of Lesbos. Phylis lent us her estate so that we can recover."

"Us?"

"Don't worry, it's not only the two of us." He winked at her mischievously.

"Where's Violett?"

"I'm here." Her friend stormed into the room, plopped down on the bed next to her, and gave her a big hug. "I heard your voice. How do you feel?"

"Fine, how about you? Are you completely healed of the forgotten curse?"

Violett gave Georg an admiring look. Her ears turned bright red. "Yes, Georg saved me. He took me to a healer in the hospital and told her about the spell and Tom and Andrew's explanation of how to stop it. The healer consulted with her colleagues and together they brewed a powerful potion that helped me."

Georg smiled at her and the look he gave her spoke volumes. He gently took Violett's hand and squeezed it.

Overjoyed, Mayla glanced from one to the other when a high-pitched squeak echoed through the room.

"Little Karl?"

At first, she only saw the short tail, the tip of which was curled. Then the little cat hopped onto her bed and sat down on her lap, kneading and purring. Love, concern, anxiety, and gratitude flowed through Mayla as she tenderly stroked the little furball's head. "It's okay, darling. Everything will be fine now." Then she looked at Georg and Violett. "Or? What happened to the others? Were the hunters caught?"

"Many were, but some are still at large. Artus is on the mend. But best of all, all laws against so-called outcasts have been repealed. The time of hiding is over. We will rebuild everything."

Mayla smiled and stroked little Karl's soft black fur. "That sounds wonderful. Where's Tom?"

Georg looked at her seriously. "He threw himself in front of you before Bertha's curse could kill you."

Mayla paled. "What? Where is he?"

"He's alive," Violett reassured her immediately, "but he's not conscious yet."

Mayla quickly sat up with little Karl in her arms. "Where is he?"

"Please don't get worked up, Mayla, think about the baby. If you want to see him, he's right next door."

A weakness seeped through her limbs, causing her to stagger for a moment before she felt steady on her feet. She immediately rushed out of her room and went next door. She didn't notice the blue sky or the afternoon sun streaming through the window and didn't have a glance to spare for the lush blooming oleander growing outside the glass or the terracotta-colored mosaic tiles — no, all she could see was the bed where lay this big man who had saved her life so many times yet threatened to disappear amidst the pillows and sheets.

"Tom..."

Without taking her eyes off him, she sat down next to him. She put little Karl next to Kitty, who was quietly curled up next to Tom, watching over him. Mayla stroked his pale cheek.

"Kitty, how is he?"

Kitty meowed, but softly, so as not to disturb his rest.

Mayla carefully stroked his dark hair, his stubble, and again his pale cheeks. "Tom, can you hear me?"

But he didn't react.

"Sweetie, how are you?" a familiar voice asked from behind her.

Mayla turned. Melinda stood in the doorway. "I'm fine, but what about Tom?"

"Do you know what he did?"

A lump formed in Mayla's throat and only now did she realize that she was wearing her necklace with the heart-shaped pendant again. Someone had put it on her. Immediately clasping the heart, she answered in a choked voice, "He caught his family's killing curse for me."

Melinda nodded. There was sympathy in her voice as she explained. "He did, with the help of a shield. But out of humility, he didn't use the full potential of the ancient magic. As a result, the shield only mellowed the curse but did not stop it. And because he threw himself in front of you, you were spared."

It was as if someone was choking her. Not a word escaped her lips, merely a croak, and she cleared her throat before asking what she really needed to know. "Will he die?"

"I don't know. Magic doesn't follow any rules. As I told you before: observe it, learn from it, but never try to fully understand it. There are no limits to magic. And that applies to every aspect."

Mayla clutched her grandmother's cloak and looked at her urgently — no, beseechingly — as if only the will of this powerful witch was enough to heal him. "Will he be okay?"

Melinda shrugged regretfully. "With the old powers, I can't say."

"Did you brew a potion like Violett's? Maybe we can use it on him too..."

"Naturally. We have done everything within our power. Now he decides, or the magic... or both."

Numbly, she watched him with one hand on her stomach where their child was growing, her heart filled with worry. "Tom... Our happy ending is so close. Come back to me, back to us. Please!"

Weeks went by and Mayla only left Tom's bedside to shower. She even ate her meals in his room. Kitty and little Karl were with her most of the time. All day long, she held his hand silently. For the first time in her life, she didn't want to talk at all and didn't long for chocolate.

Melinda tried to persuade Mayla to fly to Canada to see her parents, who had arbitrarily decided to stay there. Considering the spell broke and it was Anneliese Falk who had remembered Mayla that night, there was a chance she would do it again. Her motherly love had once been stronger than the rule that witches were forgotten as soon as they entered world folds. However, Mayla refused to leave Tom.

Georg, Violett, and Phylis eventually left. Phylis returned to her house in the Earth Circle headquarters and Georg and Violett returned to Frankfurt. Only her grandmother stayed with her and Tom, which made Mayla extremely happy. She helped take care of him so that he wouldn't die of thirst or starvation, but otherwise left him and Mayla alone, as if waiting for the magic of love to awaken him. Melinda checked several times a week to see if there was anything she could do for Tom, but the result was always the same: he had to find his way out of the darkness himself.

Today, the fourth month had started and Mayla was keeping watch by Tom's side. Little Karl sat on her lap and Kitty was snuggled up against Tom's waist to give him strength. She hardly ever left him either.

A high-pitched squeak pierced the room that didn't come from little Karl. Surprised, Mayla looked up to see a caramel-colored kitten striding into the room.

"Hi, who are you?"

The brown kitten mewed loudly and Kitty immediately jumped over and licked his head.

"Is that your other kitten?" Mayla bent down to

the little animal and carefully stroked its soft fur. "You're cute. Are you hungry?"

It cried again and jumped up on Mayla's lap next to little Karl. It snuggled against Mayla's stomach and began to purr. A moment later, an almost imperceptible burst of energy shot through Mayla's abdomen. Was that her little one?

Tears welled up in her eyes as she understood. "Are you to become our child's spirit animal?"

The little kitten squealed excitely and kneaded Mayla's thighs.

Mayla chuckled briefly, then she stroked Tom's hand. "Did you hear that, Tom? Our little one already has a spirit animal. Soon, you will open your eyes and see for yourself. Once our child is born, we will have a wonderful time together. I never thought I'd be able to start a family. But now there's a little mite on its way and you only have to wake up. We will buy a nice house and share a wonderful life together. I'd even move into the desolate cabin with you if you'd just open your eyes!"

However, Tom didn't open his eyes.

Months went by and Tom's condition did not change. Mayla stayed by his bed, growing paler and sadder. Melinda made sure she ate enough, but her grandmother really didn't have to worry about that. Despite Tom's condition, Mayla felt a smoldering happiness and she would not do anything to put her baby at risk. She ate regularly. Not a lot, but enough to survive, and she drank plenty of fluids. All she lacked was movement and distraction. Occasionally, Melinda would dare to mention that Mayla had to start living. Mayla, however, forbade her to speak of Tom as if he were already dead. Despite her grandmother's objections, she stayed in the room with him, firmly convinced that if anything could bring him out of this state, it would be love.

After some time, she received a letter from Heike, which distracted her from her worries for a moment. Her friend still hadn't forgotten her and Mayla finally found out why. The witch she had been helping out in the shop since the escape in the red Opel had given her a powerful protective amulet that prevented her from forgetting. Heike had enclosed two of these amulets, intended for Mayla's parents, with the letter. Mayla gratefully hugged the treasures to her chest as she read the letter over and over again. From then on, she wrote her friend once a week — a small ray of hope in her gloomy everyday life.

Her stomach grew rounder, her facial features softer, and then winter swept over the Greek island. Still, Tom hadn't woken up the day her labor pains started. Less than twelve hours later, the transition was complete and Mayla was the mother of a wonderful girl.

The child's screams penetrated not only the house but Mayla's mind like a wake-up call, and she stopped sitting by Tom's bed, one minute after another. She loved that the child challenged her and for her sake, she introduced a daily life that was child-oriented. After a week, she chose a name, although she would have preferred to have decided on it with Tom. However, she was sure he would not object to her choice. She named her daughter Emma Anneliese.

Whenever Emma closed her sugar-sweet dark eyes, Mayla levitated the cradle into Tom's room and stood guard at his side. She slept with him every night, but in the mornings and afternoons, she spent hours with the little one outside in the fresh air.

As hard as it was for her, the child needed to have a fulfilling life, even without Tom. She was responsible for ensuring that the little one did not grow up full of sadness, but rather hope and balance. She hid her fear for Tom and whenever she looked at her little daughter's smiling face, she thought she recognized his features in her.

For hours, she would push Emma in the stroller around the island, which she gradually explored. She hadn't known how beautiful Lesbos was since she had never been to the Greek island before. And even outside the great world fold in which Phylis's house stood, the scenery was dreamy.

With each passing day as Emma grew and prospered, Mayla became happier and calmer. Of course, Tom was missing to complete her joy, but the little girl was so delightful and full of love that no one could resist. She started laughing when she was four weeks old and hardly ever stopped. Mayla longed for Tom to see it, but she did make sure he heard it as often as possible.

It didn't take long for Emma to start walking and her magic awakened early on. A little later, she started to babble and wherever she went, the little caramel-colored kitten trailed her. It took Mayla a while to figure out the kitten's name, which Emma was able to say before her second birthday. Her spirit cat was called Karamella.

One afternoon, Emma and Karamella ran into Tom's room to play. Mayla was just waking up beside his bed and looked up sleepily when her little whirlwind swept in to see her.

She admonished them affectionately. "Not so loud, my darling, Daddy is sleeping."

Emma pressed her red lips into a pout. "When will Daddy wake up?"

"I don't know, angel, but we must never give up hope, understand?"

Emma nodded and struggled up onto the bed. Mayla helped her and the little one bent over Tom and gave him a big kiss. "Daddy, Emma wants to play!"

A tear crept into the corner of Mayla's eye and she wanted to pull Emma away from Tom. However, she couldn't bring herself to do it. The little child didn't understand that he couldn't hear her because, from the start, Mayla had encouraged her to talk to him as if he were conscious. Who could tell if their bright child's laughter might not penetrate to where his spirit was trapped?

"Daddy, wake up!" Emma pressed her tiny hands against Tom's chest and suddenly, a purple glow appeared at her fingertips. It floated out of them unchecked, enveloping Tom like a blanket, when the glow seemed to penetrate Tom. Kitty jumped up and meowed. She paced restlessly across the blanket beside him.

Mayla watched the scene in disbelief, unable to say anything or intervene.

"Daddy, wake up!" Emma's eyes narrowed and her high forehead wrinkled. The purple glow grew stronger until Tom's mouth opened slightly and the glow slipped in between his lips and penetrated his innermost being.

Mayla held her breath. Emma squeezed her eyes shut even tighter before opening them again. "Daddy?"

Her voice was so high-pitched, yet there was a sadness in it that a child so small should not yet feel. Despite all the love, had she felt that Tom was missing, felt he wasn't with her like he should be?

Tom's fingers twitched. Slowly, he raised his right hand and placed it on the tiny hands that still rested on his chest. Then he remained motionless again. Mayla watched in amazement. How could that be?

"Daddy?"

Tom blinked, but his lids drooped again. Did she just imagine it? Then, he did it again.

Mayla jumped up and bent over him. "Tom? Grandma, come quickly!"

Even before Melinda had rushed into the room, he opened his eyes. Tired at first, he peered into the small pink face with dark hair and dark eyes. Then, a tender smile appeared on his emaciated face. His gaze wandered to Mayla and his eyes shone.

"Tom? This is unbelievable. You are awake!"

Melinda had long since rushed into the room and was staring at little Emma, who happily spread her arms and threw them around her father's neck. "Finally, Daddy!"

Mayla bent over them and the three hugged until Mayla gently pulled Emma away from Tom and placed her on her lap.

"How is it...?" Tom croaked, and Mayla immediately put a glass of water to his lips. Emma jumped off her lap and helped give her father the drink. Tom laughed at her eagerness. It sounded harsh and throaty. He hugged little Emma tightly. "Mayla, what a lovely child. Thank you. You brought me back to life. I heard you all along. Everything has been gray and cold. I didn't know how to get back, but your voices and your warmth kept me alive."

Stunned, Mayla watched Emma and Tom hug

and looked at Melinda, who was running her hand through her white curls pensively. "What just happened here? It couldn't have been Emma, could it?"

"Yes, definitely. It was her."

"How is that possible? She's still so small. How can her power be greater than yours?"

Melinda leaned close to Mayla's ear so that Tom and Emma couldn't hear her words. "Tom's blood as well as Vincent and Bertha's, flows in her. As heir to the von Eisenfels family, the ancient magic is also united in her."

Startled, Mayla first looked at Emma and then at her grandmother, who was inconspicuously wiping a large tear from the corner of her eye. Mayla's thoughts raced. "But she shouldn't use it or she'll die too!"

"I'm not so sure of that. She was born with it, so she might be worthy. In any case, we must not tell anyone. This must remain our secret under all circumstances."

Wide-eyed, Mayla observed her little girl. Seeing the tenderness with which Tom and Emma were looking at each other, her heart swelled. She pushed her worries aside and hugged them both happily.

The Witches World-Folds Saga continues: "Charms & Chocolate – Protected by Water". Preorder book no. 4 now!

Charms & Chocolate – Protected by Water

Do you want to read an extra chapter about Mayla and Tom? Then join Jenny's Magic Mailing List now and download immediately!

www.jennyswan.com

Would you do me a favor?

It would be great if you could write me a review. It can be short — one or two sentences would be enough. Thank you so much. I appreciate your help, and look forward to seeing you for book no. 4.

Yours, Jenny Swan

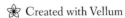